"WON'T YOU DANCE WITH ME, MISS ELFINSTONE?"

He held out a hand.

How tempting to place her hand in his, to be held the way she was held in that favorite dream.

She gave herself a mental shake. In that oft repeated dream that had begun on her first night at Mrs. Foster's Seminary for Young Ladies, she was held by a faceless stranger. Surely she was not foolish enough to give that dream figure the face and form of Stephen Ardleigh!

"I do not dance, Mr. Ardleigh," she said with suitable finality.

"You will not, Miss Elfinstone? Or"—he cocked his head and gave her a quizzical look—"you cannot?"

She sighed. "I should have known you would persist. I *cannot* dance, Mr. Ardleigh. I have no aptitude. Two left feet, you might say. And I certainly never tried my hand, ah, foot at a waltz."

"Then let me teach you."

She turned away from him once more. Was this how Eve felt when the serpent tempted her with the apple?

—From *The Dancing Shoes*
by Karla Hocker

BOOK YOUR PLACE ON OUR WEBSITE AND MAKE THE READING CONNECTION!

We've created a customized website just for our very special readers, where you can get the inside scoop on everything that's going on with Zebra, Pinnacle and Kensington books.

When you come online, you'll have the exciting opportunity to:

- View covers of upcoming books
- Read sample chapters
- Learn about our future publishing schedule (listed by publication month *and author*)
- Find out when your favorite authors will be visiting a city near you
- Search for and order backlist books from our online catalog
- Check out author bios and background information
- Send e-mail to your favorite authors
- Meet the Kensington staff online
- Join us in weekly chats with authors, readers and other guests
- Get writing guidelines
- AND MUCH MORE!

**Visit our website at
http://www.zebrabooks.com**

ONCE UPON A WALTZ

Carola Dunn
Karla Hocker
Judith A. Lansdowne

ZEBRA BOOKS
Kensington Publishing Corp.
http://www.zebrabooks.com

ZEBRA BOOKS are published by

Kensington Publishing Corp.
850 Third Avenue
New York, NY 10022

All Kensington titles, imprints and distributed lines are available
at special quantity discounts for bulk purchases for sales pro-
motion, premiums, fund raising, educational or institutional use.

Special book excerpts or customized printings can also be created to fit specific needs. For details, write or phone the office
of the Kensington Special Sales Manager: Kensington Publishing Corp., 850 Third Avenue, New York, NY, 10022. Attn. Special Sales Department, Phone: 1-800-221-2647.

Zebra and the Z logo Reg. U.S. Pat. & TM Off.

First Printing: March, 2001
10 9 8 7 6 5 4 3 2 1

Printed in the United States of America

CONTENTS

The Firebird by Carola Dunn   7

The Dancing Shoes by Karla Hocker   97

King Thrushbeard by Judith A. Lansdowne   159

THE FIREBIRD

by

Carola Dunn

One

Silent as the owl floating overhead, and as nearly invisible to human eyes, Reynata slipped along the woodland path. Though the waning moon, shining down through the trees, turned the ground into an intricate tangle of light and shadow, she had no fear of losing her way. The maze of rabbit and deer tracks was as familiar to her as the pattern on her counterpane.

She paused as a dog fox came round the bole of a gnarled oak tree. He stopped and stared, one paw raised, his nostrils quivering as he strove to catch the expected scent. Reynata looked like a vixen—but she smelled human.

Bewildered and wary, the stranger braced to turn and run.

"Good day, sir," Reynata called softly in his own language. "Do not fear; I mean you no harm."

"You're not another nasty trick to lure me into reach of the hounds?" he growled, his pointed ears pricked forward.

"No, indeed. There is little hunting in the King's Forest. It is wide, with few bridle paths, and His Majesty has no use for it, that poor madman. The trees and thickets are left to grow too densely for horses and riders to pass without more caution than huntsmen care to exercise."

"And you?" he asked, still suspicious.

"I am a wer-fox," Reynata said sadly. "At the new moon I am a girl for two or three days. At the full moon I become a vixen, willy-nilly, though in between, as now, I can choose which form to adopt."

The dog fox grinned, his long tongue lolling between sharp white teeth. "How wise of you to pick a fox's form when you can. Who would want to be a human—if these woods are truly safe?"

"As safe as anywhere."

"I've come across the moors from Somerset way, the Vale of Taunton Deane. Too many huntsmen there by half! Mayhap I shall stay a while."

"I know a true vixen in need of a mate. If you follow this rabbit path down the hill to the ivied sycamore, then turn along the valley in the direction of the setting sun, you will cross her trail."

"And with luck a rabbit's, too." Nodding his head in thanks, the fox loped off, his feet silent on the soft leaf mould. In a moment, he vanished into the shadows beneath the undergrowth, the white tip of his brush last to disappear.

Reynata gazed after him, envious. He would find his mate, settle down, and in the spring a new litter of adorable, squirming, rusty-red cubs would appear. How simple life would be if she were all fox!

Or all girl.

With a sigh, she trotted on towards Wick Towers. Lord Drake was home at last, with a company of grand friends. The heir to the earldom had been away in London for months, and Reynata had counted every day.

Tonight his father, Lord Androwick, was giving a ball at the mansion on St. Andrew's Hill. Wistfully, Reynata wondered if Lord Drake's engagement was to be announced. Had he brought home a beautiful, well-bred, blue-blooded young lady to be his wife?

Not that it would make any difference to Reynata. A

foundling brought up by a wise-woman in a cottage in the woods could never aspire to be his bride, even if she were not a wer-fox. Simply to dance with him was far more than she dared wish for. Her best hope was to watch him dancing.

Walls, fences, and hedges, meant to keep out strangers, were no barrier to a small fox. A swift shadow, she sped across the park and through the shrubbery to the terrace outside the ballroom. The curtains at the French windows were closed, but careless servants had left a slight gap at the bottom. Crouched on the cold flagstones, glad of her thick russet coat, Reynata peered in.

The ballroom had not been used since Lady Androwick died in childbirth nearly two decades ago. Reynata had once before peeked in, to see chandeliers and rows of chairs all swathed in holland dust sheets.

Tonight a thousand wax candles sparkled on crystal teardrops above and on the jewels of fine ladies below. Gowns the hues of the gayest meadow flowers swirled around dainty feet in matching satin slippers. Gentlemen in coats of black, blue, or guardsmen's scarlet bowed and skipped and twirled their partners. The lively music made Reynata's paws twitch.

Rapt, she pressed her quivering black nose to the pane. There was Master John, the earl's youngest, hopping away like mad. There were handsome Master Damon and Master Basil, smirking at the pretty young ladies promenading on their arms. There were neighbouring gentry-folk she recognized, and Lord Androwick himself, a tall, lean gentleman somewhat stooped with age, not dancing but walking about looking important.

And there was Aldwin, Lord Drake. Reynata's heart leapt. Taller than his tall brothers, golden-haired where they were merely blond, broad of shoulder but slim, and newly elegant in his London-made coat, he outshone the thousand candle flames.

Naturally his partner was the most beautiful girl in the room. Her hair was as golden as his. Sapphires glinted at her throat, and her lace-trimmed gown was the blue of the sky in midsummer. She floated down the set at his side, and when they stopped at the end, he smiled and bent his head courteously to listen to her.

A soft fox whimper rose in Reynata's throat. She had not expected this moment to hurt so much.

The music ended. Ladies and gentlemen bowed and curtsied. Lord Drake and his partner came towards the window, she laughing as she fanned herself vigorously with an ivory fan. Reynata poised to flee.

Aldwin was bored. After the London Season, he had been invited to half a dozen country house parties. He had to return the hospitality, but he longed for freedom to take up country pursuits again, to delve into managing the vast estate which would be his.

His father had suddenly decided, last winter, to permit his heir to go up to Town, to acquire a little polish and look about him for a suitable wife. Aldwin had gathered all the Town bronze he wanted, and he had enjoyed the process, but now he was tired of constant frivolity.

Lady Flavia was the epitome of frivolity. She was stunningly beautiful, and she had not an idea in her head besides catching a husband. If he stood up with her for a second consecutive dance—and the next was a waltz—he would have to take her in to supper. Her expectations would soar through the roof.

For a horrid moment he thought she would accompany him out to the terrace, which would call for an immediate declaration. But he had read her aright. As he opened the French window, a blast of chilly air entered. Lady Flavia shivered and held back.

"It is too cold by far!"

"There will be a frost tonight, I should not wonder, the first of the autumn. You must not risk taking a chill. But I am wearing a coat and desperate for a breath of fresh air. Here is your friend Lady Otterton. I shall leave you to her care."

With that, he strode out and closed the door firmly behind him. To deter her from following, he stepped to one side, out of the light cast from indoors. After a moment his eyes adjusted to the pale moonlight.

Seeing the cloaked, hooded figure of a tall woman standing at the top of the steps down to the lawn, he moved towards her, slowly, so as not to startle her into flight. "Who is there?"

"I just wanted to see the dancing, my lord." A soft, low voice. "I would have run away if *she* had come out, but I knew you would not be angry."

"Not a bit of it. You sound familiar, but I am out of touch with local matters. You're from the town? What is your name?"

"I-I think I had best not tell."

"As you will. Listen, the music is starting. Dance with me, mysterious maiden."

"Oh, yes, if you please, my lord."

He could tell she had never waltzed before, but he was a good dancer, liked to dance. She quickly followed his lead and caught the rhythm. In spite of her heavy cloak, she was light as thistledown in his arms. And oh, bliss! she did not chatter. He whirled her about the terrace.

Her face was raised to his, but in the deceptive moonlight he caught only brief glimpses of dark eyes, a tender mouth, never her whole countenance at once. As the music ended, he demanded, "Who are you? Tell me your name."

"Best not," she murmured. "I must go."

Slipping from his arms, she ran across the terrace and down the steps. He hurried after, but when he reached the top, there was no sign of her. Nowhere for a person to hide; she had vanished into thin air.

"A fairy creature?" he mused, and he returned, slightly regretful, to the mundane frivolity in the house.

Two

High above the early-morning mists twining among the tree trunks, a jay screeched a warning. Reynata raised her muzzle and sniffed the air. No scent of danger came to her nostrils. The warning was against herself.

Today she stayed on the bridle path, for her rush-woven panniers, though light and empty, were liable to catch on twigs and thorns if she strayed. In spite of the encumbrance, she moved much faster on four feet than she could have on two.

She came to the edge of the wood, where the ride debouched onto a cart track. The hedge on the far side of the track hung heavy with crimson haws, scarlet hips, and wreaths of yellow and orange briony berries. The field beyond the hedge had been reaped and gleaned a fortnight since. Most leaves were still green, but autumn was well on the way.

Huddled under a convenient bush, Reynata glanced each way along the track. No one in sight. She moved back behind a screen of undergrowth and shrugged the panniers from her back.

How she metamorphosed, she had never been quite sure. She decided to change; the universe turned inside out; and there she stood, human again and—most puzzling of all—already wearing the clothes she had put on earlier that morning. Grandmama, though she was a wise-woman, could not explain it, though she suspected it meant Reynata was not a natural wer-creature but be-witched. Reynata had long since stopped bothering her head about it.

Grandmama, Reynata's foster mother, still strove to understand the chains of magic binding her fosterling.

One winter day, nearly twenty years ago, on her way home from market, Gammer Gresham had heard a whimper and found a starving fox cub cowering behind a fallen tree trunk. She had carried it home under her cloak, to succour. To her wonder, when she opened her cloak, she found a human babe.

None of her spells sufficed to prevent the girl-child's transformation back into a fox at times. She had brought Reynata up to accept the way she was, helped her learn to control the change when possible, and loved her whatever her shape or form.

In human shape, Reynata's form was tall and slim. She bore herself with the natural grace of a wild animal. Her features were a trifle too pointed for beauty, a hint of her alter ego matched by the fox-red hair which she wore in a thick plait down her back. Eyes the translucent brown of a woodland stream completed the picture of an attractive young woman who turned the heads of townsmen and farmers' sons alike.

Yet none came courting.

The lads trudged through the woods to the wise-woman's cottage to purchase love potions for the merry, rosy, buxom village girls. To Reynata they spoke with the same polite respect and slight uneasiness as to Gammer Gresham herself. Perhaps it was because the witch had raised her from infancy, or perhaps a hint of her dual nature had somehow spread abroad.

Her aloof demeanour did nothing to lessen their wariness. As long as every full moon forced her to go upon four feet, she could never marry.

Not that she had the least desire to give her hand to

any of the lumpish fellows. Her heart she had given away long ago.

Now, on the edge of the wood, she smoothed the skirts of her high-waisted, grey, homespun woollen gown, brushing off a twig or two from the hem. She pulled up the hood of her forest-green cloak, for beyond the shelter of the trees, the air had an autumnal nip. The panniers, detached from each other, became two commonplace baskets.

Reynata stepped out onto the track and turned towards the nearby town.

Middlecombe was a small town, a large village really, but in this corner of England, cut off by forest and moor and the Bristol Channel, its weekly market was important and always busy. Here countryfolk mingled with towns-folk, and the local gentry were often to be seen. Even the Earl of Androwick, the preeminent local landowner, frequently came down from Wick Towers to greet his tenants and browse the stalls.

Lord Androwick was a passionate collector of rarities. Up at the Towers, he had cabinets filled with curious objects: tiki gods from the South Seas, an iridescent dragon's scale as hard as iron, fossilized fish and ferns, a harpy's egg, a piece of Merlin's cloak with strange patterns which changed before one's eyes, even an Egyptian mummy. In his aviary dwelt among others an archaeopteryx, a parrot who recited Homer in classical Greek, a blue-footed booby, a gryphon, and a pair of pink flamingos. His walled gardens and conservatories sheltered such novelties as the giant marigolds of Peru, rhododendrons from the high Himalayas, passion-flower vines with intricate blooms and juicy purple fruit. He had an ash grown from a cutting of Yggdrasil, the Norse world tree, and a hawthorn grafted from the tree planted at Glastonbury by St. Joseph of Arimathea, which blossomed every Christmas Day. Prized above all others was a persimmon tree from the mysterious Asiatic empire of Japan.

"Grown from a seed of the golden apples of the Hesperides," he was wont to tell visitors. "This year it has set fruit for the first time, four of them. Like medlars, they must be eaten very ripe. How I long to taste them!"

For fear of thieves, the eccentric earl allowed no strangers to approach Wick Towers. Pedlars of curiosities brought them to Middlecombe market, where his lordship condescended to inspect their wares.

With him, as often as not, came one or more of his four sons. Today, as she filled her baskets with flour, salt, yeast, and yarn, Reynata saw the fair heads of all four tall young gentlemen passing through the crowds.

Lord Drake! Would he recognize her as the girl he had waltzed with three nights ago?

She concentrated on watching the weighing of two ounces of raisins, a treat Grandmama dearly loved. The stall-holder hastily threw in a few extra, though the measure was good. Gammer Gresham had never been known to harm anyone with her spells, but it was just as well to be sure.

The purchase completed, Reynata moved on, and came face-to-face with Lord Androwick's two middle sons.

"Good day, Miss Gresham," said Master Damon, with a bow made insolent by the sneer on his otherwise handsome face. He looked her up and down in a way which made her wish she had not thrown back her hood and unfastened her cloak in the increasing warmth of the sun. "Finished your shopping? Come along to the Green Dragon. We'll take a private room, and I'll treat you to something special."

His insinuating tone betrayed his meaning, confirmed by his brother's snigger.

Meeting his sly eyes with a stony look, Reynata

bobbed a curtsy. "I have not finished my errands, sir," she said firmly, fastening her cloak as she turned away.

Master Damon grasped her arm. "Not so fast! We'll go with you, to make sure none of these louts offers to lay a hand on you. Come along, Basil."

They fell in on either side of her. Reynata racked her brains for a way to escape their mischievous attentions. None of the market people would come to her aid, for the earl's known power far outweighed the wise-woman's reputed abilities.

She started at a fast pace towards a stall selling lamp oil.

"Ha," exclaimed Master Basil, "she's in a hurry to find out what you have to give her, Damon."

"Since she's so eager, you'd better give her a little something, too."

"Damon! Basil! Father wants—" Lord Drake came to a halt before the three. "Reynata! Miss Gresham, I should say, for you are quite grown up now, are you not?"

He bowed, with a smile which made her heart turn over. Despite his words, however, it was the sort of smile a young man gives to a favoured child. Aldwin, Lord Drake, still saw her as the little girl who had joined in his and his brothers' games in the King's Forest. She had played Maid Marion to his Robin Hood, captive princess to his Sir Galahad, Flora Macdonald to his Bonnie Prince Charlie.

Was it because Master Damon had always been cast as the Sheriff of Nottingham, the ogre, or Butcher Cumberland that he had turned out such a bully?

Reynata curtsied to Lord Drake, with a shy smile. If she was still a child to him, he was more than ever the hero of her dreams. If his face had not the near-classical perfection of Master Damon's, how much pleasanter it was to look upon!

"I am sorry to deprive you of your escorts, Miss Gresham," he said. He had never believed Damon and Basil intended to distress or hurt her, putting down their nasty tricks to overexuberance, even as he rescued her from the effects. "My father wishes to show them a cockatrice he thinks of purchasing."

"A cockatrice!" said Basil in horror.

"Otherwise known as a basil-isk," Lord Drake quizzed him. "I daresay you'd be immune to your namesake's deadly gaze, but it's dead and stuffed, never fear. Miss Gresham, pray tell Mistress Gresham I mean to call upon her sometime in the next few days."

"Grandmama will be very pleased to see you, my lord."

"Come along, fellows."

A summons from the earl was not to be disobeyed. Sulkily, Damon and Basil went off with their eldest brother.

Watching, Reynata saw them join Lord Androwick and John. John was Reynata's age but seemed to her much younger. A good-natured youth, he, too, had always been prey to his middle brothers' tricks, which he fell for much more easily than she did, being not overendowed with common sense.

Common sense dictated to Reynata that she complete her errands as swiftly as possible and leave for home before Damon and Basil were free to harass her again.

Half an hour later, she turned off the cart track onto the bridle path which led through the woods to Grandmama's cottage. She walked on in human shape, for the baskets were now too heavy and awkward for a fox to carry, even if she could have set them as panniers on her own back. The path wound uphill and down, the slopes so easily covered on four feet now a wearisome trudge.

Growing hot, Reynata took off her cloak and stuffed it into the lighter basket. When she came to a brook, she put down her load and knelt on the bank to dip her handkerchief in the cool water and wipe her face.

The stream's chuckling drowned the muffled beat of hooves on leaf mould until the riders were nearly upon her.

"Another minute and we'd have caught her bathing!" cried Basil as Reynata sprang to her feet.

"No matter." Damon swung down from the saddle and pounced. "It won't be a minute's work to strip her. Well met!" he went on with an ugly grin, his grip tightening painfully on her upper arms. "There's a nice, soft bed of moss over there will suit us to perfection."

Three

Aldwin Drake moved through the marketplace, greeting his father's people, flattered by their evident pleasure in his return. At twenty-six, he had never been away from home before for more than a few days.

Though Aldwin had not won a bride, a Season under the aegis of his cynical, worldly uncle, followed by summer visits to several noble houses, had taught him to regard humanity with a discerning eye. Affectionate amusement replaced the dutiful reverence he had always felt for his father. His new appraisal of Damon and Basil was less pleasant.

He had always thought his middle brothers' manners at fault rather than their intentions. Now he was not so sure. He suspected Damon had a vicious streak, taking a positive pleasure in tormenting others, and Basil was all too ready to follow his lead.

So, as he strolled, Aldwin watched for Reynata Gresham. It was up to him to shield the child if Damon had some mischievous prank in mind. He would do the same for any female, of course, but he was deucedly fond of Reynata.

No sign of her. She must have gone home already. But no sign of Damon or Basil, either, Aldwin realized. He frowned.

John panted up to him. "Aldwin, thank heaven I've found you! They've gone after her. After Miss Gresham.

And they were talking . . ." He hesitated, blushing vividly. "They said . . ."

Aldwin's fears filled in the words all too easily. Crowds parted before him as he strode towards the Phoenix Inn, where his horse was stabled. "They told you what they were about?" he demanded of John, scurrying alongside.

"Oh, they pay me no heed. I don't suppose they even noticed I was there. I didn't know what to do except come to you."

"You were quite right, lad. I'll deal with this."

"I'd ride with you, only I came with Father in the carriage."

Aldwin forbore to point out that the inn had mounts for hire. If it came to a fight—surely it would not come to a fight, with his own brothers!—young John was more likely to get in the way than to help.

He saddled Amiga himself. In his haste, his fingers fumbled with the fine Spanish leather, patterned with inlaid silver and mother-of-pearl. The golden mare with mane and tail of silver stood still, her dark eyes rolling, aware of his disquiet. She was a palomino, of a rare Spanish stock derived from Saracen and Moorish ancestors, which seldom bred true. Aldwin had bought her at Tattersall's in London, from a wounded soldier returning from the Peninsula War. The earl coveted her, but his son managed to persuade him a menagerie was no place for a proud, spirited horse.

Amiga del Viento, Friend of the Wind, was her full name, for she had Barb and Arab blood in her and she ran like the wind.

Aldwin sprang to her back and turned her head towards the King's Forest. Out of town they galloped, up the track and into the woods. Her hooves beat a muted tattoo on the winding path, like muffled drums sounding a hasty funeral march.

It was not a matter of life and death, Aldwin assured himself. But from a woman's point of view, was not rape considered a fate worse than death? And Reynata had scarcely left childhood behind her! His heart pounded in time with Amiga's stride as he urged the mare onward.

The path curved downhill around a fallen elm, half buried in brambles. Recalling the brook just beyond, Aldwin slowed Amiga's pace a trifle.

He leapt from the saddle before he had fully taken in the scene opening before him, On the bank of the stream, Reynata struggled in Damon's arms as he strove to pull her away from the water. Basil hastened towards them from the bush where he had tied their horses.

All three stilled suddenly as Aldwin burst upon them. Basil dithered. Reynata, with a desperate lunge, twisted away from Damon, falling to the ground. Damon put up his fists and swung at his brother.

Dodging, Aldwin feinted, then connected with a left to the jaw. Not for nothing had he frequented Gentleman Jackson's Bond Street boxing saloon. Damon toppled backwards and landed with a great splash in the stream.

Aldwin turned to Basil, who backed away, shaking his head. "Not my notion," he mumbled. "Never laid a finger on her." He hung his head in shame at his own cowardice.

Damon floundered in the stream, his face a mask of humiliated hatred. "I'll get you for this," he spat.

Aldwin ignored him, giving Reynata his hand as she scrambled to her feet. "You're not hurt?" he queried. She shook her head dumbly, lustrous brown eyes huge with some unidentifiable emotion. "Come, I'll see you home."

He stooped to pick up her baskets.

"Let me." She reached for them. "It's not fitting for a gentleman—"

"I expect I can tie them to Amiga's saddle somehow." Reynata glanced at the mare, standing patient and watchful, and her eyes widened again. "She's beautiful! A gold-and-silver horse should not carry such a common burden."

"She's proud, but docile and willing. Clever, too. She answers to her name. Amiga!"

The mare's ears flickered, and she nodded twice.

"See? She won't mind playing the beast of burden for once."

"The baskets are made to fasten together as panniers." Reynata hesitated. "But they would be in your way when you mount."

"I've no intention of riding. She'll follow, even without a lead rein when it's someone she knows," he boasted. "Show me how to fasten the baskets."

Her hands trembled as she complied, he noted. Though her voice was calm, her nerves must be all aquiver at her narrow escape.

He slung the panniers over Amiga's withers. As he looped the reins out of the mare's way, he saw Damon crawling soggily out of the brook with a helping hand from Basil. He said nothing to them, hoping against hope that they had learnt their lesson.

The bridle path was just wide enough for Aldwin and Reynata to walk side by side, with Amiga following. Neither of them spoke until they had put a few windings of the trail between them and the others.

Then he said, "I'm sorry."

"*You're* sorry?" She sounded startled.

He could not look at her, shunned meeting her eyes. "They are my brothers. Their behaviour reflects on me. In fact, it dishonours the whole family. I must consider whether my father ought to know what his sons were about."

"Oh no! Pray don't tell Lord Androwick. I suffered no h-harm."

"I can only be deeply thankful that I arrived in time

to preserve you. If John had not found me quickly—It doesn't bear thinking about."

"N-no. P-pray . . ." A sob swallowed her voice.

Turning towards her, Aldwin saw tears trickling down her face. He put his arm around her shoulders to comfort her. She swung towards him, burying her face in his cravat, so he held her close.

Reynata was no child, he discovered. The playmate of his youth had vanished. In her place was a warm, soft, gently curved woman, altogether desirable, who fitted into his arms as if she had been created especially for them. He hugged her to him, his cheek against her silken, fragrant hair. It gleamed like copper in the dappled sunshine filtering through the leaves above. A sudden longing swept him to see it falling loose about her naked shoulders.

She pulled away a little and looked up at him. The way she held her head was familiar—"Good lord, was it you I danced with?"

She nodded, dark eyes brimming, and he caught her in his arms again.

"I'm s-sorry." She wept into his chest. "It was just all rather a sh-shock."

Instantly he released her and stepped back, appalled. He was no better than his brothers!

Yes, he was, dammit. He would never dream of taking her by force, nor even of seducing her. He loved her! Nothing less than marriage would suffice—his shoulders slumped—and marriage was out of the question. She was a foundling brought up by a witch. He was heir to the Earl of Androwick.

"I've lost my h-handkerchief."

He felt in his pocket. "Here, take this."

"Thank you, sir."

The hint of red around her eyes, the defiant way she blew her nose, only made her dearer to him. She was pluck through and through. He tried desperately to think of some damning fault he had observed in her over the years. He failed.

Amiga nuzzled his shoulder.

"She's growing impatient," Reynata said with a shaky little laugh. "I'm all right now, my lord. There's no need for you to come farther. They won't follow me now."

For answer he started out again, towards the wise-woman's cottage. "Cannot Mistress Gresham give you a protective spell?" he asked harshly. "Some sort of amulet? You are safe for today, I daresay, but I fear it may take greater chastisement than I administered to deter my brothers for the future, and I might not always be at hand."

"I expect Grandmama will know what to do," she said, subdued. "I never felt in serious need of protection before."

"Ask her," Aldwin commanded. "I'll ask her myself. I want to be sure you are safe before I go away."

Reynata looked up at him, and now her heart was in her eyes. Her voice trembled. "You are going away again?"

He realized the decision was made, He had no choice. Living a mere two miles from the woman he loved and who loved him, unable to express their love, would be sheer torture.

"I must go," he said. He could not tell her—or anyone—the real reason. "Lord Wellington has need of soldiers in Spain. I shall purchase a commission and do my part to save England from Bonaparte."

She was silent for the space of several paces. The sounds of the forest seemed suddenly loud, the song of birds, the rustle of leaves. Then she said, in a stifled tone, "You will be in far more danger than I. Grandmama must give you a spell, too," she added urgently.

"Perhaps." Aldwin was not sure he cared whether he

was killed or not. Was life without Reynata worth living? As he brooded, another consideration came to him. "In keeping me from harm, a magical shield might prevent my doing my duty. No, I shall take nothing."

Reynata bowed her head and trudged on at his side.

They came to the clearing where stood Gammer Gresham's cottage. The small, thatched, half-timbered building was surrounded by an orderly jungle of vegetables, herbs, fruit trees and bushes, and flowers. In this flourishing garden, chickens pecked and scratched, magically kept from destroying the desirable plants as they ate up insects, snails, and weeds. To one side, a tethered nanny goat grazed on lush grass. Before the door stood a rowan tree, proof that no wicked witchcraft lurked here.

In childhood, Aldwin and his brothers had often visited the cottage, to be welcomed with fresh-baked bread and crab apple jelly and a glass of goat's milk. Of later years, he had rarely come. Tutors kept him busy with academic studies, and then his father's bailiff with learning to run the great estate which would one day be his.

That explained how Reynata had grown up without his noticing, why she seemed to him to have changed overnight from a winsome child he was fond of to a bewitching woman he adored.

Bewitching? A love spell?

If so, he thought grimly, no doubt he would find himself unable to leave this place without committing himself to a misalliance which could only end in disaster.

Gammer Gresham was in her garden, gathering herbs. A tall woman, she straightened with an effort as her foster daughter and the visitor approached, and came to meet them. To Aldwin she had seemed ancient twenty years ago. Now he saw how stiffly she moved, how the sun-browned face had become a mesh of wrinkles. Yet her grey eyes were as shrewdly penetrating as ever, her greeting as warm.

"Lord Drake, how delightful to see you."

For the first time, he noticed the refinement of her speech. Once, long ago, she must have come of a good family. She had taught Reynata to speak well, too, he realized, but nothing could give the foundling a background to fit her to be a countess.

He bowed over the wise-woman's crabbed hand. "The pleasure is mine, ma'am. I met Miss Gresham at the market and bethought me that I had not called since I came home."

"Lord Drake's horse carried my shopping, Grandmama. Is she not a beauty?"

To his relief, Reynata had observed his reticence over his brothers' misdeeds and followed his lead. She might tell her foster mother later, but not now, when it would deeply embarrass him.

So how was he to persuade the wise-woman that Reynata was in need of a protective spell? he wondered as he disburdened Amiga of the panniers and carried them into the cottage.

"It is a long walk from town," he said, setting the baskets on the well-scrubbed whitewood table, "and a lonely one. When I am travelling far from home, I should be comforted to know Miss Gresham is defended by a charm from any possible danger. Will you not use your skills in this, ma'am, for my sake?"

"I had not considered it necessary." Mistress Gresham gave him a long, steady look. He was sure she read his mind, his deepest thoughts and feelings, even those he was not yet aware of. Abruptly she nodded. "I shall do what I can, Aldwin, though perfect safety is beyond my powers. Shall I prepare a second charm, for you?"

"No. It might hinder me in doing my duty as a soldier, and also, I should fear to rely too much upon it."

"Then God guard you and keep you." It was a dismissal. No spell bound him unwilling to the girl.

Aldwin bowed again. Reynata curtsied to him, her eyes downcast. "God guard you and keep you," she whispered, so faint he almost thought he had imagined it.

He glanced back as he untied Amiga. Through the open door of the cottage, he saw Mistress Gresham seated at the table. At her feet, Reynata knelt, her face buried in her foster mother's lap. One gnarled hand caressed the glossy chestnut hair.

A lump in his throat, Aldwin swung into the saddle and turned the mare's head homeward.

Four

"I have been remiss," Grandmama said. "I ought to have started to pass on my knowledge to you long ago, to provide your livelihood when I am gone. I have kept hoping to learn how to counter the enchantment binding you. But the best I have done after long years of study is to turn a mouse into a very surprised bat—when I had intended it to be a mole—and poor Tibb into a raven instead of a dog."

"Miaow," observed the big black bird perched on the windowsill. "Better a raven than a dog any day. Some ways it's even better than cat-hood. Talking's much easier, and flying's fun. Don't try to de-spell *me.*"

"I set the spell, so I can undo it," the wise-woman told him tartly, "and I will if you talk too much. Reynata's ensorcellment was not my doing, so it is more difficult, perhaps impossible."

Reynata essayed a smile. "It doesn't matter," she said sadly.

"I had hoped you might one day fall in love with some kindly farmer or shopkeeper, and marry, and have children."

"I shall never marry. Even if I were wholly human, Lord Drake is too far above me. He has a duty to his family. Yet however painful it would be to see him often when I can never be his, I wish he was not going for a soldier. I wish he had accepted a protective charm!"

"There is wisdom as well as pride in his refusal, my love. But tell me what happened to make him insist on a charm for you. It was not general solicitude, I think."

As Reynata related the attack and rescue, she recalled Master Damon's threat to get even with his brother. The image of his hate-filled face loomed in the forefront of her mind. Lord Drake's peril would not begin when he joined the army and went off to war.

Finishing the tale, she said urgently, "Can you not protect him without his knowledge, Grandmama?"

"It would not be right when he has rejected my help, and for good reasons."

"But that was for when he is in the army, fighting with Lord Wellington in Spain. He is in danger already; I am sure he is. You cannot imagine how wicked Master Damon looked."

"I might manage something," her foster mother said doubtfully, "something which would end as soon as he crossed the sea. I should have to have some object of his to work with, though."

"I have his handkerchief." Reynata bit her lip as the tears the square of cambric had dried threatened to flow again. "Will that be enough?"

"Perhaps. I shall see what I can do."

"Now?"

"At once," said Grandmama with an understanding smile.

Taking the handkerchief, the wise-woman rose stiffly from the bench and hobbled towards the door to the back-room, where she performed her magic. Reynata watched her with a pang of dread. How old was she? For two decades she had kept the decrepitude of age at bay with her spells, stealing time to bring up her foster daughter. But Time always won in the end.

And Reynata was old enough to take care of herself. She just could not imagine life without Grandmama.

"Meh-eh-eh," called the nanny goat from the garden. *"Mih-ih-ihlk!"*

"Coming." Reynata took up the milking stool and pail and went out into the cool of the evening.

The early-morning air was chilly when Aldwin rode down St. Andrew's Hill from Wick Towers a fortnight later. He had donned his new scarlet dress tunic, liberally laced with gold, to bid his father and John farewell—Damon and Basil being conspicuously absent. The splendid jacket was not particularly warm, but he did not cover it with his greatcoat, for he knew the townsfolk were waiting in Middlecombe to wave good-bye. He owed them the best show he could put on.

Their cheers warmed him, as did the heat rising from Amiga as he cantered out of town. Soon the rising sun dispelled the nip of frost, glinting on dew-laden spiderwebs in the yellowing hedgerows. It was a beautiful day for riding, even though he was leaving his heart behind him.

The day after escorting Reynata home from her encounter with his brothers, he had set out for London. His father had been reluctant to let him go, but gave in to persuasion. The purchase of a commission in a Guards regiment had taken less time than Aldwin expected. Returning home to take leave of his family before he proceeded to Spain, he had not been able to resist calling at the cottage in the forest.

He had an excuse. "I just came by to make sure Damon and Basil have not troubled you," he said, not dismounting when he found Reynata outside, collecting eggs. How beautiful she was in her simple, midnight-blue woollen gown!

"I have not seen them, sir," she said in a low voice, curtsying, head bowed. "Not since . . . that day."

"Good." With an effort, he managed to infuse his voice with heartiness. "And Mistress Gresham has cast a spell to protect you?"

At that she looked up, brown eyes flashing. "She told you she would. Grandmama does not break her word. Moreover, she has begun to teach me to protect myself, and others. It is past time I started to learn the trade which will be mine."

"Yes, of course," Aldwin said, taken aback by her vehemence. A vision struck him of Reynata growing old, turning into the lonely witch of the woods, while he lay dead in a foreign land. "I leave in two days' time, for London and the Peninsula," he said gruffly. "Wish me well."

"I do." She came to him, gave him her hand, and he stooped in the saddle to kiss her slender, sun-browned fingers. For a moment she clung to his hand. "I shall be thinking of you," she had whispered.

Aldwin did not want to think of her. Surely in learning his new duties, meeting new people, seeing new places, at least in the heat of battle, he would be able to forget!

He came to a crossroads and turned Amiga's head towards Long Yeoford, where the lane met the Exeter turnpike.

The lane ran downhill, into a muddy bottom with thickets on either side. Trees met above the track, forming a gloomy tunnel. A gust of wind brought leaves swirling down, but the close-knit branches still shut out the sun's light and warmth. Aldwin shivered, partly from the chill, partly from a curious sense of foreboding.

No sense in stopping to put on his greatcoat when they would be out in the sun again shortly. And useless to try to hurry Amiga through this mire. She had slowed to a walk, her hooves glugging with each step as she plodded along.

"We'll soon be out of this, my beauty." Aldwin leaned forward to pat her neck.

Shot whistled overhead as a gun cracked in the bushes behind. Amiga plunged forward.

"Damn fool!" The voice came from the bushes ahead. Damon's voice? "I told you to—" Whatever he said next was cut off by a second volley, from his position.

He, too, missed his target. Before Aldwin could react, he felt the world turn inside out around him. Without volition, he sprang into the air, beating his way upwards, instinctively folding his arms to his sides to glide through a gap in the branches, then spreading them . . .

Not arms, wings. In terror, Aldwin fled.

Below, a vixen cowered beneath bracken the rusty colour of her coat. What had Grandmama done? Her spell had saved Lord Drake's life, but by changing him into a bird! His magnificent uniform had metamorphosed into feathers of scarlet and gold, flame-bright, lighting the gloom until he burst through the treetops and was gone.

"Tibb, follow him!" Reynata called softly.

"Miaow! I mean, *grawk."* The raven took wing.

As they spoke, Damon and Basil emerged from the underbrush. Double-barrelled shotguns in their hands, they stood in the mud, gawping up at the leafy canopy where Lord Drake had vanished.

"He's gone," said Basil. "How did he do that?"

"Your fault, fool," Damon snarled, glaring at his brother. "A perfect opportunity to get rid of him when no one would miss him, and you go and shoot first. And miss!"

"You missed, too," Basil pointed out sulkily. "But didn't you see, he turned into a bird!"

"That's what it looked like," Damon admitted, his tone cautious. "Perhaps the old witch had it in for him because he didn't come up to scratch with the girl. With any luck, he's gone for good. I'll be Earl of Androwick yet!"

"What about the horse? Suppose it comes home without him?"

They turned to stare at Amiga, who stood with hanging head, fetlock deep in the morass.

"Father wants her. We'll tell him we found her wandering. No, we'll say we went to meet Aldwin at Long Yeoford, to see him on his way, and he decided to hire a horse and send the mare back to Father. He'll be so pleased he won't question it. Quick, grab her before she decides to run off."

As they converged on Amiga, Reynata gave a short, sharp bark. The golden mare started, tossed her head with rolling eyes, heaved herself out of the mud, and sprang forward. Damon lunged for her bridle. Slipping, he landed facedown in the muck. Reynata grinned a vulpine grin, mouth open, teeth showing, tongue lolling, as Amiga gathered her haunches under her and sprang again, spraying Basil with filth.

Three more hare leaps took Amiga to solid ground. She galloped off, reins dangling, stirrups swinging wildly, saddlebags thumping against her flanks.

Sliding through the undergrowth alongside the lane, Reynata followed.

"I lost her," Reynata said somberly. "She galloped into Long Yeoford, and I could not follow. She might have turned east or west on the turnpike or gone south to Dartmoor or north to Exmoor. Oh, *where* is Tibb? I wish he'd come! What went wrong, Grandmama?"

The wise-woman shook her head in puzzlement. "I cannot be sure, my love. Protective charms are always chancy, as I told you. They tend to work in unexpected ways. Possibly his is trying to keep him from crossing the seas and going to war. And then, I have been so much occupied these many years with transformation spells, perhaps there was some contamination."

"But can you change him back?"

"I believe so, since it was my own magic changed him. Not at a distance, however."

"No." Reynata shuddered. "Suppose he was flying! Surely he will come here when he recovers from the shock, when Tibb explains to him what happened, and then you can undo the spell. But he will want Amiga when he is himself again, and I lost her."

"A horse of gold with mane and tail of silver cannot long remain hidden," Grandmama consoled her. "Ah, here is Tibb now."

The raven was tapping on a windowpane with his hefty beak. Reynata hurried to let him in.

"Tibb, where is he? Where did he go?"

"*Miawk*," said the bird tiredly. "He flew too high for a poor old cat-bird like me, and into the face of the east wind, to boot. I lost him."

Reynata covered her face with her hands. Tibb hopped up onto her shoulder. He rubbed his head against her neck with a sympathetic purr.

"As you said, my love, Lord Drake is bound to come here when he recovers from the shock," Grandmama reminded her. "He cannot fail to realize what happened to him is magic."

"He didn't know you were going to put a protective spell on him. What if he thinks you changed him on purpose, to punish him for . . . for letting my humble birth drive him away?"

The wise-woman drew herself up. "If he believes I used my skills for ill, he deserves to stay enchanted! However, I daresay I could bring myself to forgive him. He will certainly go home, and we shall hear of it."

"Home! Wick Towers is the last place he would go.

Damon and Basil saw him in bird form. They would recognize him, and catch him and kill him, long before we learnt he had come."

Five

Huddled among towering rocks, high on the moor, Aldwin tried to understand what had happened to him.

He was a bird, a large bird with gleaming red-gold feathers and a long tail; that much was indubitable. Only magic could have wrought the change—equally indubitable. But was it white magic or black which had deprived him of his humanity in saving him from highwaymen?

They must have been highwaymen. However resentful his brothers might be, they would not plot to murder him! He had surely imagined recognizing Damon's voice.

Yet doubt lingered. If it had been Damon and Basil who attacked him, it was not safe to go home, at least not openly. Nor did he dare entrust his fate to Gammer Gresham, not without his father present as witness. One way or another, she was more than likely responsible for his present plight.

Could this be her revenge for his breaking Reynata's heart? Perhaps the wise-woman had given him the benefit of the doubt, hoping love would conquer pride, until his departure for Spain left no room for hope.

How petty his pride of birth seemed now! Positively bird-witted, Aldwin thought wryly. He deserved to live out his life as a bird. If somehow he escaped that fate, he would throw himself at Reynata's feet and beg her to accept his hand.

"Reynata!" he keened.

The wind whistling between the rocks was the only reply.

By nightfall, Aldwin had decided he must go home, whatever the peril. Perhaps he could attract his father's or John's attention and explain what had happened to him.

Damon and Basil often rode down to the Green Dragon in Middlecombe in the evenings to drink and gamble and wench, but Aldwin did not dare count on their absence. They always returned to the Towers by midnight, as all the doors and gates were locked then. After that, no one would be about to spot Aldwin when he tapped with his beak on the earl's or his youngest brother's chamber window.

The night was clear, with a waxing moon, and the east wind had dropped. Aldwin flew down from the moor, sailing with long, slow wing beats over the wooded combes and sleeping villages, streaked with the silver ribbons of streams. The beauty of the scene penetrated his wretchedness. He was suddenly conscious of the joy of his instinctive balancing on the air currents. If he ever escaped from his present form, he would always be grateful for the experience.

As he swooped low over the King's Forest, an owl rose to meet him. "Who? Who?"

Aldwin opened his beak to answer. "Reynata!" he cried.

Damn, that was not what he had meant to say! Apparently he was not a talking bird. He had but a single call, like the wood pigeon's "coo" or the cuckoo's "cuckoo." Or the owl's "who," of course. It had already floated away on silent wings, satisfied with his response to its challenge.

This made things more difficult for Aldwin, though.

How was he going to make Father or John understand who he was?

His home rose before him. He alighted in a tree to think. The day's blustery wind had blown away most of the leaves, and there, on the bare branches, hung four plump fruits, golden in the moonlight.

Bird instincts took over. One of the fruits smelt ripe, and Aldwin had not eaten since an early breakfast. His beak tore into the succulent persimmon. Juice dripped as he devoured a quarter of his father's precious, cherished crop of golden apples of the Hesperides, leaving not a trace.

Guilty, but feeling much better, Aldwin made up his mind to try to rouse John first. Once inside his brother's chamber, he could find a book and peck at letters to spell out his message. There was always a danger that the earl might be too eager to capture him for the aviary to give him time to communicate. He was, after all, a splendid specimen, he reflected, preening his burnished chest feathers to clean off the last drop of sweet, sticky juice.

He flew up to John's tower window. The sill was too narrow for anything larger than a thrush to perch there. Swerving, he narrowly avoided bashing his head against the glass. To tap with his beak, he'd have to hover like a kestrel. He returned towards the window and willed his wings to perform the needed action.

His earthward plunge made it plain he was not a hovering bird. Pulling up within a yard of the ground, he wrenched a shoulder muscle painfully. Disconsolate, he fluttered down to rest on the flagged path between two flower beds.

By the time he recovered enough for the effort of launching himself from the ground, a faint light in the eastern sky heralded the dawn. He must not be found here at daybreak! He longed to fly to Reynata, but fear of her foster mother daunted him. His feathers were too bright for him to hide safely in the woods during the day. The rocky refuge on the moors called to him.

Thither he swiftly flew and passed the day in exhausted sleep. When he awoke at dusk, he had an idea.

He must find a twig long enough to scratch at John's windowpane as he flew by. John would look out through the window to see what made the noise, and when he saw the fiery bird flying back and forth, he would open wide to let him in.

Wouldn't he? Aldwin had to try.

As the moon rose, wider by a sliver than yesternight, he returned to Wick Towers. Hunger gnawed at him, so he went first to the persimmon tree to see if another had ripened.

Alighting, he saw beneath the tree a curious bundle from which issued loud snores. Cautiously, he hopped down from branch to branch until he made out Damon's face under a nightcap, mouth open, eyes shut. The sleeper was enveloped in several featherbeds; on the grass beside him lay an empty brandy bottle and his shotgun. A leaf drifted down and landed on his cheek, but he did not stir. What on earth?

No doubt the earl, discovering the loss of one of his golden apples, had set his son to watch for the thief. He would be furious when another fruit was missing in the morning and Damon had no explanation!

Damon deserved to suffer his anger. Though Aldwin had qualms about distressing his father, the pangs of hunger overwhelmed his conscience. Seeking out the one ripe, fragrant, luscious persimmon among the three remaining, he gorged.

Satisfied, he looked for a twig to carry out his plan. The gardeners had swept up all debris during the day, so in the end he broke a switch off the persimmon tree. With one end clutched in his beak, he flew back and forth past John's chamber window, dragging the other end against the glass on each pass. It made a squeaky, scratchy sound, but John did not wake.

At last Aldwin was forced to acknowledge defeat. If he went on trying any longer, he would not have the strength to fly back to the moors, and he didn't feel safe passing the day any closer to human habitation.

On the third night he made another attempt. This time, he found Basil fast asleep under the persimmon tree, slumped on a chair, wrapped in all manner of greatcoats and rugs. Beside the chair stood a jug from which rose the fumes of hot flannel—a mixture of beer and gin heated with spices and sugar which Basil favoured. A shotgun lay under the chair, where it could only be retrieved with great difficulty.

Aldwin ate the next to last persimmon, with mental apologies to his father. Then he left the walled garden and flew to the gravel pathway winding through the rhododendron shrubbery. He picked up two clawfuls of gravel.

Without the hitherto unappreciated aid of his feet, he rose into the air awkwardly, with much flapping of wings. Flying to John's window, he tried to fling the gravel at the glass.

His legs were not made for throwing. Two or three small stones landed on the sill, but the rest dropped to the ground below.

A second attempt was more successful. Most of the gravel hit the windowpanes with a satisfactory rattle. But though Aldwin flew back and forth before the window for several minutes, John did not appear. Nor did a third shower of stones rouse him. Either he slept extraordinarily soundly, or he was cowering under the bedclothes.

For which he could hardly be blamed, Aldwin admitted reluctantly. His brother's window was at least forty feet from the ground. Small wonder if John was afraid of anything capable of tapping on it!

Discouraged, Aldwin returned to the moors.

* * *

"Do you think the thief the earl makes such a fuss about is Lord Drake, Grandmama?" Reynata kneaded the dough vigorously, putting into it all her frustrated energy. She was making enough bread to last for several days, for tonight or tomorrow she would become a fox, and the old woman no longer had the strength for kneading. "It's odd that he has come two nights in a row but only taken one fruit each time. Why doesn't Lord Androwick pick the rest?"

"The golden apples are very astringent until they are completely ripe. A bird smells when fruit is ripe before it is apparent to a human."

"Grmmm," agreed Tibb, whose great black beak was stuck together by a bit of dough he had pinched.

"So the thief is probably a bird," Reynata concluded, "and very likely—"

"Hush!" Grandmama held up her hand. Someone knocked on the door. "Come in, John," she called.

The youth entered and bade them good day with an awkward bow. John Drake was as handsome as his brother Damon, his looks marred only by a slightly vacuous air. Though by no means as thick as two planks, he was not—his eldest brother had been known to say tolerantly—the brightest star in the firmament.

"I need a charm, ma'am, if you please," he blurted out. "Something's been trying to get in at my bedchamber window in the middle of the night."

Reynata and her foster mother exchanged a glance. Had Lord Drake tried to attract John's attention?

"Take a bunch of rowan berries from the tree by the door," advised Mistress Gresham. "Hang it above the window and it will ward off evil."

"Will it work in my pocket? I'm to stand guard in the garden tonight," John informed her, proud but anxious.

"Did you hear, a thief's been stealing Father's golden apples? Damon said he was invisible, and Basil swears he didn't come last night, but a branch was broken, and now there's only one fruit left. *I* think they just fell asleep. Father's going to let me watch tonight. *I* shan't fall asleep. I'll stand up all night."

"You will not shoot the thief, will you?" Reynata asked fearfully.

"Oh no, I don't want to hurt him, just catch him. They all think I can't, but I'll show them. So, will the rowan berries work in my pocket, ma'am?"

"Yes, but do not leave them there longer than need be. They will last better hanging up."

"Thank you, ma'am." Blushing, the lad stammered, "Wh-what do I owe you?"

"Half a crown." She would have charged a poor man sixpence for the same charm, which could be picked free in any copse. As she had explained to Reynata, people had no trust in a free charm, and belief was an important part of magic. "Half a crown and a report tomorrow on what occurs tonight," she amended.

Business concluded, Reynata offered a cup of tea. Since her hands were covered in dough, John obligingly lifted the kettle from the hearth and poured it over the herbs in the pot. He even held a cup of the brew to Reynata's lips so that she could drink. Though the fragrant tea was obviously not to his taste, he politely swallowed it down.

"A good lad," Grandmama observed when he had departed.

"You did not want him to know the thief is his brother?" Reynata asked, shaping loaves.

"The fewer the better. He might let it slip to the others. Besides, we cannot be sure."

"No, but I shall watch in the gardens tonight. I cannot

see into the walled garden, though. You must come with me, Tibb."

"*Grawk,*" said the raven grumpily, having at last cleaned his beak. "Smells good but sticks like a burr. Fresh mouse flesh never does that. *Miaow!*"

"Listen, Tibb! You will have to persuade John to bring Lord Drake here instead of taking him into the house, where he would be in dreadful danger from Damon and Basil."

"If it is Lord Drake," Grandmama reminded her, "and if John catches him."

"I don't know whether to hope it is and he does, or not," Reynata said wretchedly. "If not, we may never find him."

John was determined to prove he was not the fool everyone supposed him. He dined lightly, taking no wine, and followed the meal with several cups of black coffee, though he liked the drink no better than Gammer Gresham's herb tea. Putting on warm clothes in dark colours, he went out to the walled garden.

The earl had decided against having his servants patrol the area. He wanted to catch the thief, and a troop of men were more likely to scare him off. So the head gardener gave John the key to the door in the wall. John went in and locked the door behind him.

It was eerie out there by himself in the dark. He wished for a lantern, but of course that would warn the thief of his presence. Thank heaven it was another clear night, for the only light came from the stars. The flagstone paths were barely visible, and tall plants loomed all around. John felt in his pocket—yes, he had remembered the rowan berries. At least black magic could not touch him.

He walked around the paths, then decided that however

softly he placed his feet, he made too much noise. Going over to the persimmon tree, he stood under it, leaning against the trunk.

The moon rose, all but full. Instantly the garden became a place of enchantment, painted silver and black by the pale light. The broken glass on the surrounding wall glittered. Above John, in the nearly leafless tree, the sole remaining fruit gleamed like the golden apple Father believed it to be.

John padded around the tree to stand in the moon-shadow. The wait was dull and chilly, but he was patient, moving as the shadow moved.

After a while, he heard the distant sounds of Damon and Basil returning, merry, from the Green Dragon. All the gates and doors and windows would be locked now. Everyone went to bed. Alone, John stood waiting for the mysterious thief.

And the thief came. Soaring over the wall, its lustrous feathers shimmering like flame in the moonlight, the bird flew straight to the persimmon tree and alighted on a high branch,

John held his breath as the magnificent marauder turned its crested head this way and that, crystal eyes alert for danger. Then it hopped down through the boughs towards the last golden apple. It stopped, amber beak stretching towards the fruit.

Its long tail dangled almost within John's reach. He leapt from the shadows and grabbed.

Startled, the bird sprang up, its great wings beating the air. It wrenched its tail from John's grasp and fled with a cry of alarm, speeding into the night until even the radiance of its moonlit feathers disappeared from his sight.

But it left a feather in his hand.

Six

With a despairing cry—"Reynata!"—the resplendent bird soared over the wall, flying high, fleeing eastward.

Lord Drake had called her name! Yet he could not have guessed Reynata was near, and if his bird vision had seen her as he arrived, he would not have recognized her in the vixen crouched outside the garden with ears pricked. She had tried to change back, hoping he might come to her, but the moon was near full, and she was caught in her fox form.

At least his cry roused Tibb. The raven had fallen asleep, perched in a tree with a view over the wall. He had seen nothing of what occurred, but waking he recalled his duty. A black shadow rose and winged after the fiery bird.

Reynata heard the click of a key turning in a lock. John was coming out of the garden, but in her present shape she dared not reveal herself to ask him what had happened. Sadly she turned homeward.

Fallen leaves crackled underfoot as she raced through the forest. A west wind arose, tossing the branches and making moon-shadows shift and waver, but to vulpine senses the way was plain. So was the presence of the big dog fox when she met him face-to-face. She stopped.

"Good even, little sister."

"Good even, brother."

"You run noisily," he said with reproach, "as though

all the hounds of hell were on your trail. Take care!
Hounds are rarely seen hereabouts, as you told me, but
poachers are no observers of the proprieties and sometimes shoot at foxes. Besides, you scare our prey. Go in
silence."

"I'm sorry," Reynata apologized. "Did you find the
vixen I told you about?"

"Yes, and I thank you. Windflower and I will mate
when the time is right. My name is Cobnut, by the way.
Yours is Reynata, I believe?" He sniffed at her in the
vulpine equivalent of "How do you do?"

The moonlight was bright enough for Reynata to see
the effort he made not to wrinkle his nose at her human
scent. Fortunately, she had no equivalent distaste for the
fox scent.

She went on, making an effort to move quietly.

When she reached the cottage, unable to open the door
and unwilling to disturb the old woman, Reynata curled
up outside. She had no heart for roving the woods and
fields as she usually did at this phase of the moon.
Though she was a nocturnal animal, she slept, tired out
after a busy day and the hopes and fears of the past few
hours.

In the morning, when Grandmama called her in, she
was full of energy and ready to set about rescuing Lord
Drake. Unfortunately, seeing him had not suggested any
useful course of action. Tibb had not yet returned. Until
he brought news of the enchanted bird's whereabouts,
Reynata was stymied.

There was still no sign of Tibb by mid afternoon, but
John Drake turned up, though it had started to rain. Again
the wise-woman was aware of his approach before he
knocked, giving Reynata time to hide in the small back-
room. From there she could hear everything that passed
in the main room, and no one ever ventured into the
chamber where Gammer Gresham kept her spells.

"Good day, ma'am!" John sounded remarkably cheerful. "I've come to tell you all about it. The thief was a magic bird, a firebird, that lit up the night with its glitter and glow. I didn't manage to capture it when I jumped out of the shadows, but I pulled a feather from its tail."

No wonder Lord Drake had flown off so swiftly. Taken by surprise, he could not have seen who attacked him, and he must have feared it was Damon or Basil. Would he ever risk another visit to his home?

"Did you bring it with you?" Mistress Gresham asked eagerly. Reynata guessed she might hope to be able to disenchant Lord Drake with the aid of his feather.

"Lord, no! Father's locked it in the cabinet with his greatest treasures. He wouldn't part with it for ten thousand guineas. It's the most beautiful thing you ever saw, long and curling and gleaming like red gold but soft as silk. You should have seen Father's face when I gave it to him, ma'am. And Damon and Basil this morning, green with envy because Father's so pleased with me."

Reynata heard the smile in Grandmama's voice. "You have certainly taken them down a peg or two."

"Well, yes," John said disconsolately, "but it would have been better if I'd caught the bird. Now Father has the feather, he's simply wild to have the firebird for his aviary. He said he'd give Winworthy Manor—it's not entailed—to Damon or Basil, whichever brought him the firebird, but he won't let me go! He doesn't think I'm old enough or have enough sense. It's not fair!"

"I daresay he does not care to be left alone, without any of his sons," the wise-woman soothed him.

"He's given them two hundred pounds each for expenses. I wish Aldwin had not gone for a soldier. I'd still be the one left at home, I expect, but I wouldn't mind him winning. If Damon catches the firebird and gets to be rich, he'll be unbearable. He's leaving in the morning to start the search."

"And Basil?"

"Damon told him to wait a day before he sets out," John said with scorn, "and he always does what Damon tells him. They're both going to go towards London. They say, because I saw the firebird fly off to the east, but *I* think it's because they've both wanted to go to London this age, only Father wouldn't let them."

"Very likely, my dear." A fey note entered the wise-woman's voice, telling Reynata her foster mother had had one of her occasional flashes of premonition. "I am inclined to believe you should not give up your desire to take part in the search. Keep pressing the earl for permission to go and in the end he will relent."

"Will he? I'll keep asking, then, ma'am. Where is Reynata—Miss Gresham? I wanted to tell her about the firebird. Its cry sounded a bit like her name."

"Birdcalls often sound like words. Reynata is running an errand."

"Oh, maybe I'll meet her going back through the woods. Thank you for the rowan charm, ma'am. If I hadn't had it in my pocket, the firebird might have burnt my fingers!"

John went off, and Reynata emerged from the backroom.

"Poor Lord Drake, losing a tail feather. I hope it did not hurt him badly. Grandmama, is John going to find him?"

"Not without your help, my love."

"Of course I will help!" Reynata cried. "What must I do?"

"I shall explain, but I warn you that the end is unclear. You will find many difficulties along the way, and I cannot be certain all will be overcome. Nor am I sure that if the firebird stood before me at this minute, I could change it back into Lord Drake."

"We can but try," said Reynata soberly. "Tell me what I— Oh, here is Tibb at last!"

Her foster mother opened the window, and Tibb sidled in, keeping one black, beady eye on Reynata. He had not been a raven long enough to be quite convinced she would not absentmindedly snap him up when in her fox form.

"Where did he go?" she demanded of the weary, bedraggled bird. "Did you manage to keep him in sight?"

"Long enough to tell which way he was heading," Tibb said sourly. "Straight into the rising sun—if it hadn't been the middle of the night—so I followed as best I could. I nearly caught up with him over Exmoor, but he outpaced me again."

"You lost him?"

"Wait a bit, wait a bit, *grawk!* He was flying up from the ground when I spotted him."

Aldwin had landed in his usual place among the rocks, but hunger would not let him rest. He flew on as swiftly as his tiring wings would carry him, until the moors were behind him. As the sun rose, he came to the orchards of Somerset. No golden apples grew here in the Vale of Taunton Deane, but from the cider apples liquid gold was pressed. Though most of the orchards had been picked bare, at last Aldwin passed over one where the ripe apples still hung. Their sweet savour rose with the morning mists.

Without a second thought, he dived, then spread his wings to slow as his feet stretched out to grip a laden bough. Too late he saw the net. His claws were already entangled.

With desperate strength he beat the air. The net billowed, but the mesh held him fast. Three rough-clothed men ran up to surround the tree. Despite the awe in their faces, the shotguns were steady in their hands.

"They shot him?" Reynata asked, aghast.

"Niaow! Had more sense than that. You should have seen him with the morning sun shining on that plumage! Gaudy, some might call it," Tibb remarked, preening his sober black feathers, "but I must say it was a sight to be seen. They bundled him up in the net and carried him off."

"Did you follow?"

"Frankly, I was fagged out. I went to roost in a nearby elm and had a chat with a local rook. Junior branch of the family to which I now belong, don't you know, and properly respectful, I must say. Brought me some grain and a dead mouse—wouldn't have touched 'em as a cat," he mused, "but I've quite a taste for seeds and carrion these days."

"I shall turn you back into a cat if you don't come to the point, Tibb," Gammer Gresham threatened.

"Miaow! Cousin Rook told me how his-feather-brained-lordship plunged in without so much as glancing around for danger. Seems those apples were something special, Cherry Normans left on the trees to reach the peak of sweetness before making into cider for the baronet's own table."

"What baronet?" Reynata cried. "Was Lord Drake taken to him?"

"Reckon so. Sir Rex Dolmat's the name."

"Then we can find him. Bless you, Tibb!"

But the raven did not hear. His tale told, he had tucked his head under his wing and was already fast asleep.

The next morning, as Grandmama instructed, Reynata waited in the ruins of an abandoned cottage at the edge of a copse just before the lane from Middlecombe reached Long Yeoford. Still in fox form, she sat on her haunches with her black-tipped ears pricked forward, listening for hoofbeats.

What Grandmama had told her to do seemed odd. However, the wise-woman was certain it was necessary, though there was no guarantee of success. She would not have insisted if she were not quite sure, for it involved some danger for Reynata. The spell protecting her only worked when she was human.

She had asked whether they could not tell Lord Androwick what had happened to his eldest son. The earl would surely be willing to ransom his heir. Grandmama thought it too risky. In the first place, she might be blamed for his metamorphosis. And then, the only way to persuade his lordship to keep the news from Damon and Basil would be to inform him of his younger sons' attempt on the life of their brother, which he would surely disbelieve. If those two found out Lord Drake's whereabouts, he would once again be in deadly danger.

Reynata's wait was lengthy, for Damon Drake was a slugabed to whom a morning departure meant shortly before noon. At last Tibb flew up to report his approach. Then she saw him, astride a grey gelding with a fat saddlebag slung on either side. His shotgun he held across the saddlebow before him.

As soon as he caught sight of Reynata, he raised the gun, cocked it, and took aim.

The dastard would shoot a fox? She had not thought him so utterly lacking in gentlemanly instincts as to commit such an appalling impropriety! He might as well be one of the common poachers Cobnut had warned her against.

"Don't shoot me!" she cried.

He looked a little taken aback when she addressed him

in the King's English, but he said truculently, "Why the devil not?"

"Because I can give you good advice."

"How can a paltry beast give good advice?" he sneered, and raised the gun again.

"Wait! I know you seek the firebird." That gave him pause. "This evening you will come to the town of Crediton. As you enter the town, you will see two inns opposite each other. One, the Pair o' Dice, is a smart, busy posting house, but you should go to the other, the Pheasant, though it is a quiet, rather shabby place."

"Pair o' Dice? Paradise! And for once I have a decent stake in my pocket," said Damon, and fired his gun.

Tibb squawked an alarm just before Damon squeezed the trigger. Reynata skipped back among the trees barely in time to escape the hail of shot. As Damon rode on, whistling, followed by Tibb, she ran home.

"You did not warn me that he would shoot at me, Grandmama!"

"I did not foresee it, my love. I have never sought to develop what foresight I have, and it is erratic, as you know. Who would guess he was blackguard enough to shoot a fox!"

"You were right about the rest, though. He seemed determined to ignore the advice I gave him."

"He is contrary by nature," said the wise-woman with a nod of satisfaction, "and a gambler to boot. With any luck, the two hundred pounds the earl gave him will keep him busy a long time, so Aldwin will be safe from him."

"And I am to do the same by Basil tomorrow?"

"Yes, child. Basil is less stubbornly perverse, but he will doubtless choose to join his brother."

Tibb returned to report Damon safely ensconced in the Pair o' Dice, already settled at a card table with the gamesters who frequented the inn.

On the next day, all fell out as Mistress Gresham predicted. Basil pointed his gun in a rather halfhearted fashion at Reynata. She advised him to stay at the Pheasant Inn. When he dithered, she told him Damon had stopped at the Pair o' Dice and was likely still there, which persuaded him to do likewise.

She did not expect him to shoot at her, since his brother was not there to egg him on, so she was taken by surprise when he fired. Luckily, his aim was shockingly bad.

However, the second narrow escape dispelled the feeling of safety she had always felt in fox form. Now she understood what Lord Drake had meant when he refused a protective spell on the grounds that he might come to depend upon it too much. How right he was! After all, the spell she had begged Grandmama to put on him was the cause of his present predicament.

In the course of the next fortnight, thrice young John rode through the woods to tell the wise-woman his father would not let him go after his brothers. Thrice she urged him to keep trying. A few days later, he came again, with a joyous face.

"Just as you said, ma'am, Father has relented!"

"You underestimated your persuasiveness," Reynata told him with a smile.

"Oh, no," said the youth, blushing, "he just grew tired of me pestering him. And he badly wants the firebird. He takes the feather out every day to look at it."

"He has not heard from your brothers?" asked Mistress Gresham.

"Not a word, so I'm to hunt for them, too, as well as the bird. Surely I'll find one of the three! Not that I want to find Damon or Basil. I'd much rather find the firebird."

"When do you leave?"

"First thing tomorrow morning. Wish me luck."

They did so gladly, and Reynata gave him a sprig of

lucky white heather she had found on the moors. He stuck it in his lapel and went off happy and excited.

"You still don't want him to know the firebird is his brother?" Reynata asked.

"Best not. It cannot be told without revealing how Damon and Basil attempted to murder Aldwin. Besides distressing John—if he believes it—it might perhaps make him take unnecessary risks to rescue Aldwin."

"Will John come to harm?"

"Not if he does what you tell him," said the wise-woman austerely. "He is willing but foolish. You must watch over him and counsel him. You will be too far from home to run to me for advice. Listen carefully, now, for there are any number of pitfalls you may have to extricate him from if Aldwin is to be saved."

"I'll do anything!" Reynata said with fervour.

Seven

A heavy hoarfrost sparkled in the early sun when Reynata once more took up her post in the ruined cottage near Long Yeoford. Her blood was warm from running, but she curled her white-tipped tail around her black feet, glad to be clad in thick russet fur. A human would have frozen, sitting there.

John did not keep her waiting. He sang as he rode along the lane on his sturdy brown mare. Reynata wondered what had become of Lord Drake's golden mare, Amiga. How sad he would be to find her missing when he took his rightful shape again—if Grandmama managed to change him back, if John and Reynata succeeded in rescuing him.

Too many ifs. She felt like howling.

The sprig of white heather was pinned to John's lapel, Reynata noticed. Then she caught sight of a shotgun slung across in front of him. Instinct took over, and she jumped up to flee.

"Don't be afraid, little fox!" he called, drawing rein. "I shan't hurt you. The gun is to shoot a rabbit for my supper, for my father is so certain I shall be cheated, he has given me very little money."

The earl might well be right, for what could be more addlepated than to explain himself to a fox? However, this time the fox responded.

"In return for your kindness, I shall give you good

advice," Reynata said, and told him about the inns at Crediton. "Spend the night at the Pheasant, and don't go near the other."

John laughed. "With what I have in my purse, any respectable inn may be too dear for me. Forty pounds will be stretched thin if I need to go to London. But I shall try the Pheasant, since you recommend it."

"You will not be sorry. " All Reynata wanted was to keep him out of the Pair o' Dice. "And don't go on to Exeter in the morning," she added. "Leave Crediton by the Tiverton road."

"Why not? All roads lead to London, and I don't know where my brothers went or where the firebird is." He tipped his hat to her and rode on.

Reynata and Tibb followed. Tibb kept John in sight, flapping from tree to tree along the way. Reynata had to make her way through fields and woods, by hill and dale, detouring around villages. She was tired by the time she reached the outskirts of Crediton.

Though the days were growing shorter, John had set out early, so it was still light. Reynata did not dare enter the town until dusk. She found a deserted badger's set dug into the rich red soil and slept for a while. Then, like a ruddy shadow in the rosy afterglow of sunset, she slipped through the back streets to the churchyard, where she had arranged to meet Tibb.

Of course, the rooks saw her. They flew up with a great racket from their roosts in the elms round about and circled, cawing. No human heeded them. Rooks were always making a fuss about something.

The great red sandstone church was much the same colour as Reynata's coat, and there were plenty of buttresses to lurk behind, as well as the tombstones. Blending into the background as dusk darkened, she vanished from the rooks' memory, and they settled down at last.

She waited anxiously, afraid John might have decided to go farther while daylight lasted.

"Grawk?" A black shadow circled the church. *"Grawk?"*

Reynata barked once. A sleepy rook roused and called an alarm, but the others disregarded it. Tibb swooped down to land on the head of a stone angel on a nearby tombstone.

"No angel could possibly fly with wings like these here," he said in disgust as Reynata joined him. "Well, our boy stopped at the Pheasant—stupid birds, pheasants, waiting around to get shot!—as instructed. Never so much as glanced at the Pair o' Dice. T'others are still there, by the way, win a little, lose a little."

"Good. Did John get a room at a price he could afford?"

"Miaow, the cat I gossiped with told me the landlady fell in love with his pretty face and gentlemanly ways and his tales of firebirds and talking foxes, though she didn't believe a word."

"Oh, dear, I should have told him to keep quiet."

"Don't fret; these townsfolk are all cynics. She thought him a traveling player. He asked if she'd cook a rabbit for him if he brought one, and she said he could have a free bed if he brought two, so he went out and bagged a couple on the common."

"I hope she doesn't mean to . . . to corrupt his morals," Reynata exclaimed.

"Shouldn't think so," Tibb reassured her. "She's as old as the mistress if she's a day. And speaking of day, tomorrow's going to be another tiring one. I'm going to roost."

"In the morning, I'll wait for you on the Tiverton road, just outside town. If he goes off towards Exeter, come and tell me."

"Never a moment's rest," grumbled Tibb, and went to join the rooks.

Reynata had no money for lodging, so she stayed in fox form and spent the night curled up in the badger's set. Her sleep was troubled, haunted by dreams of her beloved shut up in a cage, forlornly calling her name. She *had* to save him.

Before dawn she was stationed near the lane to Tiverton. Though quieter than the Exeter road, even so early it was busier than the lane where she had awaited the Drake brothers before. From where she lay hidden in a patch of bracken, she watched three farm carts and a herd of cattle pass by.

At last she heard the sound of hooves with no accompanying creaking of wheels. A moment later, Tibb *grawked* from the hedge opposite. Reynata emerged to trot along beside John's horse.

"Good day to you, sir."

"Well met, little fox! You were right, I did very well at the Pheasant." John grinned. "What good advice have you for me today?"

"I know where to find that which you seek." She prayed it was true, that Sir Rex still held Lord Drake captive.

"The firebird?" John cried, astonished. "Tell me, where is it?"

"Let us journey together, and I shall show you."

"I'll be glad of your company," said the young man, so they traveled on together by hill and dale.

Without giving away that she knew him, Reynata turned the conversation to Lord Drake. John told her the earl had not wanted to let his eldest son go off to war. Aldwin was needed at home, to help run the estate. He ought to be setting up his nursery to provide the next generation, not gallivanting around in a fancy uniform.

"Aldwin said Lord Wellington needs soldiers to stop

Boney taking over all of Europe so that he's invincible next time he decides to invade England. Father agreed, but he thought it was up to Damon and Basil, as younger sons, to volunteer. Of course, they both refused. See them risking their precious skins!"

"They are cowards?" Reynata asked.

"Not when it comes to bullying those weaker than they are. Facing the Frenchies' bullets is another matter. I'd go, but Father says I'm too young and ignorant, as though half the soldiers in the army aren't younger than I!" John said indignantly. "Anyway, Aldwin insisted, and Father gave way in the end. The awful thing is, if he's killed in battle, Damon will be the next earl."

Contemplating this dreadful prospect, they went on in silence for a while.

"I don't know why Aldwin suddenly decided to go a-soldiering," John said with a sigh. "He never talked of it before."

Reynata's heart sank. She held on to a hope that his departure was a long-considered plan just coming to fruition. Now she was forced to believe he had seen the love in her eyes and fled rather than having to hurt her with a blunt rejection. It was her fault he was in desperate straits.

She *must* rescue him.

Whenever they came across other travelers, Reynata dodged out of sight behind the nearest hedge or wall, and she gave villages a wide berth. Thus she covered considerably more ground than her companion. By the time she had made a wide circle around Tiverton, which included swimming across the River Exe, she was growing weary.

Finding shelter in a hazel thicket close to the Taunton road, she lay down to rest her tired limbs. Tibb found her there.

"He's on his way," the raven croaked. "Stopped for a bite to eat in the town."

Reynata was hungry, ravenous in fact. She did not like to hunt and kill, let alone to eat raw meat. Luckily, foxes were omnivores, so even on her fox days she ate well at home. Since setting out on this journey, she had had nothing but hips and haws from the hedges and the odd tart, shrivelled crabapple.

Remembering Cobnut, the dog fox, she looked about for nuts. Squirrels had stripped most of them from the hazels where she hid, but a few lay on the ground among the yellow leaves. Their red-brown shells were just the colour of Cobnut's fur. She cracked them with her teeth and crunched the meats in between talking to Tibb.

"When we get closer to the Vale of Taunton Deane, you will have to fly ahead," she said. "You know where Sir Rex's land lies. Find out exactly where his house is. From on high, you can spy out the way there and come down to tell us which roads to take."

"More hard work, *grawk!* It doesn't matter if John hears me?"

"Grandmama did not warn against it, but it might be useful to keep you up my sleeve—if I had one." Ruefully, she raised a paw. "I'm not sure John's capable of holding his tongue. Still, talking ravens are commoner than talking foxes."

"Niaow, who are you calling common?" Tibb protested.

Reynata laughed at the teasing gleam in his beady eye. "You know what I mean. No one will wonder if John babbles about you. Besides, he has already met you, at home. Oh, but . . ." She hesitated as a dismaying notion struck her: Tibb's link with Grandmama might make John wonder about a possible link between Grandmama and the talking fox—and between the fox and Reynata. He was not very clever, but he just might guess that they were identical.

"No, Tibb, on second thoughts," she said hastily, "it doesn't matter if he sees you, but don't let him hear you talk. Here he comes now."

John rode up with a cheerful greeting. "Good morning, friend fox! I've brought you some bread and cheese," he continued. "You can't have had time to hunt. I should have saved some rabbit last night, but I didn't think of it, and I didn't like to buy a chicken, not knowing how long my money has to last. Do foxes eat bread and cheese?"

"This fox does," said Reynata gratefully. She wolfed it down.

They journeyed on, by hill and dale. The road was busy, for a new canal was under construction nearby. The traffic had the advantage that it gave Reynata an excuse to seek concealment frequently. Hidden by hedges, she could consult Tibb without John's knowledge.

Directed by the raven, they came at dusk to the gates in the high wall surrounding Sir Rex Dolmat's manor house.

The gates stood hospitably open. Gossiping with the stable cat, Tibb had discovered that Sir Rex had invited his neighbours to dine and to view the wonderful golden bird his orchard guards had caught.

The firebird was kept in a gilded cage in a conservatory at the back of the house. Reynata's heart bled at the thought of Aldwin Drake caged and exhibited like a wild beast.

"Wait until the guests have finished marvelling and gone to dinner," she told John. "Later, after they all leave and the household retires to bed, the conservatory's outside door will certainly be locked. Earlier in the evening, with luck you may find it unlocked. Let the bird out of the cage and leave the cage there."

John agreed, not questioning her knowledge or her advice. After all, he had set out from home with no notion of where to search, and she had led him to the firebird.

Aldwin knew from the dozens of wax candles lighting the conservatory, their glare doubled by their reflection in the glass wall, that he was to be displayed this evening. He shuddered at the prospect of another humiliating session. It was bad enough being confined, with no prospect of release but death; worse being so cramped he could not even stretch his wings; but the horrible indignity of being gaped at like a fairground freak was worst of all.

Perhaps he deserved to be transformed for hurting Reynata, but not this, not this!

The first time it happened, he wanted to cower on the floor of the cage, making himself as small as possible. Pride forbade such abject cringing. Instead, he drew himself up on the perch and glared fiercely, like a mewed falcon he had once seen.

Here they came now, trouping past the orange trees, grapevines, and pineapple plants. Sir Rex led the way, a small man with a red, choleric countenance at present beaming as he showed off his prize.

Aldwin endured.

"Magnificent, isn't it?" the baronet said, chuckling at the oohs and aahs of his guests. "Look at that shine, like real gold. Had a thief after it the other day. We caught the fellow by sheer chance. There's a little surprise waiting for the next who tries."

At last they all went away. No one came to snuff the candles, so Aldwin could not lose himself in sleep. His thoughts turned, as they did so often these endless days, to Reynata.

How could he have brought himself to leave her? Now, when it was too late, he knew all he wanted from life was Reynata at his side, her children at his knee. What an arrogant addlepate he had been to consider for a moment that her obscure birth was more important than the reality of the woman he had held so briefly in his arms!

Father would cut up rough when he presented the wise-woman's foster child as his bride, but he'd come round, relieved to have his heir safe at home. Aldwin's insistence on going off to war had distressed and angered the earl. In the end, surely he must welcome the daughter-in-law responsible for his eldest son's return—if Aldwin ever returned.

For a moment he had lost sight of the present. What brought him back was a sound, the faint click of a latch, the fainter squeak of hinges, barely audible to his sharp bird senses.

Footsteps followed, someone clumsily attempting to tiptoe in boots. And there was the blurred reflection in the glass, a man moving stealthily between the plants. Another would-be thief! Aldwin was not sure he wanted to be stolen. He might get a chance to escape. On the other hand, it could materially worsen his prospects, for at least he was warm, dry, and well fed here.

Approaching the corner where the cage hung, the thief came into sight. Great heavens, it was John!

Aldwin suddenly recalled Sir Rex's precautions against theft. Desperate to warn his brother, he opened his beak, but all that emerged was a whispered "Reynata!"

John contemplated him with satisfaction, which changed to a frown of doubt.

"Friend fox said to take the firebird out and leave the cage," he muttered to himself. Aldwin's hopes flared. "But I'm not such a lobcock. It's a very fine cage, and how am I to carry the bird without it? I daresay it's heavy, but I'm no weakling."

Not without difficulty, he lifted the cage from its hook.

At once bells began to peal, rung by well-concealed cords attached to the back of the cage.

John stood frozen as half a dozen hefty footmen rushed in.

Eight

After a wakeful night locked in a cold, damp back scullery, John was grateful for the crust of bread and mug of ale he was given for breakfast. He had just finished the last crumb and drop when a beadle came to fetch him before Sir Rex.

The baronet strutted up and down the room like an angry turkey-cock. "I am the local magistrate," he announced, "and I've a good mind to transport you. Who are you, who come creeping into my very house to steal my property from under my nose?"

John hung his head. Somehow he had not thought of it as thievery. "I'm John Drake," he said, mortified, "youngest son of the Earl of Androwick. The firebird came and ate the golden apples from my father's most precious tree and broke the branches, too. Father sent me to find it. He wants it for his aviary."

"The Earl of Androwick, eh?" Sir Rex gave him a hard look, then softened. "Sit down, sit down, my boy. Why did you come as a thief in the night? If you had asked me for the bird, I'd have been glad to give it to you for your noble father's famous collection. Now, word of your breaking and entering is bound to get about. What will the world say of the *Honourable* John Drake?"

Crestfallen and thoroughly ashamed, John was silent.

"However," the magistrate continued, "I just may be

able to keep the business quiet. There's something you can do for me in return, if you will."

"Anything!" said John eagerly.

"Lord Afron has a golden mare in his stables, with a silver mane and tail, the most beautiful horse in the world, that runs like the wind. He's too heavy to ride it. It's wasted on him, but I would appreciate it properly, make good use of it. I offered two thousand guineas, yet he refuses to sell it to me! Bring me Lord Afron's golden horse and I'll make sure none of my people mentions the burglar's name. In fact, I'll even give you the firebird to take to Lord Androwick. It's good for nothing but to look at, after all."

"I'll do my best, sir, I promise."

"You'd better," snapped Sir Rex, "for if you fail, I'll write about your misdeeds to all the newspapers."

Crouched under a hawthorn on the other side of the lane, Reynata stared at the manor house at the end of the avenue beyond the gates. She had lurked right by the gates as long as darkness lasted, waiting in vain for John to return with his enchanted brother. The guests had left, the gates were closed and locked, and daybreak came, bringing no sign of youth or firebird.

John had failed. He must be a prisoner somewhere in the house, and Lord Drake was still a captive.

If only Reynata had gone herself to free him! But she would have had to change back to human form, and she could not have concealed it from John.

What was she to do next?

Tibb came winging swiftly above the carriage drive, squawking excitedly. *"Miawk! Griaow!* He's coming, he's coming!"

"Lord Drake?" Reynata demanded, springing to her feet. "John and Lord Drake?"

The raven sadly shook his head. *"Niaow,* just Master John. And he doesn't look happy."

She saw him coming then, a drooping figure plodding down the drive. At his side marched a stout man in the dress of a beadle. Reynata slid back among the trees to where John had left his horse tied.

Gate hinges creaked. "His Honour's allus as good as his word," said the beadle sternly, "so don't you go making a mull of it, or your name'll be mud from here to kingdom come."

A moment later John appeared, dishevelled and bristle-chinned, his neckcloth obviously tied without the aid of a mirror. When he saw Reynata, he looked ready to cry.

"You waited for me! You were right; if I hadn't tried to bring the cage, too, we'd have been clean away. How did you know it would set off alarm bells?"

It was not the moment to explain that she had merely wished to give Lord Drake his freedom as soon as possible. If John found out the firebird was his brother, it would not help and could only make him feel much worse about his failure. "What happened?" Reynata asked.

He told her. When he came to describe the steed coveted by Sir Rex, she pricked up her ears.

"A golden mare with silver mane and tail?" she exclaimed. "She can only be your brother's!"

"Aldwin took Amiga to Spain with him," John objected.

"Amiga never left England," Reynata said emphatically. "Believe me. Have I not proved right so far?"

"Y-yes, but . . ."

"Reach the mare and you may easily discover whether she is Amiga. You know how she answers to her name?"

"She nods, twice." John nodded in demonstration and agreement. "Yes, that's it!"

"You know where to find her?" Reynata asked.

"Lord Afron has her. They gave me directions to his

house." He frowned. "How do you suppose the baron came by her? Aldwin would *never* have sold her."

"There's no knowing." She sniffed the air. "It will rain before dark. Come, let us be on our way. The sooner we go, the sooner Sir Rex will deliver the firebird."

They set off again, leaving the vale and crossing the Black Down Hills towards Lord Afron's estate.

Reynata seized her first chance to send Tibb to reconnoiter. Returning, he described the viscount's stables. He had seen the golden horse and was certain she was Amiga, though he had no opportunity to utter her name to her.

With only fifteen miles to go, by hill and dale, they arrived in mid afternoon. A steady drizzle increased John's respect for Reynata's omniscience, but left him bedraggled and muddy.

"I don't want to try another burglary," he said, regarding with dismay the closed gates in the high wall surrounding Lord Afron's mansion.

"It's your brother's horse," Reynata argued, "and as you said, he would never have sold her. It will not be stealing, especially if Lord Afron stole her from Lord Drake." Nor would freeing the firebird have been theft, though she could not tell him so. "Lord Afron refused to sell Amiga to Sir Rex for two thousand guineas, so he will not sell to you for the few pounds you carry, far less give you the mare."

"I can but ask," John said obstinately.

"Once he has refused you, he will be on his guard," she pointed out, but John was already knocking on the door of the lodge.

"I wish to speak to Lord Afron," he said to the gatekeeper who answered his knock.

The man laughed heartily. " 'Is lordship don't talk to beggarly whippersnappers," he said, and slammed the door.

Red-faced, John said in an angry voice, "You're right, friend fox, it's no use trying to do things right. How shall I get over the wall, though, and bring Amiga out?"

"If we follow it around, we shall come to a place where it is crumbling," said Reynata, who had told Tibb to look out for just such a spot.

They found it, and John agreed it was low enough for Amiga to jump with ease.

According to Tibb's chat with the stable cat, the baron's grooms all went to the kitchen for their supper at the same time.

"Go as close as you safely can, and watch for them to leave," Reynata instructed John. "The kitchen is quite close, but if you are quiet, no one will hear you. When Amiga recognizes you, she will follow you without a halter. Whatever you do, don't stop to saddle her."

"I can ride bareback," boasted John, retrieving his self-respect after the humiliation of the gatekeeper's laughter.

Climbing over the wall, he trudged towards the mansion. It was twilight by now and still raining, so there was little chance of his being seen. He was not at all surprised to find everything just as the fox had described it. Soon after full dark, he watched the coachman, grooms, and stableboys troop off for their supper. He sneaked into the stables and walked along the row of stalls, looking for the golden mare.

There she was. "Amiga!" he said softly.

She nodded her head twice, with the nearest thing to a smile a horse can manage. It *was* Aldwin's mare. John opened the stall, and she stepped forward eagerly, quite ready to follow him, just as the fox had said. He stroked her nose. What a beauty!

Aldwin had had Spanish harness and saddle worthy of her. He would be sorry to lose it. John decided to take a peek in the tack room to see if it was hanging there, easy to abstract.

Amiga came after him, the sound of her hooves muffled by the clean straw on the floor. He lifted down the lighted lantern by the end stall and opened the door. The room was already lit, and there was Aldwin's splendid tackle hanging on the wall. With Amiga peering interestedly over his shoulder, John put down his lantern and reached for the saddle.

The disgruntled stableboy, left behind to polish a skimped harness, recovered from his astonishment sufficiently to jump up from his bench in a corner and let out a piercing yell: "Stop, thief! Help! Hoss-thieves!"

By the time John reached the stable yard, faithful Amiga still at his heels, grooms were boiling out of the kitchen.

At least the scullery in which he was locked this time was near enough to the kitchen, with its hearths, ranges, and ovens, to be warm and dry. Taking off his greatcoat and boots, John gradually dried out. He found a scrubbing brush on a shelf, clean enough to smooth his hair—he was in no position to be fussy—and then to turn upon the dried mud on his buckskin breeches and top boots. Once he was as respectable as he could make himself, he huddled miserably in a corner and tried to sleep.

The night seemed to go on forever, yet morning came all too soon. Breakfastless, John was haled before Lord Afron.

The baron, clad in an elegant dressing-gown, was seated at a breakfast table from whence rose mouth-watering smells. From Sir Rex's description of him as too heavy for Amiga, John had imagined him fat, but he was a powerful man of thirty or so, tall and robust, with a darkly handsome, rakish face.

He looked John up and down and said sardonically, "Well, well, what have we here? A would-be gentleman and would-be horse-thief. Before I turn you over to the courts to be transported, tell me who the deuce you are and how the deuce you thought you'd get away with stealing my golden horse."

"My name is John Drake," said John, "and I'm the Earl of Androwick's youngest son. Your gatekeeper refused to admit me when I wanted to come and speak to you about the mare. She belongs to my brother Aldwin, Lord Drake."

"The devil she does!" Lord Afron burst out in a fury. Then he noticed the listening servants, all agog, and waved them out. "Lord Androwick's son? You'd better sit down," he said grudgingly, "and help yourself. What makes you think the mare is your brother's?"

"She answers to her name," John told him, heaping a plate with cold sirloin, eggs, and muffins. "Besides, are there any other golden horses with silver mane and tail? Aldwin rode off on her to fight in Spain. How did you come by her, sir?"

"I bought her from a horse-coper. Might have guessed such a magnificent beast was stolen, but I paid for her fair and square. Still, I might have given her to you to return to Lord Drake if you hadn't played the horse-thief. I could have you transported, you know, or even hanged."

"I tried to see you," mumbled John around a mouthful.

"So you said." Lord Afron regarded him consideringly. "I'll tell you what: I'll make a bargain with you. There is a young lady, a duke's daughter, who's madly in love with me. I've a fancy to marry her, but her father won't hear of it. Bring Lady Helen to me and I'll give you the mare, free and clear."

"Abduct a lady?" John quavered.

"She'll be willing enough, never fear. But if you fail, I'll hunt you down, and I've witnesses enough to see you hanged, earl's son or no."

Nine

Reynata listened in dismay to John's account of his new disaster. With an effort, she bit back the "I told you so!" hovering on her lips. For the sake of a saddle, Aldwin must remain a captive!

Still, while she was no readier than John to abduct the girl, if Lady Helen were truly in love with Lord Afron and willing to elope, perhaps there was yet hope.

John gazed at her with pleading eyes. "I know I came to grief through ignoring your advice," he said humbly, "but you will help me, won't you?"

With a sigh, Reynata nodded. "The first thing is to clean you up a bit," she said, "or Lady Helen will never agree to run off with you. Even to a fox's eye you are a walking scarecrow."

"Grawk," Tibb muttered in agreement from a branch nearby.

Sending John to the nearest inn with instructions to spend whatever it cost to return himself to respectability, Reynata despatched Tibb on another reconnaissance mission, Despite his grumbles, the raven apparently had the easier task. He returned first, to report that Lady Helen walked alone every morning in the shrubbery at her father's castle, unless it was raining.

The rain had already thinned to a few spots and dashes. The western sky was clearing. Reynata sniffed the air.

"Fine and frosty tonight," she announced. "A good omen."

John rejoined them, once more a handsome, presentable young gentleman, and they set out by hill and dale for the duke's demesne.

The castle stood on an isolated hill surrounded by the marshy Somerset plain. On the slopes once kept clear to allow sentinels and bowmen to descry invaders, terraced gardens, shrubberies, and a few large trees now flourished. The thick stone walls, proof against any weapon before gunpowder's invention, had been pierced for windows so large as to horrify a medieval chatelain. Nonetheless it was an impressive sight as Reynata and John approached Duke's Curry, the village at the foot of the castle mount.

"There are dungeons, I wager," John predicted gloomily. "No scullery for me if I'm caught this time. What's more, always supposing Lady Helen doesn't scream for her servants as soon as I open my mouth, even if she comes with me at once, there's no cover for our escape. From the castle they'll be able to see us for miles."

"Terrible country for foxes," Reynata said. She had to skulk along behind the osier willows which lined the many streams and drainage channels. Worse, to avoid the frequent bridges, she had to ford or swim across the watercourses. Even her thick winter fur was beginning to grow sodden. She shook vigorously and drops flew, but she was still chilled.

Coming to a decision, she stopped in a spot screened by willows. "John," she said, "have you never wondered at meeting a talking fox?"

He looked at her in surprise. "Why, not really. All the old books are full of talking animals, and I don't see why they should have died out. In fact, I know they haven't. The wise-woman in the King's Forest at home has a talking raven."

"Tibb!"

The raven flew down to land on her shoulders, his talons hooked in her fur. He, too, was pretty disgruntled. An osier willow with a head of pliant withies was not a comfortable place for a large bird to perch. *"Grawk,"* he grunted. "What's going on?"

John stared. "You're Mistress Gresham's raven?"

"I live with her," Tibb said sourly. "Ravens and cats belong to no one."

"Do you, er, live with Mistress Gresham, too, friend fox? I've never seen you about."

"You just don't recognize me. Close your eyes."

He opened his mouth, paused, then closed it and his eyes. Reynata hesitated for a moment, but apart from other considerations, she badly wanted a night in a warm, dry, comfortable bed. She metamorphosed. Her grey stuff cloak was damp.

"You can look now."

John opened his eyes. His mouth fell open. He blinked several times and glanced around in bewilderment. "Miss Gresham? How did you come here? Where's my friend the fox?"

"I am your friend the fox," Reynata said bluntly.

"Truly? By Jove, a mighty good disguise! I never guessed. How do you . . . ?"

Reynata explained as far as she considered necessary. John was admiring, even envious, and willingly agreed to keep her secret. "But why did you tell me now?" he asked.

"Good question," said Tibb.

"Because I have come up with a plan. For a start, we shall arrive at the inn in Duke's Curry as brother and sister, John, so you must remember to call me Reynata, as you did when we were children. Drake is not an uncommon name, but we shall use Gresham to be sure you cannot be traced."

"All right," John agreed compliantly, "but my sister can't arrive on foot when I'm on horseback. We only have one mount and no sidesaddle, so you'll have to ride pillion. It won't be very comfortable, I'm afraid."

As he dismounted, Reynata eyed his horse with misgivings. She had never ridden anything bigger than the ponies the Drake brothers had as boys, but he was right. He was using his brain at last. Perhaps he would not make a mull of things this time.

She let him boost her up awkwardly onto the horse's croup, where she clung to the back of the saddle, trying not to look at the ground. Once she was there, he could not mount by swinging his leg over. He scrambled up still more awkwardly in front of her.

"Miaw-haw-haw!" Tibb cackled. John's ears turned red.

Reynata frowned at the raven. "Go and do something useful," she said. "Find out exactly when Lady Helen usually takes her walk so we don't have to spend hours lurking in the shrubbery."

"Stable cat can't tell the time. *Grawk!*" he squawked as Reynata glared. "All right, all right, I'll see what I can do."

He flew off. Reynata gingerly put her arms around John's waist, and they followed.

At the tiny inn, the Duke's Head, John took the only two chambers. Reynata went up to her room and opened the window, despite the chilly air, so that Tibb could find her. He soon appeared, with a decidedly smug look in his bright, black eye.

"Who's a clever bird, *miaow!*" he said. "I talked to the young lady herself."

Reynata blenched. "That was risky!"

"This whole affair is about as risky as it can get, if you ask me. Remember why we're doing it."

"Aldwin," Reynata whispered, tears in her eyes.

"Better for me than you to raise the subject of elope-ment," said Tibb bracingly. "I could have flown away if she'd taken it amiss. Which she didn't. The silly girl's wild to run off with Lord Afron. She'll be in the shrub-bery at eleven. What's more, having talked to me, she won't be so startled by you."

"I hope not," Reynata said. That part of her plan wor-ried her, but she could not remain in human form. "Well done, Tibb."

Next morning, after paying his shot at the Duke's Head, Mr. "Gresham" had his horse saddled. He left it tied in the yard while he strolled with his sister, in her grey cloak and hood, up the hill to take a closer look at the castle. No one saw them climb the wooden fence surrounding the gardens. They disappeared into the shrubbery.

A few minutes later, the young man and a girl muffled in a grey cloak and hood slipped out of the shrubbery and down to the fence. This time the girl had to be helped over the fence, but she made it safely. They continued down the hill to the inn, where the young man lifted the girl onto his horse's withers. He mounted nimbly behind her, and they rode off.

Back in the shrubbery another girl, muffled in a rose-pink velvet cloak and hood, strolled up and down the paths. For half an hour or so she was visible intermit-tently from the castle, if anyone was watching. Then, hearing approaching footsteps, she ducked behind a lau-rel bush.

A maidservant came down the path. "Lady Helen," she called, "your aunt says it's too cold to stay out any longer." When there was no response, she called again, "My lady?" Still no answer. "Bother," she said, "she's gone in already. Hiding from her auntie again, I shouldn't wonder." And she sighed.

Meanwhile, a fox slipped out of the shrubbery and made off down the hill.

Reynata caught up with John and Lady Helen just after they left the fenny lowlands and rode up into the well-wooded Black Down Hills. John introduced the fox to the lady as if it were an everyday occurrence, and Lady Helen accepted it as such. She thanked Reynata profusely.

"I am excessively glad Lord Afron changed his mind," she said. "He told me he would not elope, even though he loves me excessively, because my father would cast me off. Was not that excessively noble of him?"

"Unless he didn't care to lose your dowry," John grunted. He seemed rather downcast considering their success.

"Oh," said Lady Helen uncertainly. She rallied. "No, he would not care for that. He is an excessively fine gentleman, a Corinthian of the first stare, and excessively handsome besides."

"Handsome!" growled John. "Oh, well, if you like that dark, brooding look."

Lady Helen glanced up at the fair hair visible beneath his beaver. "Fair hair is excessively nice, too, and I like blue eyes, but you look just as brooding as Lord Afron now."

"Do I?" said John with a sheepish grin. "Sorry!"

"You look nicer when you smile." Lady Helen produced a singularly sweet smile of her own. She appeared to Reynata to be an absolute peagoose, but a very pretty—her hair as golden and her eyes as blue as John's—and quite amiable peagoose. Her smile obviously dazzled John. "Lord Afron hardly ever smiles," she went on. "I daresay it is because he is a rake. I am not sure what a rake is, but I know it is excessively romantic. You are excessively kind to take me to him."

"*I* think it's the most totty-headed thing I've ever done."

"Why?" asked Lady Helen with a slight pout.

"Because you're much too innocent, and sweet, and pretty, to marry a—"

Reynata missed the rest as a gig came towards them and she had to dart into the woods. When she joined them again, she was dismayed, though not very surprised, to find them gazing besottedly into each other's eyes.

"Oh dear!"

"Reynata," said John, "Lady Helen isn't going to marry Lord Afron, after all."

"*Miawk!*" Tibb groaned.

"I simply couldn't, when he was so excessively cruel to dear John." The girl shuddered. "Why, he threatened to hang him!"

"She's going to marry me," John announced proudly.

"But what about the golden mare?" Reynata tried to stay calm, though her blood ran cold. "Without Amiga, Sir Rex will not give us the firebird."

"Father won't mind, when he meets Helen. He'll be pleased she's the daughter of a duke, though *I* don't care a bit."

Sweet nothings followed, which Reynata ruthlessly interrupted. "That's all very well, John, but Sir Rex will publish your attempted theft to the world. And Lord Afron will hunt you down and have you prosecuted for a capital offence—hang him," she explained bluntly when Lady Helen looked blank.

"Oh, John!" Tears filled her lovely eyes and overflowed down rose-petal cheeks. "I don't want to marry him!" she wailed.

"What shall we do, Reynata?" John asked helplessly.

"Keep riding towards Lord Afron's house, and let me think."

They went on by hill and dale. After a few miles, Reynata said, "John, you did not mention Sir Rex and the firebird to Lord Afron, did you?"

John screwed up his face in an effort to recall. "No, for all he knows I just tried to take Amiga because she's Aldwin's."

"Good. I have a plan, but all depends on your both doing exactly as I say. Lady Helen, you and I must exchange cloaks again."

Confused, Lady Helen blinked at the fox. "But you have not got my cloak, ma'am."

"I shall have. Pray don't ask me how. I shall go as your abigail. Now listen closely. You too, Tibb."

They listened. Reynata rehearsed all three until they were word perfect. Whether they would remember her instructions in the stress of the moment . . . But she refused to conceive of failure.

By hill and dale they approached Lord Afron's estate as dusk fell. Reynata transformed to human shape, wearing Lady Helen's rose velvet cloak, and exchanged it for her own grey stuff. With Lady Helen perched precariously sideways in the saddle and John and Reynata on foot, they went up to the gates. This time, the gatekeeper admitted them to the park at once.

So did the butler, into the mansion's splendid hall. Lord Afron came hurrying to greet them there.

Lady Helen threw back her hood as he bowed over her hand with polished suavity. She stammered a bit, but that was excusable in a young lady who had taken the drastic step of elopement. "Mr. Drake has told me about the golden horse with the silver mane and tail," she said. "I should like excessively to see such a wonder before he takes it away."

"Of course, my dear," Lord Afron acquiesced. "Let us go to the stables at once. You, girl," he addressed Reynata, who curtsied, "a footman will show you to Lady Helen's chamber."

"My maid came to see me safe here, but she will not stay. Mr. Drake has excessively kindly promised to take her home."

"You shall choose a new abigail, my love," the baron promised, and led the way to the stables.

Amiga was brought out into the yard, lit with lanterns by now, for it was dark between the buildings, though the gibbous moon was rising. "I'll show you how she answers to her name," said John.

"Yes, do," Lord Afron. "Then I shall believe she belongs to Lord Drake."

As John stepped forward, with everyone's eyes on him and the mare, Lady Helen and Reynata stepped back into the shadows. Swiftly they exchanged cloaks again, pulling the hoods close about their faces.

Amiga nodded twice. Reynata, now clad in rose velvet, clapped her hands and exclaimed in Lady Helen's girlish tones, "How clever, and how beautiful!"

"Now I credit your claim, Drake," said Lord Afron, and ordered the Spanish saddle to be brought.

John mounted, and a groom lifted Lady Helen, swathed in grey, up before him. As they rode out of the stable yard, Lord Afron turned towards Reynata. At that moment, a cry came from above. "Lady Helen, *grawk!* Lady Helen, who's a clever bird?"

"Oh, you *naughty* bird," laughed Reynata. "I wondered where you had got to. It is my pet raven," she told Lord Afron. "He flew off on the way here. I am excessively glad he has found me. Come down, Tibb!"

Tibb hopped down from the weathervane to the roof and started down the slope. Suddenly he took wing. "Lady Helen!" he screeched. *"Miaow, miaow."* He flew off over the wall, in the opposite direction from the park gates.

"Oh no, he must have seen a cat." Reynata ran out of

the stable yard, and after her came grooms and stableboys and Lord Afron.

Tibb flapped ahead, letting out an occasional *"Grawk!"* to prove he was still there. After him sped Reynata, calling him, careful to stay in sight of the rest in the moonlight until she was sure wind-swift Amiga must have borne John and Lady Helen well away. Then she slipped into the black shadows beneath the trees.

No one saw the vixen who raced to the low spot in the wall and scrambled over. Behind her, fading, she heard shouts: "Lady Helen? Where are you? Lady Helen!"

Ten

Reynata caught up with John and Lady Helen well on the way towards Sir Rex's manor. Both mounted on Amiga, leading John's horse, they had galloped until the mare tired under the double load; then John switched mounts. They were very pleased with themselves and relieved that Reynata had got away safely.

"Lord Afron is probably still searching the dark woods," she told them. "When he discovers Lady Helen is missing, he will look for you on the road to the Earl of Androwick's lands."

With Reynata once again playing abigail, they stopped at an inn for the night. John's funds were running low, but Lady Helen, warned by Tibb of her impending elopement, had brought every penny of her substantial pin money.

Man and beast well rested and well fed, they set off in the morning, having hired a sidesaddle for Lady Helen. By hill and dale they came to the Vale of Taunton Deane.

In vain Aldwin had listened to what little servants' gossip he could catch: No one mentioned the fate of his youngest brother. Was poor, silly John languishing in a prison cell? What had happened at home to lead to his attempted burglary? The earl was right; Aldwin ought never to have left.

Another endless day dragged by. The sun was setting, a red ball veiled by mists, when Sir Rex's largest footman came into the conservatory and lifted down the cage.

"Y're off to a new home, my fine fellow," he said.

He carried Aldwin out to the carriage sweep in front of the manor. Sir Rex stood on the steps, but Aldwin had no eyes for the baronet. There on the gravel stood Amiga, with John on her back!

"Bring the cage here," he ordered. "I want to be sure this is the right bird." At a nod from Sir Rex, the servant obeyed. "Speak, firebird!" cried John.

Though Aldwin had no idea what was going on, he stretched out his neck and called, "Reynata!"

Stooping in the saddle, John opened the door of the cage and said softly, "Go. Quickly. Follow the raven."

With two hands needed to hold the cage, the aghast footman hesitated too long. Aldwin ducked through the opening, spread his wings, gleaming ruddily in the dim evening light, and rose into the sky.

"What the devil?" yelled Sir Rex below.

"The firebird is a man under enchantment," John told him, even as he wheeled his mount. "He belongs to no one—and the horse belongs to my brother." Amiga raced away down the avenue.

Glorying in his freedom, Aldwin swooped after his brother. He soon lost sight of John in the darkening lanes, but a raven rose to meet him.

"This way, your lordship. Keep low or they'll spot you, with those flashy feathers of yours. Don't want 'em catching you again after all the trouble Miss Reynata's had freeing you."

"Reynata?" Aldwin put a questioning note in his voice. The raven told him a tale that froze the marrow of his bones. That she should have taken such risks for him! But what was this about her turning into a fox?

"She didn't see how to keep it from you any longer," said the raven, "since Master John knows. He doesn't know you're you, though, if you see what I mean. Miss Reynata didn't want him to be distressed by your other brothers' villainy."

Aldwin disagreed. He thought John should be put on his guard, but he could not say so. He followed the raven down into a bare orchard. A horse and two cloaked females waited there. One of the women ran towards him as he landed on a low branch nearby. The rising moon showed a glint of tears on her cheeks.

Stopping a pace away, she started to curtsy, then glanced back at the other girl—Lady Helen, the raven had said. Reynata moved closer to Aldwin and said softly, "She does not know who you are. Oh, how happy I am that you are free!"

He longed to take her in his arms and hold her close, but he had no arms. Leaning forward, he gently brushed her wet cheek with his head. "Reynata," he murmured.

She stepped back. "No, you must not . . . You don't know . . ."

"Miaow, he does," said the raven.

"You told him, Tibb?"

"Everything. Couldn't tell him how you saved him without explaining your other form, *grawk.*"

Trying to put all his tenderest feelings into his voice, Aldwin said again, "Reynata!" and caressed her with a wing tip.

"Shape he's in," the raven observed acidly, "he can't very well take exception to yours!"

"Oh, if only Grandmama can change you back!" said Reynata passionately.

Swarms of questions floated through Aldwin's mind.

Unable to utter them, he was glad to hear galloping hooves and John's triumphant voice: "I did it!"

The next evening, the travelers reached the outskirts of Crediton. When Reynata tried to change to become Lady Helen's abigail, she found to her dismay she was stuck in vulpine form. Grandmama had given clear warnings about the last part of the homeward journey. Reynata wanted to stay with John, to point out the perils, for he was still cock-a-hoop over his success in freeing the firebird and she feared he would not follow her advice.

However, there was nothing to be done. Lady Helen could not be expected to sleep outdoors.

"Stay at the Pheasant again," she told John, "and whatever you do, pay no debts but your own. We shall meet you again tomorrow. In the meantime, don't sit down to rest on the edge of any well." If only Grandmama's visions were more precise!

John laughed. "I cannot imagine why I should pay anyone's shot but mine and Helen's, and there are more comfortable places to rest than the wall around a well. See you tomorrow!"

Reynata, Tibb, and the firebird left the road to avoid the town, and he and Helen went on to the inn.

The friendly landlady welcomed Mr. Drake and his "sister." She was full of gossip about a couple of rogues who had stayed at the inn opposite, the Pair o' Dice. These two had gamed away their last pennies and then made to depart without paying the landlord for several weeks' room and board.

"Fine scoundrels," she said, "and impudent? Well! Would you believe, they told him to send to the Earl of Androwick for his money? In the town gaol they are now, and in the morning they'll be off to the debtors' prison in Exeter. May they rot there for trying to cheat a landlord of his due! Credit's long in Crediton, but we're not fools."

Guessing at once that the rascals were Damon and Basil, John confided Helen to the landlady's care and crossed the street to pay his brothers' debts. The landlord of the Pair o' Dice promised to go with him to the gaol on the morrow to see the prisoners released. Well satisfied, John returned to the Pheasant.

In the morning, Tibb brought the news to Aldwin and Reynata, hiding in a thicket by the road: "They're coming, and guess who's with them? Master Damon and Master Basil, large as life and twice as nasty!"

Aldwin exchanged a horrified glance with Reynata. "We'll have to keep out of their way," she said, "and try to watch over John and Helen from a distance."

Unable to utter his disagreement, Aldwin shook his head. If he was close, he might see danger coming in time to find a way to warn his heedless little brother. He flew out of the bushes and alighted on John's shoulder.

"Ah, there you are," said John. "Look, Damon, I told you I found the firebird. Isn't it magnificent with the sun shining on its feathers? Father's going to be happy as a grig."

Damon and Basil looked at each other, a look Aldwin did not like at all. After a while, they fell behind, speaking in hushed voices. Aldwin kept an eye on them, but they soon caught up and rode on as before.

Though Aldwin caught occasional glimpses of Tibb, he saw not a sign of Reynata. He assumed she was not far off. They passed through Long Yeoford and turned off towards Middlecombe.

Damon stretched and said, "Let us stop to rest and eat the nuncheon we brought. We can shelter in that ruined cottage. There are plenty of fallen stones to sit on."

Dismounting, they all found seats. Perched on a roof

beam, Aldwin scanned the scene. The mossy stone John
sat on was part of a low wall built in a circle. A well!

Aldwin swooped down, intent on seizing John's sleeve
in his beak and pulling him away from his perilous seat.
Damon and Basil jumped up. Damon gave John a mighty
shove, sending him backward into the well, while Basil
threw his greatcoat over Aldwin.

Helplessly muffled in the heavy cloth, Aldwin heard
Lady Helen scream.

Reynata crept out of the undergrowth. She cast a longing glance after Damon and Basil as they rode off with
their plunder. Lady Helen, cowed into submission by
their threats, was to be Basil's bride, while Amiga was
Damon's share of the booty. They intended to give the
firebird to the earl, who would reward them with joint
ownership of Winworthy Manor. When Aldwin failed to
return from war, Damon would be heir to the Androwick
estates and could deed his half of the manor to his
brother.

They were going to tell Lord Androwick that the firebird had knocked John into the well, advising their father
to keep it safely caged. Overhearing their plans, Reynata
knew Aldwin was in no immediate danger, though bundled in a greatcoat and tied on behind Damon's saddle,
he was undoubtedly uncomfortable.

Reynata hurried to the well and looked down. She had
heard no splash and smelled no water, so she was not
surprised to find it dry. But nor had she heard a sound
from John since he fell. At the bottom far below, on the
accumulated leaves and twigs of decades, he lay on his
back.

Gasping for breath, he feebly moved his arms and legs.

"John! Are you hurt?"

"Winded," he choked out.

"We shall get you out of there," Reynata assured him.

"We?" said Tibb, alighting on the wall. He eyed John. "Looks like a big, juicy grub, squirming away down there. What do you want me to do, throw down a few more twigs, *graw-haw?"*

"No, go and tell Grandmama. It is not far now."

"Far enough," the raven grumbled, but he flew off.

"Ouch!" said John, gingerly standing up and feeling the back of his head. "Did those dastards hurt Helen?"

"No, just terrified her with threats."

"Wait till I lay my hands on that precious pair! My own brothers! How will you get me out? Er . . . Reynata, I know it's my own fault I'm down here. I'm truly excessively sorry I didn't do as you said."

"I believe you," Reynata said dryly. "If only I were in human form! What we need is a rope. Failing that, I shall try to find a fallen bough you can use as a ladder to climb out."

Searching the copse, she found a perfect bough, well branched to form steps. She gripped the broken end in her teeth, but it was too heavy to move. She tugged and tugged with no result. About to give up, she was startled by a voice behind her.

"Good day, little sister." It was the dog fox, Cobnut, from the King's Forest. "I see you do indeed need my aid. I had not sighted you for a long time, nor crossed a fresh scent, so I went to the wise-woman to ask after you. She sent me here to help you."

Between them, they pulled the branch to the well and lowered it, careful not to hit John. It made a precarious ladder. Reynata watched anxiously as he clambered up, swaying from side to side. As he neared the top and reached for the rim of the well, he almost fell, but she reached down and grabbed his sleeve in her teeth to steady him. A moment later, he was out, sprawling on the ground.

"Whew!" He sat up and looked around, then rubbed his eyes. "Funny, I must have been seeing double." Cobnut, ever wary of humans, was gone. John went on humbly: "Reynata, I don't know how to thank you. What shall we do now?"

"Hurry home!"

They set off, John on foot now, hatless and looking distinctly the worse for wear after his sojourn in the well. As they went, Reynata told him his wicked brothers' plans. She saw no further reason to keep the firebird's identity secret.

"It's *Aldwin?*" John was aghast. "Can Mistress Gresham change him back?"

"I hope so. You had best go straight to the Towers while I go home and fetch Grandmama there."

"Oh yes. You run ahead; don't wait for me. I'll go as fast as I can."

Reynata ran fast, but the wise-woman moved slowly, so they caught up with John at the gates of Wick Towers, arguing with the gatekeeper. Scruffy as he was, bareheaded and tousled, his coat torn, his face scratched, he scarcely resembled the Honourable John Drake, who was, besides, rumoured dead. At last the gatekeeper was persuaded to admit him, but as for the old woman in the shabby cloak . . .

Gammer Gresham threw back her hood, drew herself up, and looked at him. Hastily he apologized and hurried to open the gates. Reynata slipped through unnoticed while he bowed to the wise-woman and Master John.

They came to the massive, iron-bound oak front door of the Towers. John opened it and stepped in, Mistress Gresham on his arm, Reynata close at his side.

In the great hall, a tableau met their eyes. Lord Androwick sat in an ancient carved chair by the fireside. In its twin, across the hearth, Lady Helen wept bitterly. Damon and Basil, hearing the door open, had swung round and were gaping at the newcomers. Several servants also turned and stared.

In spite of the drama, and though she had never entered the mansion before, Reynata had eyes only for the firebird, confined in a wicker cage to one side. As she moved towards him, the earl demanded, "Who the devil . . . ?"

The butler recovered from his surprise and directed several footmen to eject the intruders. As they converged on John and Mistress Gresham, Lady Helen raised her golden head. "John!" she cried, and ran to him, to be folded in his arms.

"What the devil . . . ?"

Working at the cage latch with her teeth, Reynata did not listen to the muddled explanations which followed. She was aware that Damon and Basil tried to slink out, to be stopped by the footmen on the earl's orders. Then Grandmama joined her and pulled the latch pin.

Aldwin stepped out of the cage. "Reynata," he whispered, and brushed her foxy face with his feathery head. Then he spread his wings and launched himself into the air, to alight on the arm of his father's chair just as John at last got around to telling the earl who the firebird really was.

"My son!" the earl lamented.

From an obscure corner, Reynata watched her foster mother approach the hearth. She carried herself with pride and dignity, ignoring aches and pains. Lord Androwick rose to meet her, silent, holding out both his hands. She gave him hers.

"It has been a long time, Stephen." She spoke softly, but Reynata's vulpine senses heard every word, and wondered.

"Now will you marry me, Rosa?"

Mistress Gresham shook her head. "No, my dear. It is too late. I am content in my cottage. But you may visit me there."

"I shall!" vowed the earl. "Rosa, can you help my son?"

"I believe so. But first I must dispose of the miscreants who are still a danger to him." She turned to Damon and Basil and said thoughtfully, "Black beetles, I think."

"Grawk!" came a voice from the roof beams. "I *love* crunchy black beetles!"

The wicked pair fell on their knees. "Have mercy!" they cried.

"Had you any? Well, I daresay it would be an embarrassment to your family to have to own two beetles as relatives. Perhaps you would prefer to enlist as soldiers. Though your presence will scarcely compensate the army for Lord Drake's absence, two sons of one family will surely suffice."

Damon and Basil sulkily consented to take the King's shilling—the earl agreed they did not deserve to have commissions purchased for them—rather than be turned into tidbits for Tibb's dinner. Their father had them confined in a scullery while a recruiting sergeant was sent for.

"John shall have Winworthy Manor," he said. "I daresay, my boy, if you write a properly contrite letter to the duke, he will overlook Lady Helen's elopement. Never thought you'd do so well for yourself. A duke's daughter and a dashed pretty one!"

Lady Helen kissed his lined cheek. "La, sir, you are excessively kind!"

Mistress Gresham turned her attention to Aldwin. By then half the Towers' staff had gathered in the great hall. Reynata lurked in the background. If the front door had not been closed, she would have made her escape, for once Aldwin was human again, there was no place for a fox in his life. Her presence could only embarrass him.

Between two twittering maids, Reynata saw the firebird perched on the edge of a long carven table. Firelight glinted redly on his golden plumage. Grandmama brought a steaming pot from the hearth and poured the contents into a porcelain bowl. The fragrance of sweet herbs drifted through the hall.

The wise-woman stared at the liquid, muttering. Then she looked long and hard at Aldwin, seeming to read his mind as, with a proud lift of his crested head, his crystal eyes met her gaze.

In both hands she raised the bowl. "Drink," she commanded, and the proud head bowed to sip.

The firebird blurred—or was it the tears in Reynata's eyes? No, a gasp went up from all the watchers as shimmering red-gold feathers blended into a scarlet uniform with gold braid. Aldwin, Lord Drake, straightened from his seat on the edge of the table and looked around, searching the excited crowd.

"Reynata?"

Had he forgotten how to speak?

"Where is my deliverer, my love, my little fox?"

The servants parted to leave a passage before her. She had nowhere to hide. Trembling in unbelief, she padded forward as he came to meet her.

The world swirled about her. She was human. She was in his arms, enveloped in a tender, passionate embrace.

"Good gad!" ejaculated Lord Androwick.

Aldwin led Reynata forward. "Father, Miss Gresham, my bride. Give us your blessing."

The earl leaned forward. "Can you do that again, Miss Gresham?" he asked eagerly.

"Yes, sir," she said, blushing. "I am a wer-fox." Now he would forbid the marriage.

But he did not. He slapped his knee and exclaimed, "A wer-fox, by Jove! There's not another collector in the country . . ."

"Father! Reynata will be Lady Drake, not an exhibit in your menagerie."

"Of course not," said the earl, covering a sigh of disappointment with an injured air. "Wouldn't dream of it. A wer-fox in the family, even better! Come, my dears." He held out a hand each to Reynata and Lady Helen. "Give an old man a kiss. We'll have a double wedding, hey?"

Each gave him a kiss, promptly repaid a thousandfold by their respective lovers.

Dizzy with happiness, Reynata jumped when Tibb landed on Aldwin's shoulder.

"My felicitations," said the raven. He peered backward at John and Lady Helen, who were gazing into each other's eyes like a couple of moonlings. *"Grawk!* Just between us birds," Tibb went on confidentially, "you got the better deal, my lord. Gives a fellow ideas. I don't suppose you could spare some of that gold braid for a nest?"

THE DANCING SHOES

by

Karla Hocker

One

She dreamed she stood in a chamber of stunning magnificence. Crimson-and-gold landscape murals, gigantic painted serpents and flying dragons, gilt pagodas, lotus-shaped chandeliers seemingly held aloft by golden dragons in flight, dazzled the eye. Softly, enticingly, the strains of a waltz filled the air, but save for the musicians positioned in front of an enormous organ, she appeared to be alone in this splendid chamber.

"May I have the honor?"

She did not recognize the voice at her back, and yet it was so familiar, so known, so apropos of the situation, that she smiled and turned immediately.

The music swelled, and then she was in his arms and whirled around the room. She, who was the clumsiest female ever to disgrace a dance floor, was dipping, gliding, floating, spinning effortlessly. It was sheer magic.

The magic of him.

"Minna," he whispered. "Dearest Minna. Do you know how much you mean to me?"

"No," she returned softly. "No, I don't. Do tell me."

But then the music stopped, and he was gone.

And not once had she seen his face.

Once upon a time, in a well-known town by the seaside, there lived a not-so-young lady by name of Miss

Minna Elfinstone, one of the mistresses at Mrs. Foster's Seminary for Young Ladies. Not that Miss Elfinstone had been raised to become a schoolmistress; no, indeed. Her parents, Sir Wilfred and Lady Elfinstone, had fondly envisioned an advantageous marriage when they permitted Minna to study the sciences with the vicar, to learn a smattering of languages and the arts from a very superior governess. From Lady Elfinstone, Minna learned all about housekeeping and needlework, and how to arrange flowers and greens most charmingly, whether it be in precious crystal, delicate china, or in an ordinary crock or basket from the kitchens. Last but not least, a highly praised Italian dancing master had been engaged to— But, no, Signor Bertelli's acclaim must have been a sham, for he did not succeed in the slightest when he attempted to show Miss Elfinstone how to appear graceful on the dance floor.

In the end, it mattered little that Minna tripped in a lively country dance or jostled her partner in the cotillion. A sudden reversal of fortune found the family moving from their sprawling country manor into the steward's cottage and Sir Wilfred earning a scant livelihood overseeing the estate he had once owned. Miss Elfinstone, then eighteen years old, could no longer expect a Season in town, or an advantageous marriage. On the contrary, what she must expect was to remain at the cottage, a dutiful daughter tending her parents, and dwindle into an old maid.

Or she could look for a suitable post.

For Minna Elfinstone, that had been no choice at all. Time enough to devote herself to her parents when they were in need of support, at which time she had better have a sizable nest egg tucked away to pay the cottage rent. Too young to be accepted as a governess or companion by any but a ramshackle family, she had pounced upon an advertisement for a "female of refinement and abilities to assist in the instruction of young ladies at a superior institute of female education."

That had been eight years ago.

"Miss Elfinstone, something *must* be done!" Mrs. Foster, ensconced in a soft, upholstered chair behind a massive oak desk, fixed the slight, gray-clad woman standing to attention just inside the warm study with a gimlet eye. "I pride myself on running a first-class establishment, one that will someday draw the daughters of the gentility—nay, the *nobility*—instead of the hoydens we harbor now."

"Hoydens, whose papas pay very well," Miss Elfinstone pointed out.

"Tea merchants! Sugar bakers! Encroaching mushrooms, all of them. Their opinions do not matter."

"But their purses do."

For an instant, Mrs. Foster looked uncertain. Then she shook her head, endangering her coiffure and the lace cap perched atop the mass of tight, iron-gray curls. "They won't withdraw their funds. They know their daughters would not find another school like this one, situated in plain sight of a royal residence and all the highborn gentlemen and scarlet coats parading around the Steyne. No, Miss Elfinstone, I do not fear losing the merchants' patronage. Not while they fancy their daughters catching the eye of some gentleman with pockets to let and willing to exchange his name and title for a fortune."

"Indeed." Miss Elfinstone's voice was dry, if not a touch acerbic. "And the school carefully nurtures those hopes with the promise of an annual dance attended by 'gentlemen of rank.' A promise rarely fulfilled, if I may be so bold—"

"Do not be impertinent." Mrs. Foster's tone was stern.

But not too stern, for at present she rather depended on her headmistress. "What I must think of is the future. I cannot afford a breath of scandal attached to my school. If anyone were to learn that young ladies from *my* school—" Her face turned a purplish red that clashed horribly with her puce gown, and she groped for the ever-present glass of "restorative" on her desk. Whatever the concoction was, it did nothing to diminish her color but did restore her powers of speech.

"We must find out what those girls are doing, Miss Elfinstone. Look at those!" She pointed to a jumble of dancing slippers in a basket beside the desk. "Another set ruined!"

Miss Elfinstone had no need to look. She had been responsible for gathering the dozen pairs of worn-out shoes and delivering them to Mrs. Foster's study.

"I daresay," she supplied mildly, "that the young ladies are practicing their dance steps. At seventeen and eighteen, there's such an abundance of energy, such anticipation of excitement and pleasures to come—and then to be sent to bed at eight o'clock! I do not doubt they're dancing all night through, pretending to be at a ball and meeting their respective Princes Charming."

"Of course they are. How else could the shoes become so tattered? The second set in four days! Young fools! As if they stood a chance . . . but that is beside the point. I want to know *where* they dance. You sleep on the same floor, Miss Elfinstone, yet you assure me you haven't heard anything. No one can sleep so soundly that she does not hear twelve rambunctious hoydens stomping and prancing just across the hall!"

Minna Elfinstone sighed. Oh, yes, she could. She was so exhausted at night that she doubted anything short of a cannon fired beside her bed would rouse her once she had fallen asleep.

"I shall keep my door open tonight," she said without enthusiasm.

"Do that. Or I shall have to set up a trundle bed for you in Miss Herring's room. I do not doubt that she's behind whatever misdeeds they're engaged in."

"Miss Herrington," Minna corrected automatically. Louisa Herrington, who was bright and mischievous, and whose father had started out in life as a fishmonger's son and now owned a fleet of fishing and merchant vessels.

"Herring . . . Herrington . . . what does it signify? She's a flighty bit, that one. And no better than she should be! She must have discovered a way to slip out at night. And, worse, she talked the others into following her bad example. If they're seen in town! It'll be the end of my ambitions."

The proprietor of the superior institute of female education fortified herself with several swigs of restorative, and Miss Elfinstone seized the opportunity to depart.

"I shall get to the bottom of this," she promised, and firmly shut the study door behind her.

For a moment she stood in the foyer surrounded by quiet and a number of closed doors: to Mrs. Foster's study, to the dining hall, the drawing room, the music room, the library, and the small parlor where pupils could entertain visiting parents.

Minna Elfinstone did not believe that the twelve senior pupils sneaked out at night. After all, the doors were bolted and locked at seven o'clock, and only Mrs. Foster and Minna kept a key. The windows on the ground floor all sported a fancy grille, installed a few years ago when a lovelorn young lady had climbed out to meet one of the dragoons stationed nearby. No tree stood close to the building; no trellis provided a foothold for someone wishing to climb out an upper window. No, if the senior young ladies danced the night away, it must be in the house.

A squeal, followed by an indignant shriek, shattered the quiet. Minna gathered the skirt of her gray bombazine gown and hurried up the stairway to the first floor, where the twelve junior girls, left without a teacher since Miss Bodlyn's elopement a fortnight ago, were taught by a senior girl under Minna's supervision.

Twelve junior pupils on the first floor, twelve seniors on the second—that was how Mrs. Foster liked the arrangement. Three bedchambers on each floor, four girls to a room. One large schoolroom and a small chamber for an instructress on each floor. After Miss Bodlyn's departure, a maid had been moved from the attic to Miss Bodlyn's chamber, since it was inconceivable that Mrs. Foster would leave the comfort of her third-floor apartments at night, and the housekeeper had declined to forego the privacy of her two rooms in the basement.

Prompted by a fresh outburst of shrieks accompanied by a wail, Minna took the last steps at a run. She rushed into the schoolroom but came to an immediate stop inside the door, just as the clatter of many feet heralded the descent of the senior girls from the floor above. The sight before Minna's eyes defied description. There were thirteen girls altogether, eleven of whom were behaving in a manner more suited to lads cheering their favorite at a cock fight. The other two, limbs entwined, were wrangling on the floor.

One of the young ladies from upstairs bumped into Minna's back, propelling her farther into the schoolroom. A second young lady shot past her, crying, "Louisa! Your hair!"

Minna did not try to call for order. No one would have heeded her. She marched up to the two combatants on the floor, snatched each by an arm, and with a great effort, for the girls, when upright, were half a head taller than she, pulled them apart. Breathless, she glared at them, then at the others, who had ceased their shrieking at sight of the headmistress.

"Your hair, Louisa!" Charlotte Witherspoon repeated. "Oh, you poor thing. You look . . . plucked!"

And, indeed, Louisa Herrington, who had been assigned to supervise the junior pupils in doing their sums, had lost a significant number of her beautiful wheatgolden curls. But the second brawler, one of the junior girls, had a bloody nose.

"Louisa, go to my room and wait for me," Minna ordered, helping Mary up, the sobbing younger girl. "Everyone else! To the dining hall. Tell Mrs. Felt I sent you to assist setting the tables for dinner."

Without hesitation, everyone obeyed, and Minna could tend the nosebleed in the girl's chamber.

She dipped a cloth in cold water. "What happened, Mary?" she asked, gently dabbing the blood- and tear-streaked face. "Why did you and Louisa fight?"

"I cut off her hair."

"I saw that. But I don't see how it was possible for you to cut off several locks and Louisa not stopping you."

Mary remained silent.

"Well? Did you tie Louisa's hands? Did the others restrain her while you cut?"

Mary looked alarmed. "No one did anything, except me, Miss Elfinstone."

"Then don't you think you ought to tell me why Louisa sat still and let you cut off so much of her hair before she decided to fight with you? And what happened to the scissors? Don't you realize how dangerous it is to be engaged in fisticuffs when scissors are involved?"

"I didn't have them anymore when Louisa wo—" Mary's mouth closed in a firm, tight line.

Minna looked at the set young face, the stubborn chin,

and sighed inaudibly. Such misplaced nobility, not wanting to snitch. But at least the girl wasn't bleeding anymore.

"Very well, then, Mary. You may join the others in the dining hall."

In her own chamber on the second floor, Minna frowned at Louisa Herrington's angry face in the cracked mirror on the dressing table. She had cut the few remaining long curls on Louisa's head and was trying to shape what was left of the girl's once beautiful hair.

"You cannot tell me that you did not realize Mary was snipping at your hair until almost half of it was gone," she said, taking several snips herself.

The girl scowled darkly but did not reply.

"If you don't speak up, the blame for the brouhaha will fall squarely on your shoulders. You were put in charge downstairs. It was your responsibility to—"

"You need a new mirror," Louisa interrupted.

"Changing the subject won't help you. But, yes, that crack is distracting." Minna tilted Louisa's head this way and that. "Actually, this short crop doesn't look half bad. You have enough curl to carry it off."

Louisa leaned closer to the mirror and studied herself with burgeoning interest. "Pert," she announced at last, all vestige of a scowl disappearing. "That's how I look. Pert. I like it."

Minna laughed. She knew she shouldn't. She knew Mrs. Foster would have an apoplexy if she learned how familiar her headmistress was with the pupils. But Mrs. Foster was not likely to hear of it, since she joined pupils and teachers only once a month for tea in the drawing room, on which stifling occasions it was quite easy to remember to address the girls with requisite formality.

"You are not at all vain, are you?" Minna turned serious. "Louisa, I must know what went on in the down-stairs schoolroom."

The girl gave her a sidelong look. Then, with a fine show of nonchalance, she said, "I fell asleep."

"I see." Minna dusted strands of hair off Louisa's shoulder. "And why would you fall asleep in the middle of the day? You often complain that the night is far too long and you get too much sleep."

"Today I was tired."

Minna studied the eighteen-year-old. At first glance, Louisa looked like innocence personified, but Minna had learned to recognize the glint of mischief in those wide blue eyes. This time, however, she also saw the shadows of fatigue.

"Perhaps, my dear, the worn-out dancing shoes lie at the root of your exhaustion?"

Louisa rose. "Signor Fogagnolo bade us practice," she said demurely. She curtsied. "Thank you very much for the *coiffure très chic*. Papa promised me a ball when I go home next month. I believe I'll be cutting quite a dash, don't you, Miss Elfinstone?"

Minna decided not to press the matter. At least not for the present. It was almost three o'clock, the girls' dinner hour. But that night, she would be vigilant. Practicing ... what fustian! As if a bit of dancing practice could paint shadows beneath a healthy young lady's eyes.

Minna awoke from fitful slumber. All was quiet, The oil lamp on the night table beside her bed still glowed softly. Her chamber door was still open. The watch pinned to her gown showed a few minutes lacking till midnight.

The witching hour. And Mrs. Foster the wicked witch who had set her underpaid and overworked headmistress to guard twelve innocent maidens. Only, the headmistress wasn't guarding; she had been sleeping. And the maidens weren't quite as innocent as they looked.

Fully clothed, Minna rose from her bed. All was quiet, yet she was sure that something, some sound, had roused her. Taking the lamp, she peeked into the schoolroom next to her chamber. Nothing.

She crossed the hall and softly opened the first door. Nothing.

Nothing! No slumbering innocent maidens. The four beds were empty.

Heart beating in her throat, Minna rushed to the next bedroom. Empty.

And the next. Empty—no. One bed was occupied. Miss Harriette Trowe, who had been sniffling and coughing much of the day, lay snoring in her bed.

Minna was trembling—with fatigue, with anger, and, mainly, with apprehension. But there was no reason to be alarmed, was there? True, she had fallen asleep. But if the girls had left the house, she would have heard them in the hall and on the stairs. Would she not?

She shook Harriette by the shoulder. With a squeal, the girl shot up in bed. She saw her headmistress, and dove back under covers.

Without compunction, Minna flung the coverlet off the bed. "Where is everyone? Harriette! Where are the others?"

"I don't know." The girl coughed pitifully. "Miss Elfinstone, I'm sick. I'm thirsty, I'm sure I have a fever."

Minna returned the coverlet. She poured water from the pitcher on the dressing table and handed the glass to Harriette. When the girl had drunk, Minna felt her forehead. Warm, but nothing to fret about. Nothing like the absence of eleven young ladies.

"Harriette, I am sorry you aren't feeling well. Come to think of it, I'm not sorry at all. I believe it is the only reason you're here when the others are not. Now, where are they?"

"I don't—"

"And do not tell me you don't know," Minna snapped. "If they have left the school, they could be in grave danger. You must tell me *immediately* where they are."

"No danger . . . there couldn't be." But Harriette looked uncertain now. "Surely not, Miss Elfinstone?"

"Harriette, if you don't tell me *this instant* where they are, I vow I shall throttle you and lock you into the basement."

The girl hung her head. "They're at the Pavilion," she whispered.

"Where?" Minna did not think she could have heard aright. "And don't mumble so."

"At the Pavilion, Miss Elfinstone."

"Harriette!" Exasperated, Minna tilted the girl's face up. "This is not the time for one of your tales!"

Harriette sneezed. She drew a handkerchief from beneath the pillow and blew her nose. "It's not a tale, I swear it! I'm telling the truth. There's a secret passage, just like the one that's whispered about from Mrs. Fitzherbert's house next door. You know! To His Highness's chambers at the Pavilion."

Harriette sneezed again, and Minna sank onto the edge of the bed, her mind reeling with nebulous images of His rakish Highness cavorting with twelve—no, eleven—innocent young ladies.

"Only this passage—*our* passage," said Harriette, "leads straight into the Music Room. You know, the new wing that was built and that isn't even decorated yet?"

Minna could breathe again. The Music Room . . . so innocuous compared to the private chambers. And, she remembered belatedly, His Highness was not even in town.

"It'll be ever so beautiful when it is finished," said Harriette. "I saw——"

"Where is that passage?" Minna interrupted. She rose, looking sternly at the girl. "And if I find you've been telling tales, after all——"

"It's in the wall behind Louisa's bed."

With one last fierce look at Harriette, Minna picked up her lamp where she had left it beside the water pitcher, then squeezed behind Louisa Herrington's empty bed. She ran a hand along the wall, a solid interior wall, smooth and unadorned. There was no crack, no bump or catch, to give away the existence of a hidden opening.

Anger flared once more. She spun, knocking a shin against the bedstead.

"How dare you!" She spoke more sharply than she had ever spoken to any of her pupils. "How dare you play games when your friends may be in peril!"

Harriette slid from her bed. Eyes wide with apprehension, she approached the headmistress but stopped on the other side of Louisa's bed. "Please, Miss Elfinstone, put on my dancing slippers."

Something in the girl's voice and gaze cooled Minna's temper. As calmly as she could, she repeated, "Your dancing slippers."

"Yes. They should be there . . . somewhere . . . at your feet."

"Dancing slippers," Minna repeated once more, then shrugged. And why not? she thought in resignation. This whole nonsensical affair started with dancing shoes. Worn-out shoes.

"Hold the lamp, Harriette."

Minna bent and felt for the dancing slippers in the narrow space between bed and wall. She found them almost instantly. When she had exchanged her own shoes of sturdy leather for the satin slippers, had taken the lamp from Harriette, she once more faced the wall.

And she saw it immediately. The outline of a narrow doorway.

"Push on the rosette," said Harriette.

But Minna had already done so. She had pressed the faint but unmistakable elevation that wasn't there when she had examined the wall earlier, and she heard the whisper of a sound and saw the door pivot on a central hinge.

Harriette said, "It's tight up here, but once you're down the stairs and out of the house, it's not so bad."

All Minna could think was that the Prince Regent, if the passage truly led to the Pavilion, would never be able to squeeze his bulk through the half-width of a narrow opening and enter the young ladies' chamber.

"Go back to bed, Harriette. But if I have not returned with the girls in half an hour, rouse Mrs. Foster and tell her all."

When Minna reached the doorway at the other end of the secret passage, she could not, had her life depended upon it, have stated with authority whether it had taken five minutes, or fifteen, or even longer, to traverse the three flights of steep and narrow steps and the scarcely wider tunnel. She was aware only of apprehension that evil had befallen the girls, of irritation that they could have behaved in such an irresponsible manner and had stolen away in the middle of the night, and, guiltily, of a quite unfamiliar thrill of excitement.

For eight years, she had lived and worked at Mrs. Foster's school. The only change of pace had been the visits to her parents. And now, if Harriette had spoken the truth, she might step into the Pavilion, the controversial royal residence that was swallowing fortunes in additions and refurbishing. By George, it had better be the Pavilion and not some barn where she was about to emerge, or . . .

or those girls would suffer the rest of their stay at school without their treasured dancing lessons!

Clutching her lamp, Minna pressed against a carved rosette, similar to the one on the wall behind Louisa's bed. Again, the door pivoted on a central hinge to provide an opening barely wide enough to admit a slender person.

Minna heard music, the lively tune of a *contre danse,* if she correctly remembered her disastrous, long-ago dancing lessons. A violin and a forte-piano, of that she was certain, even though the sounds were somewhat muffled. She heard giggling and laughter, and Louisa's familiar voice crying, "Faster, Freddy! Martin! Play faster!"

Relief flooded her. The girls sounded unharmed, as exuberant, in fact, as they did when engaged in healthful lawn games.

Minna stepped through the opening. At first, she saw nothing save for a whitish wall swaying and rippling in front of her. Upon closer inspection, she realized that she stood beneath a high scaffold draped with sheets of coarse linen or sailcloth. The floor was covered with sheets as well; she almost tripped when she took another step.

The music stopped. There were cries for more. All the familiar voices—Helen, Sarah, Dorothea, Charlotte, Louisa, Felicity—and Edith McPhearson calling, "A waltz! Let's have a waltz!"

"Edith! Louisa!" Minna charged forward, tangled with a sheet, almost lost her balance. At last, she found an opening and burst into a vast chamber with the most extraordinary ceiling and chandeliers. But she had not come to gape, even if it was the Prince's latest work in progress dazzling her eye. Even if memory stirred gently . . . memory of a dream. Her favorite dream.

Eleven young ladies, each beside a dashing young officer, stood stock-still and suddenly very quiet in the center of the room, where the sheets had been bundled aside. They were staring at Minna as if she was a spook.

"Ladies!" Minna waved her lamp, the light of which was lost in the glow of many work lanterns lit all around the scaffold-lined chamber. "Come with me this instant!"

They all started to protest or explain. Minna did not understand a word. Then, above the female chatter, she heard a male voice. She could not be certain, but she believed the words uttered were, "And about time!"

Not one of the young officers; they stood like wax figures, their faces as stiff as their posture. She turned slightly and saw, to her left, a man rising from a stack of lumber, about fifteen or twenty paces from where she stood. The girls were silent once more. It was, Minna thought, as if they were holding their breaths.

Minna watched the man walk toward her. He was tall, very tall. He wore a shapeless, paint-streaked smock and, incongruously, a pair of highly glossed calf-length boots and impeccably tailored, cream-colored pantaloons, the elegance and expense of which items she recognized even after years of living in straitened circumstances.

She squared her shoulders. "Sir! Are *you* the instigator of this—" In a sweeping gesture, she indicated the makeshift dance floor with its silent occupants. "This outrage?"

He stopped, raised a dark brow. "Ma'am? Are you referring to these red-faced boys and schoolroom misses? At least they're quiet now. I wonder how you contrived that? But, indeed, I am extremely grateful. If you had not arrived just now, I might have been obliged to cut my throat to escape the incessant giggling and chattering."

The voice was deep and melodic and betrayed unmistakable amusement. Minna took a second look at him. A proper, carefully scrutinizing look. And her breath caught, for her gaze was met and held by a pair of eyes that, although undistinguished of color, was quite startling in expression.

It was laughter she saw in his eyes. Not the unkind, gloating laughter of a man feeling superior to the recipient. It was the sheer joy of situation, spreading warmth and inviting her to share the absurdity of the moment.

And absurd it was, she had to admit, to see the girls apprehensive and uncertain, and silent for once, some looking embarrassed, some as guilty as if they had been caught tying their garters in public. And the officers, so young they were still wet behind the ears, staring straight ahead, wooden and stoic, as if they were about to face a court-martial.

But Minna had only a cursory glance for the young people. She turned back to the smock-garbed stranger and, without the slightest hesitation or questioning of her sanity, surrendered to his smile.

Two

Minna feared that, if she spoke, she would dispel this moment of harmony, the delightful feeling of *rapprochement*. She was content to merely gaze at this stranger who had touched a chord in her, to become familiar with the lean face that looked both refined and rugged with its straight, elegant nose and forceful chin. His skin was bronzed, as if he spent a great deal of time outdoors. Yet, judging by the paint stains, not only on the smock but on his hands as well, he must be one of the painters working on the murals commissioned by the Prince Regent.

"Ma'am," he said. "Miss Elfinstone. It is not that I'm not flattered by your attention. But I feel obliged to point out that your charges have recovered from their shock."

With a start, Minna became aware of renewed giggling and chatter, of a violin humming softly. She should have known the girls would take her silence as permission to continue with their foolishness. Indeed, she had known it but had put everything, most particularly a reminder of her duties and responsibilities, from her mind to indulge in a moment of— Dash it! She was no better than the girls.

"Stop!" she cried, clapping her hands to catch their attention, then turned back to the painter. "You know my name and that the girls are in my charge. Why, then, did you not return them to the school? You must know that it is highly improper for them to be out at night. And *here!"*

"Ah, yes. The residence of the most rakish gentleman of the land." Soothingly, he added, "But he's not here, you know."

"That is beside the point." It was difficult, but Minna resisted responding in as light a tone as his. It would be irresponsible. Undutiful. Selfish. She had no right to wish for an interlude of speech that was not a report to Mrs. Foster or instructions to a pupil but might be considered pleasant banter. "The point is, sir, that these young ladies are not where they are supposed to be."

"Which is precisely why I expected you sooner. Several days ago, in fact."

"You did? But—pardon me. I must be very stupid, but you make no sense at all."

His mouth twitched, but he replied with suitable gravity, "Then it is I who is stupid and not explaining very well. No doubt, because I am taken off guard. You see, I was inclined to be annoyed with you because you did not come to remove these girls. So much . . . female vivacity! I suspect I am not equipped to deal with it."

"They can be rather a nuisance," Minna acknowledged. "But when you spoke to me, you did not sound annoyed."

"No."

He said nothing else, but his smile, the frank admiration in his gaze, were unmistakable even to one as unaccustomed as she to—what? Flirtation?

While she stood speechless, he deftly removed the lamp from her hand and set it down, then took her arm and guided her toward the young people, who were about to start dancing again. Minna forced all thought of his smile from her mind and frowned. The positions the couples had taken up! Ladies and gentlemen facing each other, the gentleman's right arm encircling the lady so that his hand actually touched her back. Her waist! And her right hand resting in the palm of his left!

Even without the lilting tune struck up by the violin and the forte-piano just inside a doorway of magnificent proportions, she would have known that she was about to witness a performance of the waltz, considered quite scandalous by some. Unless, of course, she followed the call of duty and bustled the girls back to the school post-haste.

And she would have done her duty, she was sure of it, had not the painter addressed her at that very moment.

"Would you care to dance, Miss Elfinstone?"

"No!" She took a hasty step away from him.

"A pity. Usually there's only young Martin with the violin, and he is not the best of musicians. But tonight, since one of the young ladies is missing, Freddy insisted on dragging the forte-piano from the old music room. Now, *he* is a first-rate pianist. Dancing to his music must be sheer delight."

"Well, I do not care to dance. And you should not have asked me! You seem to be a sensible man. You should be helping me herd these girls out of here. Indeed, you should have sent them back as soon as they arrived!"

"And so I would have done," he assured her, "had I the slightest notion how to go about it. I am sure you would not have wished me to march them up to your front door."

"No." Minna suppressed a shudder. There were several large houses on the Steyne where nightly entertainments were held. A gaggle of young ladies was sure to have caught attention. "But you might have sent them back the way they arrived."

"Had I but known how to go about it. This is their sixth night here—"

"The sixth!" she reproached. "And you permitted it! But I must not blame you. They are *my* responsibility.

Only I cannot help wishing you had sent them about their business."

"I tried. But not until last night did I discover where they slipped in. Had I caught the first one——" He glanced at the girls gliding and dipping enthusiastically to the waltz tune. "Alas! All but two were already on this side of the opening, and when I pushed one back into the passage and turned around to catch another one, the first hopped back out." He assumed an injured look. "They thought it great fun!"

"They would." Minna stepped closer to the waltzing couples. How graceful they looked. And decorous, despite the intimate position the dance required. "I wish it had occurred to you to close off the secret passage once they departed."

"I daresay you do. And I doubt not you'll disbelieve that I could no longer find the opening when I returned with boards and hammer and nails."

She turned to him. He looked rueful but quite sincere. And, possibly, he spoke the truth. After all, she had not immediately noticed the secret door, either. Still, he might have tried harder. He could have——

He said, "You believe I am making excuses."

"Am I so very transparent? I do beg your pardon, sir. And let me assure you, I fully realize that the girls' presence here is through no fault of yours."

"I am glad, Miss Elfinstone. I would not wish to be in your bad graces."

"Sir!" she began but, meeting his gaze, decided to leave well enough alone. If he was bent on flirtation, it was not a game she had learned in her youth, nor was it a skill she wished to acquire. Briskly, she said, "It is high time that we leave. But tell me, please, how you know my name. I am certain we have never met."

"The young ladies speak of you constantly. Miss Elfinstone this, Miss Elfinstone that. Always with affection and admiration. You must be an extraordinarily gifted teacher."

"If I were, they would hardly run off in the middle of the night."

"Of course they would. They're like a gaggle of geese," he said, amused. "One takes off, the others blindly follow suit. They'll outgrow it, never fear."

"That may be true, but it is no consolation to me. I am responsible for them."

He turned serious. "No improprieties occurred, I promise you. Their partners are all nice lads. Most of them I've known for years; they're friends of my brother. And I've been the strictest of chaperons."

"Then you have my gratitude. Thank you, Mr . . . ?" She extended a hand, which he gripped firmly and held a moment longer than etiquette prescribed. Strangely, Minna did not mind. She wondered what it would feel like to have that hand at her back, guiding her in a waltz. She, who had not experienced the slightest desire to dance since those disastrous lessons years ago—except in a dream.

And now she had missed his name. Warmth flooded her face. Drat! If she blushed, she was an even bigger goose than any of her pupils.

He was looking at her quizzically.

"I beg your pardon, sir. Would you mind repeating your name? I was thinking of the girls . . . that I must . . ."

"Herd them out of here?" he supplied helpfully. "Indeed, you must. And my name is Ardleigh. Stephen Ardleigh. Why don't we join your charges, and I shall waltz you up to each one so that you can warn them this is the last dance."

"No! I cannot." Minna spun to face the makeshift dance floor. "And that waltz has been going on for longer than it ought. Your nice lads, the musicians, have been playing the tune over and over again."

"I hoped you would not notice until we had our dance. Surely I deserve some small reward for my vigilant chaperonage of your charges?"

She did not look at him. "If you wish to be rewarded, you should not claim a dance." She clapped her hands. "Ladies! Off with you, this instant! If we do not return now, Harriette is under strict orders to rouse Mrs. Foster."

Mention of Mrs. Foster worked like a charm. Without an adieu or apology to their partners, the girls dashed off in a great rush and absolute silence. Even the forte-piano and violin were still.

Minna risked a look over her shoulder at Stephen Ardleigh. He was watching her.

He smiled, raised a hand in salute. *"Au revoir,* Miss Elfinstone."

She hurried after the girls. No, she should not read any significance into his farewell. Regretfully, they would *not* see each other again.

The secret passage was dark, and she had forgotten the lamp. But she closed the door firmly and groped her way in the wake of whispers and soft footsteps ahead of her. Poor girls. Minna felt almost sorry for them, even a little guilty. Significantly more than half an hour must have passed while she chatted with Mr. Ardleigh, and Harriette would long since have roused Mrs. Foster.

"Miss Elfinstone." It was Louisa's subdued voice. "I waited for you. We always leave a tinderbox and three lanterns behind the steps, so we'll have light soon."

"How cautious of you."

"Please do not be angry, Miss Elfinstone. We meant no harm. In any case, it was my fault alone. I discovered the secret door. Quite by chance, I assure you. I was—"

"We shall discuss it in the morning, Louisa. I see light

ahead. Let us catch up with the others before we're left in the dark again."

Helen Wilson was waiting at the foot of the three flights of steps. The others had gone. With a slightly unsteady hand, Helen passed a glowing lantern to the headmistress, then climbed the stairs. Louisa followed. Holding the light as high as she could, Minna made up the rear.

The stairs did not seem quite as steep as they had during her descent earlier. Or, perhaps, it was merely that she did not notice because she was steeling herself against the sound of Mrs. Foster's irate voice that, surely, must ring out at any moment. But the bedchamber on the second floor remained quiet, and when she emerged through the narrow opening, only twelve young, apprehensive-looking ladies faced her.

Minna glanced at her pin watch. It was well past one o'clock.

"Harriette, did you not rouse Mrs. Foster?"

Huddled atop her bed and with the coverlet pulled around her shoulders, the girl mutely shook her head.

No one spoke, but twelve pairs of eyes hung, pleading and hopeful, on Minna's face.

She turned abruptly and pushed the secret doorway shut. "We shall discuss this later," she said sternly. "Now, go to bed!"

Eight of the girls scurried off.

Perched on the edge of Louisa's bed, Minna removed the borrowed dancing slippers. As she was tying her own shoes, she happened to glance at the wall. There was no sign of a secret door. Not a crack or line, no elevated rosette.

She felt her heart pounding. She wanted to reach out and touch the smooth plaster, but immediately felt foolish.

She did not know what to think. Stephen Ardleigh had

assured her he wanted to nail the other opening shut but
could not find it once the girls had closed it behind them.
She herself had not discovered this door—until Harriette
bade her wear the dancing slippers.

Dancing slippers?

Suddenly, Minna was out of patience with the whole
silly affair. These past couple of weeks without Miss
Bodlyn had been a strain, and at close to two o'clock in
the morning, she was in no shape to puzzle out a correlation between dancing shoes and a secret passage.

And how ridiculous to imagine there even could be a
correlation. Just in case, however, before retiring to her
own chamber, she collected every young lady's dancing
shoes.

The following morning, Minna rose just as tired as she
had gone to bed. Her mind was heavy. She had not done
her duty as she ought.

But her duty to whom? To what? To her conscience?
What a jest! She had no conscience. Had she not for
years stood by and watched Mrs. Foster gull ambitious
merchants with carefully dropped hints that their daughters would rub shoulders with members of the upper class
at her establishment? Had she not watched those hopeful
papas part with large sums of money over and above the
already exorbitant school fee? She had justified her silence with her need for employment; with the excuse
that the girls received an excellent education, training in
speech and deportment as they would find in no other
school catering to the middle class; and, last but not least,
that otherwise crafty men of business should know better
than heed Mrs. Foster.

For eight years she had ignored her conscience and
done nothing to undeceive the fathers of her pupils. Yet
now, when the girls were quite literally rubbing shoulders

with members of the upper class, at least those younger sons who could be spared to a career in the army, she worried about duty, even though she had not the slightest notion whose concept of duty and responsibility would be served if she reported last night's events.

True, the girls were in the wrong. They should not have slipped away. Six times already! But they had merely indulged in an innocent romp, the sort of "impromptu hop" ladies of the *ton* carefully arranged for their daughters prior to their coming out. The sort of informal dance Mrs. Foster should arrange for them at least once a month.

No impropriety had occurred. She had Mr. Ardleigh's word on that. Minna could not say why his word carried weight with her. It simply did. She knew nothing about him except that, by the looks of it, he was a painter. And, come to think of it, that he shared the family name of her former neighbor, her father's friend, Viscount Willoughby. Which meant nothing, of course. There must be dozens of families named Ardleigh quite unrelated to the childless, elderly gentleman who had given her, for her fifth birthday, a pony called Apple Dumpling.

Stephen Ardleigh. And just how much did he have to do with her sudden inability to define duty? Not a question to bring about the certainty, the peace of mind, Minna sought.

During class, she found it extremely difficult to concentrate on the French verbs the seniors conjugated, especially since the girls were watching her like keen young hawks eyeing their prey. Eleven seniors; she had sent Harriette, sniffling much less than the previous day, to supervise the younger girls while they wrote an essay on the evils of giving in to impulse.

She knew the senior girls were burning to ask if she would report them or had already done so. But they would have to stew awhile longer. At least until she figured out herself what had kept her from going to Mrs. Foster immediately upon their return from the Pavilion. And what stopped her from going to the study now instead of waiting to be summoned.

Barely half an hour into the French lesson, a maid poked her head into the schoolroom. "Miss Elfinstone, you're to report to the study. Right away, miss!"

Outwardly calm, Minna bade her pupils start a letter in French to an imaginary friend. There were sighs and a few groans. Abruptly, Minna changed her mind. From her personal cache of books on a shelf between two of the schoolroom windows, she selected a slim volume, beautifully bound and tooled.

She said, "On second thought, I do not know how long I shall be gone, and you will need an occupation to keep you awake. I want you to take turns reading aloud. You'll enjoy this. May even learn from it. Miss Jane Austen's *Pride and Prejudice*."

On her way to Mrs. Foster's study, Minna peeked into the first-floor schoolroom. Harriette was nodding over her French verbs, but all twelve junior pupils were bent over their essay books and busily scratching away with their pens.

No more excuses to delay the interrogation she was about to face. Head held high, Minna descended the last flight of stairs, marched up to the study door, knocked perfunctorily, and entered.

Mrs. Foster was smiling, and Minna knew even before she saw the lady and gentleman, and the young girl, that she was about to meet a prospective pupil. That was the only occasion to draw a smile from the dour proprietor of the school.

"Here she is," Mrs. Foster cried gaily. "Our esteemed Miss Elfinstone! I wouldn't know what to do without her. Such a wonderful teacher! And a *lady*. Like yourself, Sir Edward, our dear Miss Elfinstone's father is a baronet." And in that vein she continued for several moments while Minna shook hands with Sir Edward and Lady Marchmont and their fifteen-year-old daughter, Elizabeth.

Mrs. Foster addressed Minna. "Sir Edward and Lady Marchmont have made arrangements to stay in town for a few days. That will give Miss Marchmont an opportunity to observe the lessons and get acquainted with the other girls."

Lady Marchmont said, "Only if it's not an impo—"

"Of course not!" Mrs. Foster cut in. She directed a smile at Lady Marchmont, and a hard, flinty look at her headmistress. "You will personally take the young lady under your wing, won't you, Miss Elfinstone?"

"It will be my pleasure." Minna gave the girl an encouraging nod. "Come, my dear. I will show you around."

There was no point arguing the unwisdom of obliging the headmistress to spend all day with the younger girls and leave the seniors unsupervised. Elizabeth's father was a baronet. That said it all. Mrs. Foster would, if necessary, pay *him* to send his daughter to her school next term. What a feather in her cap! Any self-respecting merchant would pay double for the privilege of having his daughter share a room with the offspring of "Sir Edward and Lady Marchmont."

And, at least, the Marchmonts' arrival meant a reprieve from the report she ought to make. She would not receive gratitude if she broached the topic of worn-out dancing shoes while the school's proprietor was bent on charming a baronet and his lady wife.

Thanks to Miss Austen's novel, the day passed without mishap on the second floor. Shortly before six o'clock, when the younger girls had finished their lessons and were showing Elizabeth Marchmont the bedchambers before taking their prospective new friend down to supper, Louisa and Helen burst into the first-floor schoolroom.

"Dancing lessons, Miss Elfinstone!" Helen cried breathlessly. "May we have our slippers?"

Minna looked up from the essays she was correcting. "They are in my armoire. Open the right-hand door and you'll see them."

"Thank you, Miss Elfinstone," said Louisa, turning and drawing Helen with her.

"And return them immediately after your lesson!"

The girls stopped in the doorway and looked at each other. Then, slowly, they faced the headmistress.

They curtsied. "Yes, Miss Elfinstone."

And they dashed off, giggling.

Giggles and whispers invaded her dream. Her lovely, favorite dream of effortlessly, gracefully, dancing the waltz on a blue carpet spangled with stars and creatures of eastern fable, and surrounded by painted serpents and golden dragons. Of feeling the gentle pressure of a guiding hand at the back of her waist, the hand of the faceless stranger who inspired her to dance as she had never danced before. How easy the magic of his presence made that which an acclaimed Italian dancing master had been unable to teach—the melting of stiffness, the conquering of self-consciousness, the surrender to rhythm and sound.

But the giggling was a dissonance in her dream.

And then there was absolute stillness. She no longer felt the guiding hand at her back and came to an awkward, stumbling halt in the middle of a turn.

Minna awoke with a start. She was out of breath, disoriented. It took a moment to disentangle her legs from the coverlet, to sit up and light the lamp on the night table. Not an elegant lamp like the one left at the Pavilion the previous night, and which had been a gift from a former pupil, but a utilitarian piece she had found in a cupboard in the cellars.

As on the night before, it was close to midnight. All was quiet. Tempted to simply lie down again and go back to sleep, Minna nevertheless rose to check her armoire. The slippers were there. All twelve pairs. Conscientiously, she also went to check the girls' bedchambers.

They were empty.

Minna could not believe her eyes. Heart pounding, she stood in the third bedroom and stared at the wall behind Louisa's bed. The wall was smooth, unmarred by the outline of an entryway or a rosette.

Minna dashed to her room, struggled into a gown, slid barefoot into her sturdy leather slippers—then took them off again. Calling herself all kinds of fool, she retrieved a pair of dancing shoes from the armoire and put them on.

She returned to Louisa's chamber. Her hand and arm were not quite steady when she raised the lamp to look at the wall.

There was the door. And the rosette.

Three

Minna pushed aside a paint-streaked sheet hanging from the scaffolding and stepped into the Music Room. The girls and young officers, concentrating on the figures of a cotillion on the makeshift dance floor, paid her no heed. The music was supplied by a single violin; indeed, Stephen Ardleigh had been quite correct when he said the violinist was but an indifferent musician.

"Slipped away, did they?"

She had known she would see him here, and yet the sound of his voice made her start. She turned slightly to her right and saw him rise from one of a pair of elegant elbow chairs. No paint-streaked smock for Mr. Ardleigh tonight. He wore a coat of dark-blue superfine, molded to a pair of shoulders that must inspire confidence in any damsel in need of protection. His pantaloons were of the palest champagne color, and his Hessian boots gleamed like mirrors.

All of a sudden she was painfully conscious of her own appearance, the hastily donned drab gown, hair braided for sleep but, undoubtedly, with several strands escaping the plait.

"Please join me, Miss Elfinstone. If we are to chaperon, we may as well be comfortable. Or would you care to dance?"

She sat down, stiffly, perched on the edge of the chair. She assumed her most formidable no-nonsense expres-

We'd Like to Invite You to Subscribe to Zebra's Regency Romance Book Club and Give You a Gift of 4 Free Books as Your Introduction! (Worth $19.96!)

If you're a Regency lover, imagine the joy of getting **4 FREE Zebra Regency Romances** and then the chance to have these lovely stories delivered to your home each month at the lowest price available! Well, that's our offer to you and here's how you benefit by becoming a Regency Romance subscriber:

- **4 FREE Introductory Regency Romances are delivered to your doorstep**
- **4 BRAND NEW Regencies are then delivered each month (usually before they're available in bookstores)**
- **Subscribers save almost $4.00 every month**
- **Home delivery is always FREE**
- **You also receive a FREE monthly newsletter, which features author profiles, discounts, subscriber benefits, book previews and more**
- **No risks or obligations...in other words, you can cancel whenever you wish with no questions asked**

Join the thousands of readers who enjoy the savings and convenience offered to Regency Romance subscribers. After your initial introductory shipment, you receive 4 brand-new Zebra Regency Romances each month to examine for 10 days. Then, if you decide to keep the books, you'll pay the preferred subscriber's price of just $4.00 per title. That's only $16.00 for all 4 books and there's never an extra charge for shipping and handling.

It's a no-lose proposition, so return the FREE BOOK CERTIFICATE today!

A
$19.96
VALUE...
FREE!

No
obligation
to buy
anything,
ever!

PLACE
STAMP
HERE

REGENCY ROMANCE BOOK CLUB
Zebra Home Subscription Service, Inc.
P.O. Box 5214
Clifton NJ 07015-5214

sion, but inside she quaked, feeling as vulnerable, as ignorant and unsure, as she had at seventeen, in the throes of a violent crush on the new young curate.

But she was not seventeen. And she did not have a violent crush on Ardleigh—or such was her profound hope.

In an admirably steady voice, she asked, "When did they get here?"

"About fifteen or twenty minutes ago." Stephen Ardleigh adjusted the second chair so that they were partially facing each other. "Yesterday I was not certain I would see you again. So I must admit I am rather glad they gave you the slip."

She did not look at him but at the dancers. "I took away their dancing shoes. Where, I wonder, did they find new ones?"

"Freddy—you may remember, he played the forte-piano last night—is the brother of one of your charges. Helen, I believe."

"Helen Wilson?"

"That would be right. Her brother is Freddy Wilson. And if I understood *my* brother correctly, Freddy and some of his friends scoured the town for dancing slippers today."

"That would explain their easy submission when I ordered the old slippers returned to me after their dancing lesson." She frowned. "But I do not understand. The Wilsons are farmers, are they not?"

"Snobbish, Miss Elfinstone?"

Disconcerted, she finally looked at him, saw that he was teasing, and relaxed against the canvas-padded chair back. "I did not expect a farmer's son with the dragoons."

"Freddy is in the guards. He and four of his friends are merely visiting here. You're not familiar with military uniforms, are you, Miss Elfinstone?"

"No. But never mind my ignorance. Just tell me about Freddy and how come he's an officer in the guards."

"A mere cornet, Miss Elfinstone. But not a *mere* farmer's son. The Wilsons are what you might call landed gentry. An old family." He gave her a sly look. "Came over with the Conqueror, no doubt."

"Indeed." She relaxed even more. "With a name like Wilson!"

"At least it made you smile. And you're still smiling, though a bit mischievously. What are your thoughts?"

She shook her head. "I cannot—must not—say."

"That Mrs. Foster does not know of her catch but refers to Helen as the 'farmer's daughter'?"

Her smile faded.

"My dear Miss Elfinstone, there is no need to blanch. You must realize that Mrs. Foster's sentiments are not unknown in town. But that particular bit about the 'farmer's daughter' I have from my brother, who had it from Helen herself."

She could not speak.

Leaning forward, Ardleigh looked at her with concern. "Now what? You are even paler than before. What have I said?"

"I did not realize that the girls know how Mrs. Foster speaks of them. I—" Minna felt ill.

Stephen Ardleigh took her hand between both of his. "My dear girl—"

She withdrew her hand, but he recaptured it immediately.

"Hold still." He chafed her hand. "You're cold, and I am warming you. That is all. And before you say it, I do know you're not my dear girl. Not yet."

The challenge in his gaze was so deliberately provoking that, instead of raising her hackles, it made her relax once more. Odd, how comfortable she felt with him, a stranger.

"I haven't been called a girl in a great many years, sir, but I shan't quibble on *that* point."

"That is much better." With a final vigorous rub, he released her hand. "Now tell me what you could have done, or could do, to stop Mrs. Foster from disparaging her pupils and their parents. Without losing your post, that is."

"There is much I can do," she said with more assurance than she felt, since she could not think of a single measure that would stop the school's proprietor from voicing what she wished. "And if I am dismissed, I would simply take up another post."

"Without a reference?"

"There's that," she conceded.

"And leaving the girls without their Miss Elfinstone?"

She looked at her hand, missing the warmth of his touch. "In eight years I have not had as many perturbing thoughts or doubts as these past twenty-four hours." She raised her head and met his gaze squarely. "I have not reported the girls."

"I should hope not."

"But it is my duty."

"Your duty is to the young ladies. You're fulfilling it by chaperoning them."

She gave a short, wry laugh. "Hardly. It is not at all the thing for young ladies to slip away at night."

"Then insist that they must be accompanied by you from the start."

"What? And become a part of this—" Agitated, she rose.

"This outrage?" he supplied, rising as well. "I believe that is the term you used last night. But are you not the headmistress, responsible for the lesson plan, et cetera? At any other school, would they not have the opportunity to mingle with young men and practice their steps at small, informal dances?"

He said nothing she had not told herself. The lone violin had started a waltz tune. Involuntarily, Minna began to sway in time with the music but caught herself and said with a great deal of asperity, "I wish you would not speak in such a nonsensical manner! You're making my head spin."

He held out a hand. "Won't you dance with me, Miss Elfinstone?"

How tempting to place her hand in his, to be held the way she was held in that favorite dream.

She gave herself a mental shake. In that oft-repeated dream that had begun on her first night at Mrs. Foster's Seminary for Young Ladies, she was held by a faceless stranger. Surely she was not foolish enough to give that dream figure the face and form of Stephen Ardleigh!

"I do not dance, Mr. Ardleigh," she said with suitable finality.

"You will not, Miss Elfinstone? Or—" He cocked his head, gave her a quizzical look. "You cannot?"

She sighed. "I should have known you would persist. I *cannot* dance, Mr. Ardleigh. I have no aptitude. Two left feet, you might say. And I certainly never tried my hand, ah, foot at a waltz."

"Then let me teach you."

She turned away from him once more. Was this how Eve felt when the serpent tempted her with the apple?

The waltz tune ebbed and flowed all around her, invading her mind. Badly played as it was, it was the tune of her dream, the music that inspired graceful movement . . . a dance she had not even recognized in the early years of the dream. Slowly, as if propelled by an invisible force, she turned to face him again.

He held out a hand, and still without a will of her own, she placed her hand in his. He stepped close, bringing his right arm around her until his hand rested at the back of her waist. They did not touch except where his hands touched her, and yet her whole body was affected by his proximity. All over, her skin felt warm and tingling, her breathing was labored, and her pulse raced.

"What madness!" she gasped out, freeing herself and stepping back to a safe distance.

For a moment, he seemed disconcerted. Then he nodded. "But of course," he said gravely but with an unmistakable twinkle in his eye. "Madness, indeed, to attempt the waltz on these sheets." With the tip of his boot, he caught a fold of protective floor covering. "Proper fools we'd have looked if we had taken a tumble."

She was grateful for his light tone. "And what an example it would set if I were to dance with you."

"An exemplary example. As in everything you do."

She gave him a startled look, wondering if, unaccountably, he had resorted to irony. But she was mistaken.

He said, quite seriously, "Anyone observing your charges must perceive that it is so. Never mind what I said about their vivacity. They are delightful. I have observed no simpering, no unbecoming forwardness. I've had sufficient speech with them to know that you've not made them ashamed of their background but have infused pride in their heritage. You have instilled sufficient knowledge so they can actually form an opinion on a topic and hold up their end of a conversation. They show—in the bud, I concede, but it's definitely there— the same quiet dignity you present to the world."

"Sir!" Again she felt that warm, disturbing tingle. "Are you determined to put me to the blush?"

He smiled but said nothing.

To cover her confusion, she prattled on. "Do tell me, are you related to Viscount Willoughby?"

He cocked his head and studied her for a moment. "And if I am, will that count against me? Or for me?"

"What a question! I asked merely to make polite conversation."

"A pity. I had hoped kinship would be a point in my favor and that you were checking my pedigree."

"Your—" She gave a choke of laughter. "Can you never be serious?"

"But of course." He offered his arm. "Pray take a turn about the room with me, Miss Elfinstone, and I shall gladly expound on the twists of my family's connection with that of Willoughby."

She glanced at her pupils, completely absorbed in the dance. Envy shot through her. If only—

"Very well," she said briskly. "Just until the dance is finished."

She accepted his arm with utmost caution, but no disturbing sensations overset her equilibrium. On the contrary, she basked in a feeling of extreme well-being and was able to proceed at his side with the dignity he had praised.

"Pardon my curiosity, Mr. Ardleigh, but are you a painter?"

"Yes." He grinned. "Though some I could name accuse me of boasting. They call me a dabbler. I did, however, convince Prinny and Mr. Crace to let me 'dabble' at one of the smaller murals. The large ones, painted on cambric, are done by Lambelet in the ballroom at the Castle."

Prinny? An oddly familiar term for a painter to apply to his regent. She carefully stepped around a coiled rope and a wooden box filled with paints and brushes. "May I see your painting?"

"Next time you come I shall make sure it is not hidden by shrouds."

Next time. But there would not be a next time.

A lowering thought. Perhaps she ought to make the most of the occasion. Minna slowed, stopped to look up at the ceiling that had first caught her eye. There was the tentlike octagonal cornice, and stained-glass windows above that, but the light of the work lanterns did not reach high enough to show any detail. Still, as on the previous night, the view of the ceiling was sufficient to stir a memory, which slowly crystallized into a picture.

"Are those chandeliers in the shape of lotus blossoms? And a golden dragon in flight underneath each one?"

"You have good eyes, Miss Elfinstone. Quite spectacular, aren't they? The upper leaves are made of white ground glass, edged with gold. And the lower leaves, a pale crimson."

Her heart pounded. "I have no sense of direction in this shrouded room, but on one side, behind the scaffolding and sheets, are five windows, are there not? And between them four pagodas of Chinese porcelain, beautifully colored and gilded. And the murals are landscapes, all with Oriental motif, and there is a white marble and ormolu mantelpiece, a smaller pagoda on each side of it. An organ—"

She broke off, embarrassed, when she saw Stephen Ardleigh staring at her. "You must think me mad! I apologize. I do not know what made me blurt out these fantastical notions."

"But you're quite correct. That is, there is no organ yet, but it will be built. And the pagodas have only just arrived; they're still in crates. The mantelpiece is here, though. But no one has seen it yet. How do you know all this?"

She hesitated. "Would you disbelieve me if I said I saw it in a dream?"

"It would stretch credulity. But no," he said slowly, pensively. "No, Miss Elfinstone, I would not disbelieve you."

"A carpet," she murmured, gazing at the center of the room. "Brilliant blue, spangled with stars and creatures of eastern fable . . . and there's dancing. Waltzing." Warmth stung her face. If she said much more, he'd have the whole of her dream.

He quirked a brow. "Well? Did you? Dream of Prinny's Music Room last night?"

"I did." No need to speak of the other times she had dreamed of the Music Room. But he appeared to believe her. Would he believe as well if she told him what she had come to suspect as the magic of dancing shoes and the secret passage?

The music had ceased. One of the young officers was approaching with Louisa on his arm. "I say, Stephen! Could we not have some refreshments tomorrow night? It's a bit hard on the ladies without even a sip of lemonade once in a while."

Ardleigh said, "Miss Elfinstone, allow me to present my rapscallion brother, Lieutenant John Ardleigh."

The young man bowed. "I beg your pardon, ma'am. I've heard so much about you, I forgot we needed introductions. Honored to meet you, Miss Elfinstone."

She shook hands with Lieutenant Ardleigh, liking him immediately for his open gaze and unaffected manner. There was a marked resemblance between him and his older brother, but John's face was softer, his coloring lighter than Stephen Ardleigh's. And although John's smile was as warm and infectious as his brother's, it did not give Minna a single disconcerting flutter or a moment of breathlessness.

Louisa said, "Please don't be angry, Miss Elfinstone."

Thus reminded of her duty by her very own pupil, Minna opted for frankness. "I *was* angry when I discovered you gone, but, I must admit, as soon as I arrived here, my mind was preoccupied with . . . other matters." No point taking frankness too far. "So, I suppose, I am as much in the wrong as you are. And it *is* wrong to slip away."

"But is it so very wrong that we wish to dance a little?" For once, there was no mischief in Louisa's wide blue eyes, only uncertainty. "And meet young gentlemen?"

"It is not wrong to wish, Louisa. Only to go behind the backs of those responsible for you."

"Then, please, Miss Elfinstone, won't you be our chaperone?"

John and Stephen Ardleigh had withdrawn a little and were conversing in low tones, but at Louisa's plea, Minna became aware of Stephen Ardleigh's gaze on her. That she should accompany the girls had been his suggestion as well.

She should say no. Immediately and with finality.

"Miss Elfinstone?" Louisa pleaded.

Minna met Stephen Ardleigh's gaze. She made a wry little grimace. So I am exemplary, am I?

He smiled, giving her the uncanny feeling that he had read her thoughts.

Shaken, she looked at Louisa. "I'm sorry to say that I am in a quandary about this. So let us return to the school now, and I shall give you my decision tomorrow."

All day, the twelve senior pupils behaved with the utmost decorum. They studied quietly, apparently totally absorbed in French verbs, a Shakespeare sonnet, and Miss Austen's *Pride and Prejudice*. Contrary to Minna's expectation, they did not once approach her to plead their cause. But if they believed that decorum and studiousness would ease their headmistress's decision making, they were sadly mistaken.

After supper, while the older girls were at their dancing lesson, Minna at last went down to the foyer, knocked on the study door, and entered.

"Miss Elfinstone!" Mrs. Foster spilled a drop of the

restorative she was about to pour. She did not look too pleased at the interruption. "What is it? Have Sir Edward and Lady Marchmont not yet picked up Elizabeth?"

"They have." Minna closed the door. "And they asked me to convey their appreciation and to let you know that Elizabeth won't be coming tomorrow. They're returning home."

"What!" Mrs. Foster's voice rose shrilly. "But they're sending her next term, are they not?"

"Oh, indeed." Minna was all too aware that it was her presence at the school that had influenced the decision; Sir Edward had told her so personally. "Mrs. Foster, I have come to speak about the senior girls."

"Not another set of worn-out dancing slippers, I trust! Whatever it is, you take charge, Miss Elfinstone. I have one of my headaches and was hoping to retire early for once."

Minna watched the proprietor of the superior institute of female education pour a generous measure of restorative and down it. There was no question that Mrs. Foster needed to retire to her private apartments immediately rather than the usual eight o'clock. But first she must consent to a number of innovations her headmistress planned to introduce at the school.

She stepped close to the desk. "Mrs. Foster, the senior girls will leave in a month. It is time to hold a few informal dances."

"*A few!* What nonsense. We've never had more than one dance."

"None at all these past two years."

"None were necessary. And neither is there a need for one now. Not until next year, when Sir Edward and Lady Marchmont must be impressed." Mrs. Foster rose. "That will be all, Miss Elfinstone."

Minna stood her ground. "No, Mrs. Foster. That is not all. I remember distinctly your promise to Mr. and Mrs.

Herrington that their daughter would have all the benefits
of a first-rate academy. Those benefits should include
informal dances, teas, musicales, *in the company of
young gentlemen of good family*. I will gladly arrange
for twelve young gentlemen—"

"No!" Mrs. Foster's color rose alarmingly. "You will
not arrange anything at all, Miss Elfinstone. I have no
desire to spend several evenings—without good reason—
in the company of hoydens and pimple-faced, stammering youths." She brushed past Minna. "And you, Miss
Elfinstone, would do better to consider what tone to take
with me!"

Minna clasped her hands to keep them from reaching
out to shake the older woman. "The school has an obligation to these girls."

Mrs. Foster spun, an unwise move that made her sway
unsteadily. She glared at Minna, who felt certain she was
about to be dismissed on the spot.

"Perhaps, Miss Elfinstone, you labor under the belief
that you are too valuable to be dismissed as long as
there's no second teacher? You're mistaken, I assure you.
I taught hoydens years ago, and I will not hesitate to
teach again if necessary." A crafty look flitted across
Mrs. Foster's sharp features. "But I need not say more,
do I?"

Minna did not speak. She could not.

Mrs. Foster, looking pleased with herself, said, "For
some reason, you love those girls. I know you will not
put yourself in a position that must cause your dismissal.
And neither would you consider resigning. Good night,
Miss Elfinstone. Don't forget to lock up and to keep
those hoydens in their rooms."

For quite a while Minna stood there, in Mrs. Foster's
study, unable to quiet her seething emotions. Employ-
ers—with very few exceptions—always took advantage

of their staff. But to use her attachment to the girls! What a rotten, black-hearted thing to do.

When the reversal of fortune had sent her family from the manor to the steward's cottage, Minna had not wasted any time or emotion bemoaning fate. Now, for the first time, she wished she had wealth, or at least sufficient means to rent a small property to start her own school. Without a qualm, she'd coax or bully her pupils' parents to let the girls go with her.

Alas! That was impossible.

At eight o'clock, Minna had the house locked and barred, the younger girls in bed, with permission to keep the lamps lit another hour. Sally, the maid who had been moved to the first floor after Miss Bodlyn's departure, would make sure the lights were doused.

On the second floor, the senior girls' doors were closed. Minna gave them a pensive glance but proceeded straight to her own chamber.

From her armoire, she took the gown reserved for visits at home, where always a dinner invitation from Lord and Lady Willoughby awaited her. The gown, too, had come from Lady Willoughby. Minna loved it. The rich honey tone made her skin glow and her hair glisten with golden highlights. With the gown, she wore a pair of softest kid slippers. She brushed her hair, then, instead of fastening it in the usual tight chignon at the base of her neck, piled it atop her head, fastening it with a gold ribbon and amber-tipped pins.

After a final look in the cracked mirror, she sat down at the small pedestal table that served as a writing desk and as a worktable when she did sewing or mending. Several stockings and the hem of a petticoat needed attention, but Minna did not pick up her needle and thread.

She merely sat, hands folded in her lap, and let her thoughts roam.

At eleven o'clock, she rose, doused the light, and in the dark went to Louisa's chamber. She knocked and entered.

Twelve young ladies, gowned and wearing dancing slippers, sat perched on the four beds. None of them spoke, only gazed at her expectantly.

Minna cleared her throat. "Is it too early to leave?"

Smiles and glowing eyes acknowledged her question as the girls bounced to their feet.

"Not at all," said Amelia Trollope, picking up one of the lanterns, already lit and placed in readiness on the floor behind Louisa Herrington's bed. She opened the secret door, then stood back and looked at her headmistress.

"Go ahead," said Minna. "I'll follow."

The girls started filing through the narrow opening. Suddenly, Louisa said, "Miss Elfinstone, you're not wearing dancing shoes!"

"Won't kid slippers do? They're the best I have. Besides, I'm with you, and——"

"It won't work! Only satin or silk will do," cried Edith McPhearson. "I tried when I broke a ribbon on my dancing slippers. The door shut in my face!"

Minna did not argue but, with Louisa lighting the way, returned to her room and donned a pair of the girls' old dancing slippers.

"Do the young gentlemen at the Pavilion know where the secret opening is?" she asked as she followed Louisa and Edith down the steep stairs to the underground passage.

"No," the girls answered in unison. Louisa added, "It is magic, Miss Elfinstone. Only young ladies wearing dancing shoes can see and open the secret entrance. It's a bit scary, isn't it? But so deliciously thrilling!"

"Indeed," said Minna, guiltily acknowledging a *very delicious* thrill of excitement. She would no longer fret about the right or wrong of this venture, or how much her own desires had influenced her decision to provide for the girls what Mrs. Foster denied them. The young ladies *should* have some experience at social intercourse with young gentlemen before they left school. And thus, at present, her own wishes were inextricably linked with the girls' need. No point, then, to wallow in guilt. That would be dealt with when her seniors had gone home.

The Music Room was dark and quiet when she finally stepped through the opening and the shroud of protective sheets. It would have been better to carry the lanterns all the way instead of leaving them under the stairs, but never before had they been needed.

"No one is here," one of the girls whispered.

Minna was aware of such heavy disappointment that it was like a physical ailment, leaving her weak and low of spirit.

"We'll wait, won't we?" Louisa urged.

"I don't like the dark." That was Helen Wilson. "Can we hold hands?"

A light appeared suddenly, and Lieutenant John Ardleigh bore down upon them. "My apologies, ladies! But Stephen has not yet returned, and I promised him I would not bring my friends unless he is present. That was before Miss Elfinstone made an appearance, but Stephen is such a stickler for propriety, I feel I ought— In fact, not even I should be here. But I did want to let you know at least—"

Minna said, "We appreciate your brother's concern, and yours, Lieutenant Ardleigh. Perhaps tomorrow night we shall find Mr. Ardleigh returned?"

"Can you not wait? He said he'd be back by nine. It's not like Stephen to be late, but he rode—not far, only to see his cousin Willoughby not many miles past Rottingdean. His mount may have cast a shoe. Please wait, Miss Elfinstone!"

He looked so eager, her young ladies so pleading, that Minna relented, gladly, even. "Just for a little while. Half an hour at the very most, mind you."

There was a collective sigh of relief. John Ardleigh made the circuit of the Music Room, lighting all the work lanterns, then addressed Minna once more.

"Shall I leave, ma'am? Or do you think Stephen would wish me to stay with you?"

It occurred to Minna that there was yet another consideration she had not taken into account. And how she could have overlooked such an important point was more than she could say. The point that neither she nor any of her pupils had any right to be in the Pavilion. But they were here, and that was that.

"I cannot speak for your brother, Lieutenant. But I would most definitely prefer if you stayed. Tell me, have you been here often? I mean, prior to these dances? Or are you and your friends trespassing . . . like my pupils and I?"

"Not a bit," he said airily. "And neither should you worry that *you* may be trespassing. Not as long as Stephen says it's all right." And with a murmured excuse and a bow, he turned to the young ladies.

Minna raised a brow. *As long as Stephen Ardleigh says it is all right?*

As she watched the young people, she had to admire John Ardleigh's manners, his deft way at drawing each of the young ladies into the conversation, never singling one out or snubbing another. If it had not been for the fact that Minna had nothing better to do but observe him very closely, she would never have noticed that he was singling one young lady out, after all. But only in the way he looked at her, never that he paid her more attention than another. Before she could start to worry about yet another unforeseen situation, she caught the sound of firm footsteps approaching rapidly.

Stephen Ardleigh.

How was it possible that the mere sight of a man she had met but two nights ago could send her spirits soaring higher than the lofty ceiling of the Music Room? But it did. And his smile warmed her heart and made her take an involuntary step toward him.

As on the previous night, he wore a dark coat and palest champagne-colored pantaloons and was followed, she noted absently, by John Ardleigh's red- and blue-coated friends.

"Miss Elfinstone." He bowed over her hand. "How very beautiful you are."

She wanted to laugh off the extravagant compliment, but when she met his gaze, she could not. He made her *feel* beautiful, and she said simply, "Thank you."

"I apologize for my lateness. Two factors are responsible. My mount cast a shoe."

"Your brother warned us that may have happened."

"Kind of him. 'Twas speedily fixed, though. The longer delay must be laid at your parents' door."

"My parents?" She gave him a startled look. "How—oh! Your brother also said you were visiting your cousin Willoughby. Viscount Willoughby, then? My father's old friend?"

"The same. And from Willoughby Hall I proceeded to your parents' home. You're very like your mother, you know. Such a gracious lady. And kind and beautiful."

She could only stare at him.

"She invited me to dinner. Later, your father, after a stern and thorough interrogation, very generously granted permission that I may pay you my addresses. So, my dear Miss Elfinstone, will you marry me?"

Four

Minna wanted to pinch herself. Somehow, when she sat down on the hard little chair by the pedestal table in her room, she must have fallen asleep. And now she was dreaming—as vividly and fantastically as in the dream of waltzing in the full, if future, splendor of the Prince Regent's Music Room.

"Miss Elfinstone." Stephen Ardleigh placed a supporting arm around her. "You look about to swoon. Allow me to take you to a chair."

"No. I do not wish to sit. Thank you." Minna did pinch herself and, for good measure, Mr. Ardleigh's wrist as well.

He looked startled, then laughed. "I know the feeling well."

"You do? I mean, how could you? You cannot possibly know what I am feeling."

"Perhaps not. But I know what *I* am feeling. When your young ladies appeared the first time here in the Music Room, I was beset by a strong sense of expectation. I had not the vaguest notion what it was that I expected to happen, and it drove me to near distraction. Then, when you fought your way through those sheets two nights ago, *then* I did know." He grimaced ruefully. "I have wanted to pinch myself ever since to make certain I was not in a dream woven in protest of what I cynically called the vain quest for the perfect woman."

Minna found it difficult to breathe, impossible to think clearly. "Are you making sport of me, Mr. Ardleigh?"

"Only of myself, Miss Elfinstone. I had to learn to be practical at an early age in order to take charge of a younger brother and sister. That so painstakingly constructed practical side is forever warring with the other side of me."

"The romantic in you," she said when he fell silent. "I should have thought of it before. You could not be an artist if you were not also a bit of a romantic. And you may let go of me. I truly am not about to swoon."

His arm tightened. "What if you're wrong? No, Miss Elfinstone, I dare not risk letting go."

The violinist was playing a waltz tune, and the music, combined with the heady experience of a strong arm supporting her, only served to heighten the sensation that she was living in a fantasy. In *her* dream, with the faceless stranger miraculously changed into the man at her side.

She drew a deep, fortifying breath. "Mr. Ardleigh, will you teach me the waltz?"

"Yes!" His voice held a triumphant note. "Yes, indeed, I will."

And she was whisked into the center of the room, onto the makeshift dance floor.

"Trust me," he said. "Allow me to hold you close. It'll be easier that way."

Aware of her pupils' interested gazes upon them, she inclined her head in a barely perceptible nod. But he saw, and before she could reflect upon the wisdom of her decision, he held her in the proper waltz position, or rather, *improper* position, for they were far too close. How warm he was, spreading that warmth to her. Stiffness melted, self-consciousness ebbed as she stepped and dipped and whirled under his expert guidance.

The girls were forgotten as the music, the feel and

scent of him, filled her mind. She danced as she had danced in her dream, gracefully, effortlessly, and it all was possible because she had consigned decorum to perdition. It was not merely his hands that guided her, but a touch of his shoulder against hers, the length of his leg leading her into the next step—a gentle wooing into the delight of the dance. Into awareness of self.

With my body I thee worship . . .

She stumbled, stopped, gazed at him in consternation, unsure whether the words had been in her imagination, or whether he had uttered them.

The music stopped, and into the stillness, he spoke. "You have not given me an answer, Miss Elfinstone."

Once more she was aware of her pupils' wide-eyed attention, of grinning young officers, of John Ardleigh leaning close to Louisa and whispering something that made the girl's eyes grow even rounder.

"Pray let us take a turn about the room, Mr. Ardleigh." To the girls, Minna said, "One more dance, then we shall leave."

Heart still racing—from the exertions of the waltz, of course!—she accepted the proffered arm. For a few moments they walked in silence along the scaffolded, shrouded perimeter of the Music Room.

"Did I rush you?" he asked at last.

"How can you ask? Two days ago we did not know the other existed!"

"Did we not?" he said quietly. "Now that I have met you, I know I've been waiting years for you. And at the same time, as impossible and illogical as it seems, I feel as if I have known you forever."

She thought of her dream, of the ease she had felt in his company from the very first moment of meeting him, and admitted, "It does not seem so impossible. I, too, feel as if I have known you for a very long time. But is that enough?"

"It is for me. I am three-and-thirty, and not once have I felt about a woman the way I feel about you. I want to be with you morning, noon, and night. I cannot offer you riches at present. But I can give you an adequate home and all the comforts you may desire. Unless—" The lightness was back in his voice, and the look he gave her was quizzical. "Unless, of course, your notion of comfort is outrageous?"

As lightly, she replied, "Dear me! Have I come across as mercenary? But all I want, I assure you, is a school of my own."

"Then you shall have it. In fact, I shall purchase Mrs. Foster's school for you. It will suit admirably, since I shall be engaged for a while longer with Prinny's decorations."

She stopped and gave him a puzzled look.

"What? Do you not believe me capable of persuading Mrs. Foster?"

"Capable, yes. But, surely, you're funning." She frowned. "Mr. Ardleigh, why do you refer to the Prince Regent as Prinny?"

"Ah! What a disrespectful wretch I must seem to you," he said with a smile that warmed her from head to toe. "But, faults or not, I like the man. He counts me his friend. Miss Elfinstone, won't you call me Stephen?"

"Are you deliberately changing the topic?"

"Not at all. I am trying to keep our conversation on track. What about calling me Stephen?"

Turning slightly, she gazed absently at the dancers, engaged in yet another waltz. How they enjoyed the dance . . . and did not hesitate to flaunt their pleasure for all the world to see.

"Miss Elfinstone?"

"Very well." She did not look at him. "My name is Minna."

"I know. A name derived from the old German *minne*.

Love. Your parents could not have chosen a more suitable name for you."

How caressing was his voice.

How tempting to turn and accept his offer of marriage.

Instead, she said, "I do believe Louisa and your brother are developing a tendre for each other. I must not permit theses dances again."

"Why? They do not sit in each other's pockets or behave in any way improperly."

No, indeed. Lieutenant Ardleigh was waltzing with Charlotte Witherspoon. However, no one could miss the looks and smiles exchanged when he and Louisa danced past each other.

Stephen said, "And if something more serious grows out of this calf's love, I do not think Mr. Herrington would object. As I warned you, we have no fortune, but neither are my brother and I reduced to fortune hunting. John won't have a title, but someday—in the very *distant* future, I hope—he'll be closely related to a viscount. Would you like being a viscountess, my dear Minna?"

She spun. "Willoughby? You are the heir?"

"You sound disapproving. Do you mind? I can always decline, you know."

"Not disapproving. *Astounded!*"

He gave her a quizzical look. "Perhaps I should not have mentioned it at all? I have a most difficult time figuring out what will or won't sway you in my favor. Do tell me it's not important!"

She could not help but smile. "It is not at all important. But what—just supposing, mind you, that I did accept your offer and you were a viscount later on."

"Indeed, let us suppose."

"What would you do with a viscountess who runs a boarding school?"

"The same, I would hope, that you will do with a viscount whose main occupation is painting."

Stepping between her and the makeshift dance floor, he took possession of her hand, raised it, then gently brushed his lips across her wrist.

"I would adore the viscountess with the boarding school. Love her. Dearest Minna, do you not know how much you mean to me?"

His broad shoulders shielded her from her pupils' view, so it could hardly be embarrassment that heated her blood, her skin. How was she supposed to think? To weigh the alternatives before making a decision when all she wanted was to hold him close and feel his arms around her?

But giving in to impulse, surrendering to the lure of the moment, was hardly the way to decide over the rest of her life.

Mustering resolution, she withdrew her hand from his clasp. "Mr. Ardleigh . . . Stephen . . . lud! I am stammering like the veriest schoolroom miss! This will not do at all. I must have time—time to consider your offer."

"What is there to consider? Tell me your doubts, and I shall lay them to rest."

"But that is precisely the point," she said with some asperity. "I do not have any doubts while I am with you. I must be alone—"

"Why?" he interrupted. "If you have no doubts when you're with me, then you are safe from them forevermore. Just say the word, and we shall be married immediately."

How persuasive he was. But reason prevailed. "Where, sir, is your practical side when it is needed? Marry immediately! Indeed, I have never heard anything more nonsensical."

"Not at all. You may remember that I mentioned a sister?"

"So you did." Purposefully, she started for the dance floor to summon her pupils.

"My sister is married to a rector, and yesterday I sent

him word that I would require a special license. He obliged by posting up to London, to Doctors' Common."

She stopped and looked at him. There was no laughter in his eyes to assure her he was teasing. But then, marriage was a serious matter, and if he had spoken in jest only, she would have been greatly disappointed.

"Shall I send for him?" he asked.

"No," she said weakly. Then, more firmly, "Most definitely not. I do not know whether to cry or laugh or stomp a foot in exasperation, and if ever I needed a moment alone, it is now. I feel . . . bowled over by your ardor. I never expected an offer of marriage. And now this! You make me feel . . . loved. Cherished. Desired." Tears welled in her eyes. "But how do I know that this . . . feeling is not a spurious thing. A moment of madness. Of self-deception?"

He stepped close. With his thumb, he gently caught a teardrop escaping down her cheek. "Send the girls away," he said, his voice low, urgent. "Let us be private just for a little while. A single minute would suffice! And I shall convince you—"

"Indeed!" she cut in. "I do not doubt that you could convince me. Of anything you wished! That is precisely what makes me . . . well, not frightened, but . . . and besides," she added inconsequentially when she could think of no specific term to describe her feelings, "when I marry, I would wish to see my parents there. My pupils. I—"

She broke off, feeling like a simpering miss, a prattling fool, even though she knew herself to be a most rational being. And seeing him smile did not help a bit.

"Say no more, my love." Cupping her elbow, he steered her toward her pupils. "Go. Take all the time you wish. I shall wait here for you tomorrow night."

* * *

Tomorrow night.

Tonight.

Take all the time you wish, he said. . . . and expected her tonight!

She knew her answer . . . she knew it not. . . .

She knew . . . not.

"Miss Elfinstone?"

Minna looked up from the stack of sonnets written by her pupils and to be evaluated by her. Alas, not a single one had had the benefit of her full attention.

"Yes, Amelia? What is it?"

"Should I not spell Louisa with the younger girls? She has been down there for over three hours."

Guilt-stricken, Minna glanced at the watch pinned to her gown. "Yes, go at once. And I thank you for reminding me, Amelia."

When Louisa stepped into the second-floor schoolroom, Minna apologized.

"It's quite all right, Miss Elfinstone," the girl replied airily. "Are you and Mr. Ardleigh getting married?"

Minna could feel the other girls' eyes on her. "I beg your pardon?"

"I asked if you and Mr. Ardleigh—"

"I heard the question. But whatever makes you think so?"

Louisa cocked her cropped head. "You may think me impertinent, but, Miss Elfinstone, we've known from the first night that Mr. Ardleigh is head over heels in love. And you seem to be quite taken with him."

But Minna was not interested in the girls' perception of her. In truth, she should not encourage such talk at all.

She asked, "What makes you think Mr. Ardleigh is in love?"

"He was different before you appeared. Not precisely grumpy, because he was always polite and conversed with us. In fact, the greater part of our conversations was about *you*. He was keenly interested in anything we could tell him about you. John—Lieutenant Ardleigh—was teasing him that he was trying to paint a picture of you. Not your face or form. But your inner self."

Minna was silent.

After a moment, Louisa said, "You should have seen his face when you stepped into the Music Room the first time, Miss Elfinstone! When I was a child, two of my father's ships were reported lost in a typhoon. Close to sixty men lost! And, of course, the cargo. Months later, the harbor master sent a messenger that the ships had been sighted. My father's face had a look then that resembled Mr. Ardleigh's when he saw you." Bestowing a sunny and infinitely wise smile upon her teacher, the eighteen-year-old sat down at her desk.

The rest of the day dragged interminably. Minna was glad of the rigid structure of lessons, meals, and outdoor activities Mrs. Foster had imposed upon pupils and teachers and which had by now become an ingrained habit. Whenever her attention wandered, the girls unhesitatingly recalled her to her duties.

She did not see Mrs. Foster that day. Mrs. Felt, the housekeeper, confided at dinner that the lady had been closeted with her solicitor since noon. But Minna had no interest in speculations about Mr. Greyson's visit. She had more weighty matters to mull.

Minna had planned to wait until eleven, but at ten o'clock that night she could sit still no longer. Once more wearing her beautiful honey-gold gown and a pair of the girls' dancing slippers, she went to Louisa's room.

The young ladies were dressed and waiting.

Minna looked at them, her heart swelling with pride. Yes, they were boisterous at times, and silly, and mischievous. But, as Stephen said, they were delightful, and she loved them all.

"I am sorry." Her voice caught, and she had to clear her throat. "I know you'll be disappointed, but tonight I must go to the Music Room alone."

The girls exchanged looks.

Louisa said, "We suspected as much. Look—" She raised the hem of her gown, showing off her feet clad only in stockings. "No dancing shoes."

"Miss Elfinstone, I would like you to try these on." Amelia Trollope handed Minna a pair of silk slippers matching the color of her gown. "My mother sent them when I complained how quickly my slippers wear out. She never wore them because they pinch."

Tears stung Minna's eyes. Was she now, on top of everything, turning into a watering pot? Fumbling, she untied the ribbons of the old white slippers and exchanged shoes.

"Thank you, Amelia. They fit perfectly."

Dorothea handed her one of the lanterns. Helen stepped forward and, winking, dabbed a drop of rose water on Minna's wrists.

Louisa embraced her. "Do what's right, Miss Elfinstone," she whispered. "Right for you."

After hugs from the other eleven, Minna stood before the secret door. She was the only one in dancing shoes, the only one to see the rosette.

Taking a deep breath, she pressed the rosette. The door pivoted on its central hinge, and she stepped through the narrow opening.

Stephen was waiting when she emerged in the Prince Regent's Music Room. The look on his face told her everything she needed to know.

She was breathless all of a sudden, as if she had run

the length of the secret passage. "You're here! I feared
I might be early."

He grinned. "Hardly. I've been waiting since eight-
thirty." He took her hand, kissed it, sending a delicious
shiver up her arm. "My love, I was terribly remiss last
night. Before you say anything, allow me to rectify an
omission."

"What?" She felt so light, so carefree, when she
looked at him that it was difficult to concentrate on his
words. "Did you omit to tell me that the Prince Regent
sent out the guards to arrest us for trespass?"

His arms closed around her. "I did not tell you that I
love you. Minna, even if you have never believed in the
magic of love at first sight, you must believe it now.
Because I fell in love the moment I saw you. Nay, I was
in love when I first heard of you. Minna, my dearest
Minna! I love you."

And then she was crushed to his breast; his mouth
covered hers in a kiss that sent her spinning into a diz-
zying whirl of the most pleasurable sensations. The taste
and feel of him awoke a hunger that could not be as-
suaged by a kiss alone. She wanted more. All of him.
Forever. Cupping his face in her hands, she kissed him
back, loving the feel of his skin, the slight roughness that
made her wonder how he would feel in the mornings, in
need of a shave. She traced the strong line of his jaw,
then buried her fingers in his hair . . . and felt him re-
ciprocating, caressing her back, the curve of her neck.
But his hands seemed hesitant, or carefully held in
check—which his mouth was not. And so she took her
fill from that which he offered, until at last, panting, they
broke apart.

"Sir!" she said, gasping for breath. "I think you had
better marry me."

Immediately she was caught in his arms again. But he

held her loosely, looking down at her with the laughter in his eyes that had first captured her heart.

"To make an honest woman out of you? Or to save me from turning into a ravisher? Minna, my love, you are a delight! But I wish you had not caused me twenty-two hours of agony before you made up your mind."

"I should apologize. I was missish last night because, even though I would not admit it, I did want to marry you even then. But, you see, I never expected an offer of marriage. There is no dowry, you know. And my station—"

"Hush!" His arms tightened around her. "Do you love me?"

"I love you, Stephen. I love you with all my heart."

"No reservations? No doubts because we know each other such a short time only?"

"None. Only . . ."

"What, my love?"

"Only, I will always feel a little guilty for deserting the girls."

He raised a brow. "Oh, ye of little faith!" he said with mock severity. "I told you I would purchase the school."

"But that was in jest!"

"Was it?" Removing one hand from her waist, he reached inside his coat. "Mrs. Foster drove a hard bargain, but here it is. The deed to your school."

Minna stared at the piece of parchment he unrolled for her perusal. And there it was, the name of the deed holder: Mrs. Stephen Ardleigh.

"If all else failed and you still refused to marry me, this, as a last resort, was to be the lure. I am glad I had no need to bribe you."

"So I learned something new about you. You, sir, are an unprincipled rogue!"

"And you, madam, are all I ever dreamed of in the woman I will cherish to the end of my days."

They gazed at each other. No words were necessary in this moment of commitment.

Softly, at a distance, the notes of a forte-piano rippled out. A waltz tune. The tune of her dream.

"Minna, will you dance with me?"

She placed her hand in his, and he led her to the center of the room. For the first time, she noticed that no work lanterns were lit, but the central chandelier, in the shape of a lotus blossom, had been lowered and was shedding its soft, slightly rose-hued light over the makeshift dance floor.

Stephen said, "I moved the forte-piano outside the room and told Freddy to play when I gave him the word. He must have grown impatient. Or, perhaps, he believed me a slow-top who needed a nudge."

"But this was perfect timing."

"Perfect. And we shall marry as soon as possible?"

"As soon as my parents can be notified." A thought occurred to her. "Stephen! What are we to do about the secret passage? We cannot leave it as it is."

"Why not?" A glint of mischief lit in his eye. "We just won't put any curious young ladies into that room. You'll make it your study. Then, when the fancy strikes us, we can sneak out and do . . . this!"

He whirled her around the dance floor, and she was caught up in the magic of the waltz. In her mind, the room transformed itself into the magnificent chamber she had visited in her dream: the carpet beneath her feet a brilliant blue spangled with stars and creatures of eastern fable, the gilt pagodas between the windows, the mantelpiece of white marble and gilt, the painted serpents and flying dragons. The Prince Regent's fabulous Music Room . . . as it was to be, someday in the future.

KING THRUSHBEARD

by

Judith A. Lansdowne

One

Once upon a time in the midst of the scamper and the scramble, the dashing and the darting, the sheer exhilaration and the considerable excitement—adequately hidden beneath masks of ennui—that comprised the London *ton* in the midst of a Season, a gentleman arrived on the doorstep of Number 4 Hanover Square and sent the servants into a tizzy. James, the first footman, was so stunned to discover who stood upon the doorstep that he slammed the door he had just opened right in the gentleman's face and dashed down the corridor bellowing for the butler.

"It be Himself!" James bellowed, skidding into the butler's pantry. "Oh, gawd, Mr. Tempest, it be Himself at our very door! You must come. I cannot possibly answer the door to Himself!"

Tempest studied the first footman calmly. "You are mistaken, James," he said. "Madam would have advised us to expect him."

"It be Him. I be knowing Himself, Mr. Tempest!" responded James, swiping in agitation at his wig and setting it madly askew. "You must come. He cannot be adequately met by such a one as I am."

With quick steps, Tempest traversed the long corridor to the vestibule. He drew aside the curtains on the window to the left of the door and peered out at the doorstep. "By Jove, it *is* Himself," he whispered hoarsely, allowing the curtains to fall back into place. "I must speak with Henri at once," he muttered, abruptly beset with nerves. "Henri must abandon the pheasant."

"Himself will not abide a pheasant on the table," agreed James. "We will require beef. And baked bread pudding. Himself delights in baked bread pudding."

"Just so," agreed Tempest. "I will tell Henri at once. James, you must go directly to Mrs. Sarsenet and say that his lordship's chambers must be aired and the special linen got for his bed. And flowers. Flowers in every room. And I must fetch the best of the wine from the cellar for dinner this night. And his hearth must be cleared of coal! Have we wood enough at the stable to use in his hearth? Himself cannot abide coal!"

Elias Ezekiel Thoroughgood, Earl of Lanningsdale, placed one gloved hand upon the door frame and the other on his hip and stood patiently waiting for the door to open a second time. He had every confidence that it would. His smile flickered like candlelight in a tiny breeze as he studied the perturbation on the countenance of his valet.

"I cannot believe he done that," muttered Bertram, setting the third of his lordship's portmanteaux on the step and drawing himself up to his full height of five feet, one inch. "The audacity of some personages!"

"It is not audacity, Bertram. I have known James since I was in leading strings. There is not an audacious bone in his body."

"The fellow closed the door right in your face, lordship."

"Yes, I know, but only because he was nonplussed. Tempest will open it for us soon."

"When is soon?"

"I am not certain. Apparently Tempest is nonplussed

as well. That was Tempest peering out at us a moment ago. I ought to have sent Mama word to expect us."

"Ought always be expecting of the master of the house," growled Bertram quietly.

"Yes, well, but the London staff does not expect me to appear without notice, Bertram. I have never done so before."

Lanningsdale shifted his hips so that more weight came to rest upon the right one than the left and grinned patiently down at his ruffled valet. "Come, Bertram, smile. The door will be opened to us soon. It is not as though we stand here shivering in the winter wind, you know."

Bertram could not fail to note how his lordship's smile continued to flit about his lips and how mirth sparkled in his kind blue eyes. Never been one to grow angry at nothing, thought the valet. Do I not be angry for him when 'tis necessary, he will not be getting nowhere in this world.

"I do beg your pardon, Mama, for not sending word," Lanningsdale sighed as he settled into the puce armchair in the drawing room. "I received this invitation at Rosehill five afternoons ago, and since then I have thought of nothing but being reunited with Missy."

"Madness," replied Lady Lanningsdale, frowning over the invitation he handed her. "If Lady Artemis did not wish to be reunited with you last Season or the Season before that, why should she wish it this Season? Ah, but then, it will not have been Lady Artemis invited you, Elias. It will have been Miss Waithe. In her desperation, Miss Waithe's reach has extended itself all the way to Rosehill."

"Last Season? The Season before that? You do not mean to say, Mama, that this is Missy's third Season?"

"Exactly so," harrumphed his mama.

"And no one thought to invite me to even one of her entertainments until now?"

"Likely Miss Waithe thought it unorthodox to ask you to travel such a distance for but one evening, Elias. But, the poor woman is desperate for gentlemen this year, I expect. Perhaps Lord Breckenbridge convinced her that as the families were once neighbors, you might be counted upon to make the effort."

"Well, I am pleased he did. I should hate to think of Missy grown, married and gone forever without my having had so much as one opportunity to court her."

Lady Lanningsdale gazed worriedly at her son. His sweet blue eyes glistened with happiness. Dark hair curled about his ears, whispered across his brow and cuddled against the back of his neck with a charming nonchalance. Tall, broad-shouldered, slim-waisted, he had grown into the very image of his late papa.

"What is it, Mama?" Lanningsdale queried. "You are staring at me in the most unnerving manner."

He not only looks like Giles, but he sounds like Giles, Lady Lanningsdale thought. That voice could charm the birds from the trees. Doubtless his merest whisper will set a young lady's heart to shuddering right down inside of her.

"Mama?" insisted Lanningsdale. "You are staring yet. Have I dirt on my face? Is my neckcloth soiled?"

That figure, Lady Lanningsdale thought. That face. That voice. What will I do if Lady Artemis cannot resist him?

"Mama, will you not say one more word to me? What have I done? What have I said?"

"What? Oh, it is nothing, darling. You do not actually wish to—court—Lady Artemis, do you? You did not mean precisely that? I realize the invitation must have stirred your memory and therefore your imagination,

Elias, but you are not truly in the market for a wife? You cannot be. You are far too young."

"I am two and twenty."

"Just so. Much too young."

"Mama! Father was merely one and twenty when he asked you to be his bride."

"But we were so much more versed in the ways of the world, Elias. We were not as frivolous as young people today. And ours was an arranged marriage, darling. Your father and I knew we were to marry each other from the time we were children."

"Yes, and you were not at all happy about it," offered Lanningsdale with a teasing glint in his eyes.

Lady Lanningsdale smiled the most pleasing smile in response. "I admit I was rather intimidated by your papa at first. After all, Elias, to marry a man enamored of the study of wizardry? But he proved to be the kindest, most humorous of all gentlemen."

"Just like me," Lanningsdale observed with a grin.

"There are times I think you as alike your father as two nips in a tuck."

"And so you are pleased to have my company, Mama, and will be delighted to have me escort you to the Breckenbridge ball."

"No. I do not believe that I shall be at all pleased by that, Elias."

"But whyever not?"

"Because you have not come rushing to London simply to escort me to a ball, my dear. You intend for me to smooth your reception into Breckinbridge house," replied his mama with a most cognizant shifting of her eyebrows. "And once I have done so, my darling, you will have all to do with Lady Artemis and nothing to do with me."

"Never!" protested Lanningsdale, running a nervous finger around the inside of his neckcloth. "Do you say

I will abandon you to the dowagers and the old men? I think not."

"You will," declared his mama softly. "I see it in your eyes, Elias. Drat Miss Waithe for remembering your name! This invitation has set it in your mind again to marry Lady Artemis. I thought you had abandoned that idea years ago. Do not attempt to marry her, Elias. Do not so much as attempt to court her. Heed my words. Lady Artemis is no longer the charming Missy with whom you played. Take yourself back to Rosehill or off to the Continent or to the colonies if you wish, but do not place yourself within sight of Lady Artemis, I beg of you."

"But I have dreamed of finding Missy again, Mama, for all these years. Dreamed of renewing our old friendship and of the two of us coming to love one another. Well, I already *do* love *her*. I always have. And she is surely old enough to marry now. Are you afraid that she will not have me? That I will be crushed because of it?"

"No," sighed Lady Lanningsdale. "I am afraid that she will have you, Elias. Very much afraid that she will."

Lady Artemis glared at the stack of invitations resting upon the silver salver on the long table in the vestibule. "More?" she muttered. "Papa," she called as her father stepped from his study into the corridor, "are these invitations to our ball as well? Are yet more people to be invited?"

"Indeed," nodded the Earl of Breckenbridge. "Your aunt Gwen has had Rathmore writing them for days. Every unattached gentleman of rank she could think of, she has invited. The first batch were delivered to gentlemen who do not reside in London during the Season. And these will be delivered to those gentlemen who do. Ladies, too, of course. One cannot have a ball without a number of ladies. The thing will prove to be a sad crush if everyone accepts."

"I am certain that you need not suffer a sad crush on my account, Papa," replied Lady Artemis with a lift of her stubborn chin. "I doubt there is a gentleman invited whom I shall find in any way acceptable."

"Artemis!"

"I cannot lie, Papa. I will not give myself to a gentleman. Any gentleman. I promise you that I will not."

Breckenbridge gave a shake of his graying head and slipped back into his study to avoid any further conversation with his only child. Truly, he had been most remiss in her upbringing. In her eighth year, when her mama had died of the fever, he had placed Artemis into the hands of Mrs. L. Paxton-Dalrymple of the Paxton-Dalrymple School for Young Ladies, and Mrs. Paxton-Dalrymple had returned to him a prideful, willful, spoilt young woman. No gentleman was good enough for Artemis. Oh, how he regretted now his decision to place her under Mrs. Paxton-Dalrymple's tutelage. He ought to have kept the gel at home and given his sister-in-law, Gwenyth, authority over her. But he had yet had hopes for Gwenyth, had thought that he would be able to find his sister-in-law a husband. That had never come to pass.

"It is all talk," he whispered to himself as he shuffled past the bookshelves in his library. "Artemis will find a husband." He pulled out one book and then another, searching for the most ancient of the volumes—volumes that might be sold to antiquarians for a tidy profit. Artemis *must* choose this time around, he thought. I cannot afford another Season. I cannot afford this Season. But I must attempt it. Gwen is right about that, for Artemis must marry. End in dire circumstances else.

"Perhaps I ought to tell her the truth," he muttered, running his fingers through his thinning hair. "If she knew the truth, perhaps she would not remain so very headstrong."

But Lady Artemis had been born headstrong, and even then she stood complaining to her aunt Gwenyth about the number of invitations issued to the ball and the impossibility of there ever being a person in pantaloons to whom she would consent to be married. "It is such a waste, Aunt. They are all of them insufferable!" Ceasing on that exclamation to pace the sunroom, Lady Artemis stared down at the pleasant, rotund lady who sat quietly upon the striped sopha. "I will not be wed to any man, Aunt Gwenyth, not even if Papa demands it of me."

"As to that," sighed the long-suffering sister of the late Lady Breckenbridge, "your papa cannot demand that you marry anyone, Artemis. In my day, it might be done—a gentleman might force a daughter to marry whomever he wished—but no longer."

And it is such a pity that he cannot force her into marriage, Miss Wraithe thought, gazing at her niece's pouting countenance. But she knew better than to voice that particular opinion aloud. "Come, Artemis, sit down here beside me and let us discuss your problems honestly, my dear one."

"My problems?" asked Artemis, her finely drawn eyebrows rising. "I have no problems, Aunt Gwen, except for Papa's unceasing efforts to marry me off to one paltry gentleman or another. I cannot think why he is so set upon it. You never married, and only see what a fine life you have."

Gwenyth Waithe, who acknowledged nightly the great debt she owed to her brother-in-law for having taken her in as he had when Artemis's mama had died, and for having done his very best to find her a husband, only shook her greying head sadly from side to side and patted the seat beside her. "Come and sit, my dear," she urged.

"Let us discuss my fine life, then, and what you may well have to look forward to."

There followed a halting but profound sermon on the terrors and dependency of a maiden aunt that would have set any other young lady's hair to standing on end, but Lady Artemis would have none of it. "It does not apply to me," declared Artemis adamantly. "For one thing, I am not nor ever will be anyone's maiden aunt. And for another, Papa is not a mere baron, as your papa was. My papa is an earl. You will see, Aunt. I will set up my own establishment and manage my own finances and do whatever I wish once I convince Papa that I shall never marry."

"Finances? And where do you imagine that these finances will come from, Artemis?"

"Why, from Papa. He would not think to deny me anything. He has never denied me the least trinket since Mama died. I am his heart's solace. He has said so any number of times."

"But if your papa cannot afford such extravagance as to set you up in a household of your own? Or worse yet, my dear, if your papa were to die?"

"Oh, pooh, Aunt. You are nothing more than a worriting old maid. Papa to frown upon one of my dearest wishes? Papa unable to afford to set me up in a household of my own? My papa?"

"Oh, my poor dear," murmured Miss Waithe, dabbing the corner of a handkerchief to her eye. "My poor, poor dear. I understand that your papa does not wish to confess it to you, but you must know. You must be told before all hope is gone."

Thereupon followed the most horrendous tale of sunken ships and cargoes lost at sea, of misspent monies, failed crops and investments gone awry. "And so your papa cannot possibly provide you with an establishment of your own, darling. And worse yet, when your papa does die, you will inherit nothing. Everything left to us at this point is entailed and must go with the title to Mr. Robert Grandly of Lincolnshire," sighed Miss Waithe.

Lady Artemis tilted her stubborn little chin upward in defiance. "I refuse to believe a word of it," she declared. "Papa would tell me straight out if he were in such dire circumstances. You are being a worrisome rabbit merely, Aunt Gwen. If Papa were in such straits as you have chosen to believe, he would not so much as attempt to provide me with a third Season. But here I am, and so here is the proof that what you say is not to be believed." Artemis rose and, with a swish of her skirts and the whisper of her forest green slippers across the carpeting, she departed the room, her head held high and her mind filled to overflowing with anger at her aunt for telling such farradiddles and implying that she, Lady Artemis, of all people, must marry a person in pantaloons in order to have a happy and secure life. But then, most of the ladies remaining from the previous generations had been misguided in that regard. Mrs. Paxton-Dalrymple had warned that it was so.

Merely two days later Lanningsdale entered the morning room in Hanover Square. "I have sent a footman with word that we will attend Missy's ball," he announced, giving his mama a kiss on the cheek and then moving on to survey the contents of the warming dishes on the sideboard.

"I vow, Elias, you were born with the ability to select the very worst from among all other possibilities," his mama sighed, tapping the back of her fork nervously up and down against the tablecloth.

"What does that mean precisely?" Lanningsdale asked, considering the coddled eggs that stared up at him from one of the chafing dishes. "Is it likely to be a dull and boring affair, this ball of Missy's, Mama? Will you despise being obliged to sit through the thing? You have not taken a sudden dislike to Breckenbridge as well as to his daughter, have you?"

"No, no, the earl is quite nice, really."

"So I always thought. He and Father were very good friends before Breckenbridge sold Willodean, were they not?"

"Yes, but that was so many years ago, Elias."

"Still, I doubt Lord Breckenbridge has altered much from the gentleman I remember."

"No."

"Good."

"Elias, the ball is for the purpose of marrying off Lady Artemis. It is thrown precisely to find the gel a husband."

"Just so. Just why I came."

"You do not understand, Elias. Lady Artemis cannot find a husband. She is not at all as you remember her. She is twelve years older and has changed a great deal. She has undergone such an alteration that Lord Breckenbridge grows desperate."

"Bosh! Why?" asked Lanningsdale, deciding to ignore the eggs and help himself to a rasher of bacon instead. "Has Missy become deformed in some way? Has she developed spots? Does she bray like an ass when she is amused? Why do you choose such a word as desperate?" He added three pieces of toast and a strawberry tart to the bacon on his plate, poured himself a glass of ale, and carried all to the table where he took the seat opposite his mama. "Can a gentleman actually be desperate about marrying off his daughter?"

"Yes. Yes, indeed. A gentleman with daughters can be driven to do the most desperate things, especially, Elias, when his daughter is Lady Artemis."

"I do not understand, Mama, why you have taken Missy into such dislike. She was used to run tame in our house, just as I ran tame at Willodean. You delighted in having her about. 'A thankful change from the company of men,' you were accustomed to say at all hours of the day and night."

"Yes, but that was before her mama died and Lord Breckenbridge sent her away to that dreadful school."

"And that dreadful school did what? Am I to assume that Missy has become somewhat of a bluestocking?"

Lanningsdale's mama frowned a bit over that. Then, "No, I do not believe she is a bluestocking," she replied.

"What then, Mama? Why have you grown to dislike her so?"

"Because she has become cruel and insensitive!"

Lanningsdale, a bit of bacon halfway to his lips, stared at his mama in amazement. He did not believe a bit of it. Not for one moment. Something else going on here, he thought to himself. Likely Missy has insulted Mama in some way without even knowing it. Missy could never be cruel or insensitive. She was always so very sweet and gentle. Did she not help me mend a pheasant's wing and nurse it until it could fly again? Did she not go so far as to cry when I caught a trout and force me to throw it back into the stream? And she was always ready to take even the ugliest of God's creatures under her wing. Certainly she cannot have changed so drastically in twelve years as to have become out and out cruel. Mama is mistaken in that.

TWO

Though her nerves were quite on edge, the dowager Countess of Lanningsdale waited upon line with great solemnity. She had already decided that she would nod regally to the Earl of Breckenbridge, Miss Waithe, and Lady Artemis as she passed before them. She would give none of them her hand. She would introduce Elias in the most icy tones and, the warning having been given, she would move quickly away on Elias's arm.

But it will not do a bit of good, she thought. I ought not to have come, and I ought to have prevented Elias from coming. He will fall madly in love with Lady Artemis at first sighting.

As the two of them ascended to the top of the staircase and meandered toward the small receiving line, Lady Lanningsdale could not help but despair. If Elias had truly loved the girl when she was a child, he must fall in love with her again now that she was grown.

And if Lady Artemis decides to have him! thought the countess. What will I do then? How will I save my son from a monster disguised as a faery princess? And then they were before the Gorgon, and Elias was bowing over the creature's hand.

"You are come to our little ball dressed as befits a king, Lord Lanningsdale," said Lady Artemis quite loudly, taking her hand back from Lanningsdale as quickly as possible. "Papa, a veritable king bows before me. And only see how crookedy his chin has grown. Why, it makes him look like a thrush with a beard, does it not?" Artemis laughed, most pleased with herself. "You are not Lord Lanningsdale at all, sir, but King Thrushbeard!"

"Artemis!" protested her papa.

"Artemis!" echoed Miss Waithe.

"Lady Artemis," murmured Lanningsdale softly, sending shivers up and down his mama's spine, for she had heard that particular whisper on her late husband's lips often. "Lady Artemis, you do not remember me. But you will. And you will learn to long for this thrush's song, I assure you of it." Then, with another bow, he passed her by and led his mama down the corridor and into the Breckenbridge ballroom.

"There is nothing at all crookedy about your chin, Elias," protested Lady Lanningsdale as her son led her to a chair along the west wall. "Your chin is perfect."

"Thank you, Mama, but it is a bit crookedy," the earl responded, standing before her and fingering the cleft in his chin thoughtfully. "Artemis has grown to be a veritable vision, has she not?"

"Yes. And she has grown haughty and hateful as well."

"No. Merely on edge," drawled the earl thoughtfully. "Only think what it must be like, Mama, to be put through one's paces at such a ball as this, to be displayed like a hack on the block in Tattersall's. She does not at all remember me, I think. But she will. She will."

Resplendent in blue pantaloons, midnight blue coat, a waistcoat of gold embroidered in silver that glittered with every movement and black dancing slippers with gold-and-silver buckles, Lanningsdale smiled down at his mother encouragingly. "Do not fret, Mama. I do not mind to be called King Thrushbeard before all of these people. In fact, it is apt, do not you think?"

"No!" declared the countess, snapping her fan open

and plying it angrily before her decidedly warming cheeks. "I have never heard such nonsense. To make such a thing of a tiny cleft in your chin, Elias. A cleft that I have loved with all my heart since first I held you. To call your chin crookedy because of it and name you Thrushbeard!"

"Hush, Mama. It is not of the least significance. No more significant than that she titles me king because of the opulence of my waistcoat. A child's nervous prattle is all it is."

"Do not make excuses for her, Elias. She intended to insult you. She intended for the other guests to laugh at you. Cannot you see that it is so?"

"I cannot. She is on edge, as I said. I will set her at ease and remind her of her days at Willodean, Mama. Then she will call me Elias, as she was accustomed to do, and there will come an end to this King Thrushbeard nonsense."

In a gown of sleek, glowing jonquil that clung like gossamer to her exquisite figure, Lady Artemis fairly flowed around the dance floor. Exchanging partners as she traveled down the line, stepping to the figures first with this gentleman and then with that, she was never at a loss for words. "Lord Mannerly is so very round," she declared as she stood opposite Lord Davies. "Round as a wine barrel. And do you hear how his voice echoes? He is an empty wine barrel, I fear." And again, as Lord Barrett led her into a waltz, "Lord Davies is so very red. Red as a fighting cock, and he likes to crow. I cannot abide a crowing cock!" And yet again, as she curtsied to Lord Mannerly, "Lord Barrett is so tall and thin. Tall and thin has little in."

Throughout the evening not an unattached gentleman escaped the censure of Lady Artemis's tongue. But when it came to the Earl of Lanningsdale, she was the most vocal of all. "One would think that King Thrushbeard expected to attend a ball at Carlton House. How does he remain upright under the weight of that waistcoat? Surely it is formed of pure gold. Well, it proves his strength, if not his worth, that he remains standing. And his chin! I cannot help but laugh each time I see it. So crookedy it is that an elf might sit upon the top of it and tap his feet on the bottom."

Miss Waithe was thoroughly appalled by her niece's quite public comments on Lanningsdale's appearance. More so because she remembered, if Lady Artemis did not, the handsome lad who had once been the girl's favorite companion. "Will you not waltz with Lord Lanningsdale," Miss Waithe urged, amazed, as that gentleman approached them, that a glint of good humor still lingered in Lanningsdale's heavenly blue eyes.

After all these years his eyes still shine with love for her, Miss Waithe thought, and then she actually prayed for a miracle. As Lord Lanningsdale came to a halt before them, she prayed with all her heart that no sooner would Artemis waltz with the man, but the scales would fall from the girl's eyes and she would recognize in Lord Lanningsdale a true and faithful love.

"May I have this waltz, Lady Artemis?" Lanningsdale queried quite properly. "You have danced with every other gentleman, I believe. Is it not time to allow me to escort you to the floor?"

"Waltz with you, King Thrushbeard?" asked Lady Artemis with a defiant tilt of her head. "I cannot possibly. I have turned my ankle, I fear, and cannot dance one more dance this night."

"You have what?" exclaimed Miss Waithe, staring at her charge in disbelief. "Artemis, how dare you to tell such a farradiddle?"

"I dare because I do not choose to tell the truth,"

Artemis stated, sipping at a glass of champagne. "But I will be truthful if you insist, Aunt. The truth is, King Thrushbeard, that I do not wish to dance with you. Nor did I wish to dance with any of the others. I find men the most disgusting creatures."

The Earl of Breckenbridge, overhearing his daughter's remark, stuffed his hands into his pockets, muttered under his breath and stalked from the ballroom. It would serve the gel right to be married off to some beggar from the streets, he thought. That would put an end to such nonsense as she continually spouts. Married to a beggar and forced to live in the street beside him! "And she may yet be," he whispered forlornly. "If things do not turn about for me—and rapidly, too—Artemis may yet become a beggar, be she married to a beggar or not."

The dowager Countess of Lanningsdale watched as Breckenbridge stomped from the ballroom. That poor man, she thought. And then her son came to stand before her.

"Lady Artemis has declined to dance with you, Elias? She has insulted you again? Let us depart then. Even her own papa has had enough of her tongue and departed."

Lanningsdale's blue-eyed gaze, which had grown considerably cool, fell full upon his mama. She shivered in the chill of it.

"I expect every gentleman here has had quite enough of Lady Artemis," he responded. "Yes, I believe we shall take our leave."

Together they bid farewell to Miss Waithe and sought out Lord Breckenbridge in his library to thank him for the evening.

"Why you should thank me, Lanningsdale, I cannot imagine," muttered that gentleman. "My daughter has done naught but make you an object of her spiteful humor for the entire evening."

"Not for the entire evening," Lanningsdale replied.

"Although I do not doubt that she would, did I remain for the rest of it."

"I am heartily sorry. You may believe it. And I apologize to you as well, Countess. We were good neighbors once. I hope you will forgive Artemis on the strength of that. Though I do not forgive her. No, I do not. It is a sore point with me at the moment that a man is not allowed to strangle his own daughter upon his own dance floor."

"I would gladly have strangled the girl for him," commented the countess as she entered her back parlor, seated herself on the chaise longue, kicked off her slippers and wiggled her toes inside her white stockings.

"No, Mama, would you? Strangle the woman I love?"

"Elias, you are not so witless as to believe that you love such a harridan as that."

"Oh, perfectly witless," Lanningsdale assured her, stepping to the sideboard to pour his mama a brandy and carrying it back to her with a serious frown on his most intriguing face. "So witless, in fact, that I can think of no one else but Lady Artemis to take to wife."

"Elias!"

"She is beautiful, Mama. Almost as beautiful as you. And she has a fine form and a neat ankle."

"She never did display her ankle to you?"

"Indeed, and gazed straight at me when she did. Her eyes are hard as gemstones, Mama. They were never used to be that way. Only remember how lovely, soft and inviting they once were. How filled with tenderness."

"You are mad to base your feelings upon a child remembered," the countess declared, sipping at her brandy.

"Well, then, her lips—in this present time—are marvelous. They will taste like cherry wine, I think, once they cease to mock as they do."

"They do never cease to mock and never will!"

"I do not deny that she wounded me, Mama. Yet, my Missy is somewhere inside of this dreadful Lady Artemis. And because Missy exists within her, Lady Artemis remains desirable to me."

"You are moonstruck."

"Perhaps I am," sighed Lanningsdale, taking up a post by the window and staring out into the moonlit square. "Perhaps I am."

"You be wishing to marry a gel what thinks you be a bird?" asked Bertram, his green eyes wide with wonder.

"She does not think that I am a bird, Bertram. She named me after a bird. Thrushbeard, she called me. King Thrushbeard."

"Why would she do that?"

"Because she thinks my chin is crookedy like a thrush's beak, is what she said."

"Humph!"

Lanningsdale turned from his looking glass to gaze at the little valet who was busily tucking the gold waistcoat safely into the clothespress. "I gather you do not think the same."

"Humph!"

"Do not be insulted, Bertram. The insult, I am certain, was intended for me, not for you."

"A thrush's beak indeed," muttered the valet, setting his lordship's dancing slippers into the bottom of the armoire. "A perfectly fine chin, it be. Perfectly fine. 'Twere a good enough chin for your mama when your papa wore it."

"But quite possibly it is not as good as I have been led to believe." Lanningsdale in nightshirt and slippers eased down into the wing chair before his chamber fire and sipped at a cup of hot chocolate. "Mama detests the girl."

"I should think so."

"But Mama can be brought to like her if she must. I cannot understand what has gotten into Missy. She is not herself."

"Not herself?" asked Bertram, ceasing to fold down his lordship's counterpane. "Changed considerable?" he asked, gazing thoughtfully at nothing and blinking his large green eyes. "Could be," he declared after the longest pause, and then finished turning back the covers.

"Could be? What could be, Bertram?"

"Could be as someone put a spell on that gel," replied the little valet. "When your papa put the spell on me, I were most enormously changed."

"I do not think you changed much at all," grinned Lanningsdale. "I was merely four, but I do remem—"

"I were taller as a frog," interrupted the valet petulantly.

"You were?" Lanningsdale smiled to himself as he gazed into the fire. "I seem to recall that you were small. Fit in my palm."

"I never did not! It took you two hands, lordship, and even then you could not hold all of me. I were *very* tall for a frog. Emerald green. And excessively well put together," Bertram added with a sniff. "I were exquisite."

"Yes, well, Lady Artemis was exquisite as a child, and she is exquisite as a woman, too. I am not speaking of outside appearances, Bertram. You were a splendid friend to me—gentle, loyal, honorable—when you were a frog. And you are precisely the same now that you are a man. But Missy is not at all as I remember her. All the caring, the kindness and the good nature that I recall has fallen right out of her. Might someone have cast a spell to keep her exquisite on the outside but make her abominable within?"

"No," declared Bertram. "I were stupid to think it. Your papa would not never do such a thing. Besides which, he be dead now these five years."

"There are other people who can cast spells. My papa was not the only one."

"He were the only one what I ever knowed."

"I am positive there are others. If one is interested, there are entire libraries to be found filled with volumes—"

"I never seen but one," interrupted Bertram, lighting the wick on the bedside lamp with suddenly shaking fingers.

"Well, you have not gone about looking at other people's libraries. I wonder if any of father's volumes are here in this house? He could well have found use for one or two of them in London. I shall go and have a look-see, eh?" the earl added, setting his cup of chocolate aside and rising from his chair.

"Why, lordship?" asked the valet, ceasing to move at all except for his fingers, which quivered.

"Why? Because I may find them helpful, Bertram. If someone has cast a spell on Missy, perhaps one of Father's volumes will explain how to cast it off again. Or perhaps I shall discover a different spell. One that will make her the gentle, loving girl I once knew."

"No!" exclaimed the valet in a hoarse whisper. "Do not go casting no spells, lordship!"

"Why not?"

"Because you be—not good at it."

"I am aware that I have not proved adept at it in the past, Bertram, but I am older now," said Lanningsdale, strolling in the direction of the door to the corridor. "Perhaps with age has come ability. Papa was an excellent wizard. I am his son. Certainly he has passed some of his ability on to me."

"No, lordship, he didn't not."

"He must have. And if someone has already cast a spell on Missy—" Lanningsdale took the china doorknob in his hand.

"You ain't good at spells!" interrupted Bertram, seizing a pillow from the bed and fluffing it with considerable vehemence. "You be terrible. Change the lady into a pig, you will."

"I will not," protested Lanningsdale, releasing the knob and turning to stare at his valet. "What a thing to say!"

"You went and changed Lord Hardin into a pig," the valet pointed out, tossing the pillow aside.

"Yes, but I was younger then and—"

"Last year it were."

"If you will allow me to finish—I was younger then *and* I was distracted by—by—I cannot seem to recall by what."

"A pork pie."

"No, really?"

"A pork pie," nodded Bertram significantly.

"Well, I will not be distracted again, and I will not change Missy into a pig. Change her into a compassionate human being."

Bertram stared at his lordship, panic writ plain across his face. "Perhaps it do not require no spell," he offered hastily. "Lady Artemis already be a human being. It be the other part what concerns you, lordship. Ain't that correct?"

"Yes. Someone has altered her, Bertram. She has become a harridan. I find I do not like her at all, and I was accustomed to like her very well. How would you suggest that I change her back again if not with the aid of wizardry?"

"Experience, lordship."

"Experience?"

"Just so." Bertram nodded again. "I bet it were not

no spell altered the lady. Some fearful experience changed her. And some fearful experience be what will change her back."

"Experience," murmured Lanningsdale, strolling back toward his chair before the hearth. "You may have something there."

Bertram gave a tiny sigh of relief as he watched the earl sit again before the fire and take up his chocolate. "So you will not be attempting to cast no spells, lordship?"

"Perhaps not. You may go. Oh, Bertram," murmured Lanningsdale just as the valet's hand touched the doorknob. "I did change Hardin back into himself again, did I not?"

"I do not recall," Bertram replied. "You must have done, lordship, but I do not precisely recall."

Three

Lanningsdale, taking his valet's advice to heart, declined to search the library for any volumes of spells his papa might have left behind at the London house and began, instead, to court Lady Artemis assiduously in the hope that he might provide her with the precise sort of experience that would return her to the pleasant, appealing, compassionate being he remembered. He virtually haunted Breckenbridge House, calling upon Lady Artemis at every opportunity, sending her posies, paying her morning calls, taking her driving in the park, escorting her to the theatre, accompanying her to Vauxhall.

"I cannot think why you do it," his mama sighed in the third week of his rather frenetic courtship. "Elias, the girl makes a jest of you from morning till night. She accepts all that you offer and gives you nothing in return—not so much as a pleasing smile." The countess set her needlework aside and studied her son with considerable pique as he stood blocking the doorway to the Blue Saloon.

"I know, Mama," Lanningsdale agreed. "Missy does any number of things that set my teeth to aching just as they do yours, but still, I love the girl."

"How can you, Elias? How can you love such a cruel, insensitive chit? There is no other gentleman would put up with half so much as you have done. You have only to witness the absence of beaux about Breckenbridge

House since that hideous ball. They have all turned away from her one after the other. Except for you, Elias. Why do you persist? Have I taught you nothing about love and marriage? Oh, my dear, I have not, have I? It is all my fault this unfortunate attachment of yours. I have always supposed that you knew about love—that you had somehow absorbed the correct concept of it from your father and me. I did never once think that perhaps you had not, that perhaps I should speak plainly to you of what a lady and gentleman ought to expect from one another."

"You need not do that, Mama," Lanningsdale replied, spinning down with some vehemence onto an exquisite lyre-backed chair and almost toppling it in the process. "I am perfectly aware of what one ought to expect from love and marriage. I merely say that I love the girl. I do not say that she loves me. If I am correct in my estimation, she does not even like me. But then, I do not like her, either."

"And how can you love someone you do not like, Elias?"

"I can because I truly believe, Mama, that beneath the mockery and the haughtiness and the spoilt beauty who calls herself Lady Artemis lies the heart and soul of my dearest little Missy. And she calls to me, Missy does, Mama, and begs me to love her regardless of this Lady Artemis who surrounds her and holds her captive."

"You are a dreamer like your papa, Elias, and merely dream that you are in love."

"No," stated Lanningsdale with great consideration, a frown creasing his brow. "No, I do not believe so. I am in love. But she is the most frustrating person. I vow, she is. No matter what I do or say, she finds me laughable. You do not think she is *already* under some sort of spell, do you, Mama?"

The countess shuddered at his words. *"Already* under

some sort of spell? Elias, you have not—you did not think to—you cannot have attempted to place that girl under a spell yourself? Oh, my dearest, please say it is not so! Say that you have not attempted to cast a spell over Lady Artemis."

"I promise you that I have not, Mama. But it has occurred to me to make use of some of the things that Papa taught me. I was, in fact, speaking of it to Bertram some while back."

"No, no, no, you must not!" exclaimed Lady Lanningsdale a deal more loudly than ever she was wont to speak.

"But why not, Mama, if it would work to my advantage and Missy's? Surely she is not happy as she is. No one who is truly happy could be so spiteful and mocking. Someone has altered her. And such an alteration it is! Most assuredly it is a spell woven about her. Why should I not search through Father's books to discover a way to unweave it or to spin another that will return her to her very best self? Why should I not when it would serve to make her happy—and to make me happy as well?"

"Because you are not *good* at wizardry, Elias. Do you not remember attempting to make your cousin James more appealing to Lady Emily? You changed the poor boy into a pig!"

"Yes, yes, I know I changed Hardin into a pig. I have already been reminded of that, thank you very much."

"You have? Whoever reminded—'THE FROG?' " asked the countess, her countenance betraying some astonishment.

"I wish you will not call Bertram 'THE FROG' in precisely that tone, Mama. I am fond of Bertram."

"Well, of course you are, darling. He was your pet. I should not have thought him intelligent enough, however, to have heard you speak of spells and think to remind you of James."

"But I did return Hardin to his former self," stated Lanningsdale, his voice betraying his uncertainty. "I am positive that I did."

"Elias, you do not remember if you did or did not," accused his mama. "How can you not remember? I was forced to share my traveling coach with a pig! We had it hoofing and clattering about the house at Bath for two entire days until you could at last determine what had happened and undo the spell."

"By Jupiter!" exclaimed Lanningsdale, remembering with great relief. "Bath! Of course! Hardin became himself again at Bath!"

Lady Artemis sat politely in her papa's study, her back straight, her hands folded quite properly in her lap and a look of strict attention pasted upon her pretty face.

"I cannot think why!" exclaimed her papa, pacing about the room in agitation. "You were always such a sweet, biddable child. And now—now—I cannot think what has come over you. You have done everything possible—everything—to make each and every eligible gentleman in England abhor you. It is as though you have set your mind to discover how to make yourself a pariah to any man of sense, taken lessons in how to become a veritable shrew!"

"Really, Papa," protested Lady Artemis. "You are climbing into the boughs, sir, for nothing."

"For nothing?" Breckenbridge ceased to pace and stared down at his daughter, his eyebrows rising in surprise. "How can you say it is for nothing, Artemis?"

"Because I do not care to have a gentleman, Papa, so how can it make the least difference that there is not one of them will have me? I have told you over and over that it is my wish never to marry at all. You need only provide me with monies enough to set up my own establishment and I shall live most contentedly with Aunt Gwen as companion. All men are dullards, Papa—strange, loathsome beasts—and I shall not be forced to marry with one of them. Never!"

"Loathsome beasts?" asked her papa blankly, crossing to the large mahogany table he used for his desk and sinking down into the enormous chair behind it. "All men? Am I then a loathsome beast, Artemis?"

"Yes, I expect you must be," declared his daughter with a curt nod, "though I do not see it myself. I expect that I do not merely because you are my papa, and so our relationship is necessarily altered. All men are beasts, Papa—born to prey upon women, to take all that women have, make slaves of them and, in the end, rip them to pieces."

"R-rip women to pieces?" The Earl of Breckenbridge could not believe his ears. "Men?"

His daughter nodded emphatically. "Mrs. Paxton-Dalrymple herself was accustomed to say so over and over again. Men are the scourge of the world. And particularly, they are the scourge of womankind."

"This is what you learned at school?" asked her papa, tugging at the cravat that had tightened abruptly around his neck. "This is what that woman taught you?" He gasped, perspiration beading upon his forehead. "Of all the balderdash I have ever heard! Why, I loved your mama with all my heart. Never did I—prey—upon her, as you say. I have done all, given all, first for your mama's happiness and now for yours."

"That is not true, Papa."

"It is not? When, Artemis, have I denied you anything? Every frippery, every falderal, every gown and bonnet and reticule you ever desired, I have given you. And three Seasons, Artemis. I have sported the blunt for three Seasons!"

"Well, but you are rich, Papa, and I am your daughter,

and as I said, between a gentleman and his daughter, the relationship obviously alters. And then again, perhaps it does not," she added with a pursing of her lips. "After all, Papa, I have said most clearly that I do not wish to marry and yet, you continue to urge me to it. You wish me to marry so that you may be rid of me and gain more riches into the bargain, do you not? You think to regain in the marriage settlements all that you have expended on my behalf."

The Earl of Breckenbridge could not believe his ears.

"Your intention is to sell me, Papa, to the highest bidder, to some beast of a man who will pay you with monies or lands or livestock and then take me home to be his slave and bear his children. Well, I shall not do it, Papa. I will not be sold."

Lady Artemis gazed at her papa, triumph glinting in her cold emerald eyes. "You think I do not know the way of the world, Papa, but I do. Mrs. Paxton-Dalrymple has taught me well. Aunt Gwen has hinted to me about money, you know. I could tell that she did not wish to do so, but I expect you urged her to it and she could not oppose you. She has gone so far as to say that you are in dire straits. I do not believe a word of it, but if it is true that you have—through ill-luck and bad judgment wasted a significant portion of your funds, then it is also true that you think to sell me off to replenish them."

The Earl of Breckenbridge opened his mouth, closed it again, opened it once more like a carp out of water. His face, red as a cock's comb, faded to a vile pink, then to white, then changed to a fine pale gray. "Never," he whispered, his voice atremble. "Never. You are my d-daughter. I l-love you, Artemis. I h-have always loved you. A man does n-not sell his daughter no m-matter what his circum-circum-stances."

* * *

Lanningsdale leaned back into the wing chair in White's parlor and crossed one long leg over the other. He sipped at a glass of port and studied the severe pallor of the gentleman who sat across from him. "I came as soon as I received your message, sir, but you are not looking at all the thing. Perhaps you ought to take yourself home and we will meet again on the morrow."

"No, no," protested Breckenbridge. "We must have a conversation, you and I, and we must have it now. I only hope that it is not already too late."

"Too late, sir?"

A tinge of color climbed into the elder gentleman's cheeks. "By Jove, Lanningsdale, I do not know how to begin. I fear you will think me outrageous. But I am so angry and so baffled and so very desperate. And you were used to be fond of my Artemis once."

"I am fond of Lady Artemis now, sir."

"You are?" A sigh of relief escaped from somewhere deep inside of Breckenbridge. "I should have thought that by this time my Artemis would have turned you away from her completely. She has done so with every other gentleman."

"Has she?"

"Indeed." Breckenbridge felt his neckcloth growing tight again and tugged at it fitfully with one finger. "And—and—I have come to discover, Lanningsdale, that it is all caused by that dratted woman!"

Lanningsdale's ears would have perked forward with the greatest attention had he been a horse. As it was, he merely set his glass aside, rubbed one hand along the arm of the chair in which he sat and wiggled his right foot. "That dratted woman, sir? Certainly it is not Miss Waithe to whom you refer?"

"No, no, Gwenyth is the best of all sisters-in-law. It is that dratted Mrs. Paxton-Dalrymple," Breckenbridge said with great precision, in the most dangerous of tones.

"Ruined my girl, she has. Changed her from a charming child into a veritable shrew. Turned the gel against all men. Can you believe it, Lanningsdale? Even *I* am to be considered a loathsome beast. No way to talk sense to the gel now. Well, after years of—"

"Ah ha! Mrs. Paxton-Dalrymple!" Lanningsdale interrupted, tasting the woman's name on his tongue with great relish. "I knew it! Mrs. Paxton-Dalrymple. So that is the name of the vile sorceress."

"Pardon?" Breckenbridge pulled himself from his own thoughts to stare at the young earl across from him.

"I realized at once that someone had placed her under a spell," offered Lanningsdale excitedly. "I just could not think who would do such a thing."

"A spell? Yes, well, I expect that is as good a way as any to say it," Breckenbridge replied. "And my Artemis will not be changed back again to the sweet thing she was. At least, not by me. That is precisely the reason I thought of you and begged you to meet with me. Thought of you at once, my boy. That is to say, I thought of your father first, but then I thought of you. I hoped, you know, that on the strength of our old friendship, your father's and mine, that you might find it in your heart to—"

"Of course, sir. You were right to come to me. What means did she use, this Mrs. Paxton-Dalrymple?"

"What means?"

"Yes. Do you know? A potion perhaps? Or was it woven upon a lock of hair? Or did she actually perform one of the ceremonies and call on the faeries or the gnomes to do her vile work?"

The look on Lord Breckenbridge's countenance was not to be described. "C-call upon the f-faeries? What the deuce are you speaking of, Lanningsdale?"

"The means, sir. What means did she use, this sorceress, to change Lady Artemis so?"

"Her big, fat tongue," grumbled Breckenbridge angrily.

"Her tongue? H-how? I mean to say," Lanningsdale stuttered.

"Mean to say what?"

"Well, her tongue. What did she—How would—Ah—"

"Devil the woman! Had the charge of my gel for years. Spilled the most vile, insulting drivel into my Artemis's ears. Could not help but some of it dribble into Missy's brain. Vile, loathsome creature, Mrs. Paxton-Dalrymple, to change my gel from a pliable young miss into a woman who detests all men!"

"She detests *all* men? Missy?"

"Indeed. Thinks we are beasts who live only to enslave women, take all they have from them and then r-rip them to pieces! Of all the balderdash I have ever heard!"

A look of relief swept over Lanningsdale's countenance on the spot. "Words. Merely words, then. You did not actually mean that this sorceress—that she—somehow with her tongue—Thank goodness! Words are something I can easily deal with."

"Yes, so I thought. When we were young, your father had such a way with the ladies—a silver-tongued rascal, he was. And you are his very image, you know. His very image! I could not but think that you had inherited his skills."

Lanningsdale nodded.

"It is not too much to ask of you? I would not think to ask it except that I am grown desperate."

"You need be desperate no longer, sir. I shall free your daughter from the evil influence under which she has fallen."

Lord Breckenbridge breathed a sigh of relief. He had not liked to take advantage of the son of an old friend. But after his last talk with Artemis, his memory had plagued him with visions of the tall, handsome Lord Lanningsdale he had known cajoling the haughtiest misses into bubbling laughter, sweeping one after another of the country girls off their feet with gallant speeches and smiling eyes. And this son of that Lanningsdale had certainly inherited his father's particular smile and manner, that voice and those eyes. Most certainly young Lanningsdale, if any gentleman were capable of it, was exactly the gentleman to disabuse Artemis of her odd notions, to convince her that gentlemen were not beasts at all, to engage her feelings enough that she might come to wish to have a gentleman just like Lanningsdale to fall in love with her.

Lanningsdale recovered his port and smiled thoughtfully to himself. If this was not just the thing—to have Missy's own papa come to him and ask him to remove the spell under which this vile Mrs. Paxton-Dalrymple person had placed the girl. Bertram could not protest against it now. No, not even if it must involve the placing of a different spell on Lady Artemis. Even his mama would not be able to find fault with him over the doing of such a thing now. Not when he had been particularly requested to do it by Missy's own papa!

Four

That very evening found Lanningsdale ensconced in the library of the house in Hanover Square, searching diligently among the bookshelves and at last carrying three ancient-looking volumes to the reading table. He could not quite believe that three volumes were all there were. In the library at Rosehill his father had two entire shelves of volumes concerned with wizardry, sorcery and the magical arts. Still, it was an extremely long trip to Rosehill, and there was a certain necessity for haste. Indeed, thought Lanningsdale, the sooner I rescue Missy, the better. Certainly there will be something in one of these volumes that will aid me to do it. If I must drive to Rosehill, it will be a se'ennight before I can begin.

Driven by the hope that Lady Artemis could swiftly become, once again, the sweet Missy of his memory, the young earl settled himself at the table and began to peruse the volumes.

"Elias, whatever has enthralled you so?" asked his mama, peering in at him. "You have been in here all evening. Will you not join me for tea?"

"What? Oh! Yes, certainly, Mama. I shall join you in the drawing room in a moment, eh? I have merely to finish reading this one page."

"A page of what? What have you found so very interesting?" Lady Lanningsdale stepped into the library and crossed behind her son to peer over her shoulder. "Good heavens, what is it?" she asked with a slight wrinkling of her nose. "How can you read it? Is it Latin?"

"It is English, Mama. Very old English."

"And inscribed by a very shaky hand, I should say."

"Yes. I expect whoever copied it was quite advanced in years. Still, it is readable and most interesting."

"It is? What is it about, Elias?"

"Well, it is about—" Lanningsdale halted to think for a moment. Ought he truly to tell his mama what it was about? No, he thought, this is not the time. Yes, he thought, she must know sometime. She is not like to see Missy abruptly altered and simply accept it. No, he thought again. If I tell her the truth, she will protest so heartily and so reasonably that she may succeed in changing my mind.

"Elias? Are you not going to tell me what it is you read?"

"An ancient treatise on—on—cooking—Mama."

"Cooking?"

"Just so." Well, it is not an absolute clanker, Lanningsdale told himself. The potions described do require cooking in a manner of speaking.

Lady Lanningsdale studied her son with a most suspicious glint in her eyes. Cooking. Of all things. And he expected her to believe *that?* "I did never realize, Elias, that you took an interest in such things as cooking. Are you thinking to become a chef, then?"

"No, Mama, of course not. I am merely—merely—intrigued by some of the recipes. Nothing more."

"I see." And she did see. She saw very clearly. Recipes indeed, she thought. And I expect one or the other of them involves a series of nonsensical syllables uttered while dancing around a cooking pot with a willow between one's teeth. "Set it aside and come to tea, Elias," she urged, placing her hands upon his broad shoulders, her long, delicate fingers kneading them, as they had often done his father's. "I have heard a most horrendous story from a trusted friend and I wish you to hear it as well."

Two days later, Lady Artemis stared at her father, appalled. Her mouth open, her eyes somewhat glazed, she sank slowly down on the brocade sopha in the rear parlor, her shoulders trembling, her breasts heaving as she attempted to catch her breath and to still the wild beating of her heart.

"I had hoped for more time, my dear," Breckenbridge murmured apologetically. "I had hoped that perhaps— Bah! I was a fool to hope. What good has hope ever done for anyone? There is nothing left for me now but to sell out all and escape as best I can."

"Papa," managed Lady Artemis with great effort. "Papa, it cannot be true. You cannot have lost all! Surely you exaggerate your circumstances."

"Would it were so," mumbled Breckenbridge, tugging at his sleeves. "Would that it were so. But it is not. The last of my hopes has crumbled, Artemis. The *LucyAnn* has been seized by the French and her cargo confiscated. I placed the last of my blunt on those silks from Asia, my dear. The last of it. The only bit of luck is that the news has come to me before it has reached the ears of the moneylenders. We must depart for the country at once, Artemis. It is not yet so far into the Season that we cannot gain a bit of income by renting out this establishment, and we will be better able to shore up and sustain ourselves at Roebuck."

"At Roebuck? But Papa, Roebuck is the most ancient and ill-kept of all your holdings! We may as well reside in the gutters of London as reside at Roebuck! I will not do it!"

"Then you must end a governess or a lady's companion or become a schoolteacher for your blessed Mrs. Paxton-Dalrymple, Artemis. For you cannot live without monies and I have no monies to spare you. A roof over your head and food from our own gardens is all I have to offer now."

Lady Artemis could not believe it. Even as she watched her papa exit the room, his head bowed, his feet shuffling lethargically—something they had never done before—she could not believe it. Surely there was some mistake. "Papa is an earl," she whispered to herself. "An earl cannot be poor. It is some enormous jest he plays to urge me into marriage. Well, but I will not marry. I will not!"

Even Miss Waithe's sorrowful sighs and lamentations could not convince the young woman when, a mere quarter hour later, that particular lady entered the rear parlor to commiserate with her niece.

"It is all rubbish, Aunt Gwen," Lady Artemis stated succinctly. "Rubbish and nothing more. Papa cannot possibly be in such dire straits as he declares. And if he thinks that by presenting me with such a farradiddle as this, he will gain my consent to sell me off to some oaf of a gentleman, he is sadly mistaken. I shall not be intimidated by such a threat as removing to Roebuck. I promise you that I shall not!"

Miss Waithe, who knew beyond all doubt that the removal to Roebuck was a deal more than a threat and who had, in fact, begun to pack for the trip, emitted the saddest little wail and fell to twisting the fine linen handkerchief in her hands into such a travesty that it came to look more like a string than a handkerchief and proved sadly inadequate as an item with which to stem the flow of her tears.

It was a most dejected Lanningsdale who entered the house in Hanover Square on Tuesday of the following week. His handsome head bowed, his hands behind his back, his spurs jingling the most melancholy tune, he made his way slowly up the staircase and into the sunroom to stand before his mama. "Gone," he said quietly. "Without so much as a word to anyone. And damned scavengers pecking away at the house, too, Mama."

"I am so sorry, dearest."

"Yes."

"I *am* sorry, Elias. I did not like the young lady, but I cannot be happy for the ill luck that has befallen her papa. Lord Breckenbridge was once a good neighbor and always a good friend to your papa and me."

"Just so. And just as I was preparing to give him aid, this must happen."

"Fate," murmured the countess, attempting to suppress the sound of relief that tinged her voice but not at all succeeding.

Her son eyed her, askance. "You are pleased it happened," he accused softly.

"No, no, I am not. I could never be pleased to see a gentleman brought so low as Lord Breckenbridge has been, and so quickly, too. I am merely relieved, Elias, that now you will not think to cast some silly spell over the girl or conjure up some foul-tasting potion with which to lace her tea."

"And what makes you think that I will not?"

"But Elias, she is gone into the hinterlands as practically a pauper."

"And I will bring her back from the hinterlands as a countess. Have you not thought, Mama? Missy will marry me now. She will marry anyone, I should think, to escape poverty."

"And you will accept such a union?"

Lanningsdale frowned, considering. "Well, I should like a better one. I should like her to marry me because she loves me."

"She will say that she loves you, Elias, as desperate

as she must be. There is no other gentleman will offer for her, I think. She insulted them all and quite turned them from her."

With a sigh, Lanningsdale seized a china shepherdess from one of the cricket tables and, tossing it carelessly in one hand, sank down on one of his mama's new Egyptian-style chairs. It had a back shaped like a pyramid and sphinxes for feet, and it did not so much as wobble at his weight. "If there were some other way to free Missy from this Mrs. Paxton-Dalrymple's spell, Mama, I should not resort to wizardry at all. But as it is, I may persuade Lady Artemis to marry me, but marriage will not restore her to the sweet Missy I love, do you think?"

"No."

"No. I did not think so."

"The best thing you can do, Elias," offered his mama thoughtfully. "The very best thing you can do will be to leave the girl at Roebuck for a year or two. Let her do more than merely shake poverty's hand. Allow her to discover how hard and unforgiving life can be when one must hold tight to the purse strings. Such haughtiness and scorn as she possesses cannot live forever in such humbling circumstances."

"It cannot?"

"No, it cannot. She will learn what it is to be humble and dependent upon the kindness of others. And then, when you go to her, as I have accepted that you will, she will likely welcome your suit with kindness and gratitude."

"But a year or two," muttered Lanningsdale, juggling the china shepherdess from one hand to the other. "A year or two is such a very long time, Mama, when a bit of wizardry might restore her to her old self in the blink of an owl's eye."

* * *

The little valet stared at his earl in silence.

"What? You do not think it an excellent idea?" asked Lanningsdale, studying himself thoroughly in the looking glass. "I think it pure genius myself. Pure genius. You did say, Bertram, that it was experience the lady required to turn her into her sweet self once again. Mama said the same."

Bertram blinked one large green eye and then the other. He harrumphed the tiniest bit like a bullfrog with a putrid sore throat. He shook the riding coat he held open for Lanningsdale rather violently and then shook it again.

"I have given it great thought, Bertram. And I have discovered just the right spell. I was rather fearful that I should be required to resort to a potion of some kind, but luckily that is quite unnecessary. All that is required is an incantation. The right words. The right time. The right place. The correct inflection of one's voice. Merely that, and poof! The scornful, haughty Lady Artemis will be my darling Missy again."

"Instantly, my lord?"

"Well, no. Not instantly. What the incantation will do, you see, is to compress the experience of poverty which Mama thinks will cure her into four weeks. Certainly that is a much kinder thing, Bertram, than one or two years," Lanningsdale added, one finger massaging the indentation in his chin. "It is a minor alteration of time and circumstance, merely."

"Do not be doing it, lordship," Bertram warned quietly.

"But why not? There is nothing can go wrong, Bertram."

"Anything can be going wrong," said the valet.

"What?"

"You might find yourself thinking of something else in the midst of them words an' change the both of you into dickeybirds."

"No, never. It does not involve actually changing anyone, Bertram, merely altering time."

"Well, but you might be distracted an' alter time different than what you want, then. Might make the both of you ancient," muttered the valet, shaking the morning coat in great agitation. "Never know what might be going wrong."

"Nothing will go wrong," the earl stated with great self-assurance. "Turn one person into a pig," he added in a mumble, "and the entire world thinks you can do nothing right."

Bertram gulped back a reply and instead, assisted Lord Lanningsdale to don his coat, but the little valet quivered so much as he did so, that it took the earl three attempts to get his arms into the sleeves.

"Nevertheless, I have decided to have a go at this particular spell. Pack our bags, eh, Bertram? You and I are bound for Brecken this very morning. We shall take the curricle. Faster. There is an inn in Brecken. The Blue Lady, I think it is called. We will go as far as possible today and finish up at the Blue Lady tomorrow. And then I will pay a visit to Roebuck Hall. Off with you, Bertram. Pack us something decent to wear and I will have Tempest send word to the stables to have the curricle brought 'round."

I expect the Earl of Breckenbridge will be pleased to see me, thought Lanningsdale as he left a stuttering Bertram behind him and strolled confidently toward the staircase. Perhaps Missy will be pleased to see me as well, especially if I tell her that I have come to rescue her from her present situation. And once she has welcomed me, I will set about to undo the spell that this Paxton-Dalrymple person has placed on her, just as Breckenbridge requested me to do, and then I will buy up all Breckenbridge's debts and set him on a new footing in the world. Yes. Precisely. Give him a new start.

And then, when I ask for Missy's hand in marriage, he will be overjoyed to give it to me.

"Elias? Where are you bound?" asked the countess as he hurried down the stairs into the vestibule below.

"Mama? I did not think to see you here. What a charming bonnet that is!"

"Yes, it is, is it not?" agreed the countess, placing a hat pin into the wide-brimmed straw confection with cherry ribands and a circlet of flowers. She studied herself in the looking glass above the trestle table, turning her head first one way and then the other. "You do not think that I am too old for it?"

"No, never. It makes you look quite pretty, Mama, and jolly as well."

"Jolly?"

"Yes, well, gay, you know. Not sober and frowning like some frustrated old matron."

"I have never been a frustrated old matron."

"No, and now you do not look like one, either.

"Elias! Do you say that I *have* been looking like one?"

"No, Mama, not at all. I merely mean that with such a bonnet as that you could not possibly look like one. Where are you off to, Mama?"

The Countess of Lanningsdale turned from the looking glass and noticed at once how bright her son's eyes shone. "You are up to something, Elias," she said.

"No, what makes you think so? Oh, Tempest, send word to have my curricle brought 'round, will you?"

"Yes, my lord," replied the butler, turning immediately about in his tracks and exiting the vestibule into which he had just stepped.

"I do wish you would not drive that thing, Elias."

"Not drive it? But why not, Mama?"

"Because you drive a good deal too fast and pay not the least attention to anyone around you."

"Mama! I am a regular Jehu when it comes to driving."

"Just as you say. But be kind to me, Elias, and do not become an abruptly dead Jehu."

"No, I will not." Lanningsdale grinned. "I give you my word. I am off on a bit of an excursion, Mama, so you will not expect me to be about for a time, eh?"

"An excursion?"

"Yes. Into the country."

"Elias, you are not bound for Roebuck Hall? You are! I can see it in your eyes! After all I said to you! And in a curricle yet! If you must go—and I cannot see why you must—can you not take the traveling coach, and travel in safety and comfort?"

"No, no, the curricle will do, Mama. It is a good deal faster than that lumbering old coach, and I can drive it myself."

"Just so," sighed his mama, visions of her son careening up the turnpike at an astounding pace making her heart shudder. "Promise me, Elias," she said, placing a hand on each of his shoulders, "that you are just going to visit Lord Breckenbridge and nothing more. I mean to say, promise me that you are not going to Roebuck Hall to—to—"

"Mama, I merely go to see how Breckenbridge does and ask if I may be of some service to him," interrupted Lanningsdale. "He and Papa were excellent friends. And Papa would not like to know that I had deserted the fellow in his time of need."

Lady Lanningsdale nodded. "We should offer him our assistance. That is quite true."

Lanningsdale grinned the most satisfied grin and leaned down to give his mama a peck on the cheek. "I intend," he said, "to offer him all the assistance he asks of me, Mama. And to provide him with the help he asked of me several days ago."

"Lord Breckenbridge sought your help days ago, Elias? And you did not give it to him at once?"

"I could not just then, Mama. But I find that now I can. Good-bye, Mama, and have a pleasant jaunt about town in your charming bonnet," he added, giving her a hug and strolling out of the vestibule in the direction of the library.

Five

Roebuck Hall, the primary seat of the Earl of Breckenbridge, huddled innocuously just two miles beyond the village of Brecken, near Hertford. Having lost its Great Hall to a fire over a century before, its entire third floor to a lightning strike in 1775, and its kitchen to a falling oak tree two winters past, it no longer possessed the awe-inspiring aspect it once had. Hasty rebuilding by three earls careful of their monies had deprived the once-grand edifice of significant portions of its grandeur. Still, it proved sufficient for Breckenbridge's needs at the moment. The roof did not leak, the kitchen—though now housed in a separate building—was inhabited by a cook who knew very well how to make do with good English food, and a minimal staff allowed the earl to keep his chin up and face village society without the least need of apology for the straitened circumstances in which he found himself. Altogether, as he strolled through the ill-tended park, Breckenbridge thought himself lucky to have been able to preserve this much of his heritage. Though all else he possessed, none of it having been included in the entailment, must eventually go to pay his debts, still, Roebuck would survive the coming onslaught of solicitors, moneylenders and duns intact. "And a gentleman cannot wish for more than that," he told himself quietly. "After all I have wasted, I cannot truly wish for more than that."

But he did wish for more, he discovered quickly. Only one more thing—that his Artemis would marry. "Though what gentleman will have her, I cannot think," he mumbled.

"I will have her," replied a voice from out the skies. "And I will make her happy as well!"

Startled, Breckenbridge halted at once and peered up at the clouds. It occurred to him that perhaps Greek gods were not merely a myth and one of them was at last speaking up.

"No, not in the clouds, sir. I am just here, in this twisted oak."

"Lanningsdale?" asked Breckenbridge at sight of that most familiar face above him. "What the devil do you mean by sneaking about in my tree?"

"Not sneaking about," Lanningsdale replied, grasping the branch on which he sat and lowering himself to the ground. "Thinking. I have been thinking a good while, actually. Arrived in Brecken yesterday. Came here early this morning. Thought to come at once and seek your permission to marry Lady Artemis. But then I thought that I had better think it through again."

"She will not have you, I promise you that. Not unless you can disabuse her of the wild notions with which Mrs. Paxton-Dalrymple has stuffed her brainbox. By Jupiter, I should like to put my hands around that woman's throat!"

"Yes, well, that is exactly what I was thinking."

"You were sitting in my tree thinking about strangling Mrs. Paxton-Dalrymple?"

"Thinking about undoing that sorceress' spell. Neither Mama nor Bertram thinks I ought, you know. But I cannot see why I should not. I am a good deal older now than I was when I—when I made that little faux pas with Hardin."

"Hardin?"

"Um-hmmm. But, I have learned a good deal since then. I will tell you what you must do, Breckenbridge. You must convince Missy to accompany you for a stroll along the stream, eh? Just down by the willow grove. And when you reach the largest of the trees, you must get her to sit with you beneath it."

Lord Breckenbridge cocked an eyebrow in serious doubt.

"That is all you must do. Honestly."

"Merely walk with my daughter beside the stream and sit with her beneath a willow?"

"Just so. And do not fear. I shall do the rest. You will see, sir. Mrs. Paxton-Dalrymple's words will be stricken from Missy's heart."

Lady Artemis could not think why her papa wished to stroll with her by the stream, but since she had nothing at all better to do with her time than to sit and set stitches into scraps of linen, she welcomed his invitation. In a walking dress of forest green, topped by a Spanish fly-colored pelisse, a matching bonnet of shimmering Spanish fly silk on her curls, and stout walking shoes upon her feet, she took his arm and accompanied him from the house.

"I expect you have not yet changed your mind about—about—marriage," offered her father tentatively as they passed by the paddock.

"No, I certainly have not."

"No."

"Papa, you have not asked me to stroll with you in an attempt to change my mind? I shall not change it. Not ever. There is no man in all the world whose existence I value as much as I do a lowly worm's. Do not sigh so, Papa. I know the truth. I choose never to become some man's slave. I will not give any gentleman power over me."

"I have power over you," murmured her papa, staring down at the path ahead of them.

"And I have given that considerable thought," nodded Artemis. "I did think to leave you when we came here. I could not bear the thought, you know, of attempting to live in such lowering circumstances. But I have changed my mind about that."

"Why?"

"Well, because, Papa, I cannot *afford* to leave you. And though Roebuck Hall is not as elegant as it might be and once was, still, it is not some ramshackle cottage of which I must be ashamed. No, I shall remain here with you until you recover your fortune, and then you will give me enough money to set up an establishment of my own. A very fine establishment. In Town. In one of the more fashionable neighborhoods. And I shall live out my life with Aunt Gwen by my side, doing precisely as I like." Lady Artemis gazed around her, startled. "Papa, the path is a deal more dark than I remember it."

"Only because the trees have grown together overhead," replied her father. "We shall come to the stream soon, and the sun will be shining through the willows as it always has done."

"I do not remember the willows especially. I remember tall grass and wildflowers and an elm here and there."

"That would be at Willodean," replied her father. "Oddest thing. Never was a willow at Willodean that I recall. Only elms along the stream and one large oak. You were accustomed to play beneath the oak with the fifth Lord Lanningsdale's son."

"King Thrushbeard? I was accustomed to play with that overdressed, imperious—"

"Be careful what you say, my dear," interrupted Breckenbridge. "His papa was always a good friend to me, and he, a good friend to you."

"I do not recall that at all, Papa."

"You do not wish to recall it, I think. You have forgotten everything that ever happened to you before Mrs. Paxton-Dalrymple entered your sphere."

"Oh, I have not. I remember most things perfectly well, Papa. I just do not recall any sort of friendship between myself and that—that—"

"Say no more," her papa instructed as they came to the meadow and he spied the row of willows in the distance where they bordered the meandering stream. "You are wrong to call him King Thrushbeard and equally wrong to think ill of him."

"I cannot but think ill of him, Papa," asserted Lady Artemis. "He is a *man.*"

Her papa grunted in the oddest way, and then they strolled on together in silence until they reached the stand of willows. "Only see how beautiful, Artemis," he said then. "How the sunlight filters through the willows and dapples the stream."

"Yes, it is very pretty," Lady Artemis agreed, though she thought to herself that it was not quite as pretty as the ball gown she had been forced to return to Madame Constantia upon their exit from London. Nor was it worth near the price of that lovely article.

"Come, my dear, let us sit for a moment beneath that tree and gaze at the sunlight playing upon the stream," urged Breckenbridge, steering his daughter toward the largest of the willows and ducking with her beneath its outer branches. "Only see how marvelously the willow dances around us," he added, shedding his coat and placing it on the ground for his daughter to sit upon. "Come, Artemis, sit down, do, and we will ponder the beauty of the natural world for a while."

"Very well, Papa," nodded Artemis, "but I think you

would do better to ponder ways of regaining your fortune."

"Bah! Have I not a fortune here before me? A peaceful, bubbling fortune to charm my soul?"

"No, Papa, you have a stream before you, flowing noisily over rocks and doing not one thing to put monies back into your pockets."

"Money is not everything, Artemis."

"No, but it is the very best of things, and it is a great bore, Papa, to be without any."

"You do not need to be without fortune," offered a voice from above them. "Fortunes are easily come by."

"Who? What?" stuttered Artemis, staring up into the branches of the willow.

"I will gain you a fortune of your very own in a matter of moments," rumbled the voice. "A matter of moments."

"I see you, fool," announced Lady Artemis in the most exasperated tone. "Do you think I cannot see you in the branches above us? Come down at once before you fall on Papa and break both of your necks. What do you think to do up there, frighten me into believing that you are some magical being? Of all the stupid things!"

"I *am* a magical being," Lanningsdale laughed, descending gracefully from his perch. "I am the progeny of the greatest wizard of all time. Why, my father could trace his ancestry all the way back to Merlin the Magician if he wished."

"Humbug," muttered Artemis.

"No, it is not."

"It is. Pure humbug, and balderdash as well. There is dirt on your face, King Thrushbeard. How very awkward for you to present yourself in such disarray. Cannot you feel that smudge on your cheek? I should think you could, one such as you."

"Artemis, do not insult the gentleman."

"I am not, Papa. I am simply stating a fact. No gentleman so well dressed as King Thrushbeard will like to have a smudge on his cheek. The ladies will not like him half so much to see him so. And he is intent on having the ladies like him, I think."

"Only you," responded Lanningsdale, ignoring the smudge and staring at Artemis. "You are the only lady I am intent on having like me."

"Well, I do not like you. And I am not impressed by your smudge or your hanging about in trees."

"But you would be impressed and you would come to like me, too, if I restored your Papa's fortune and brought you a fortune of your own."

"Perhaps. A bit."

"Then why not let me have a go at it?" asked Lanningsdale, his heart overflowing with love for her while his brain belittled him for thinking to regain the playmate he had lost. "It does not involve much. Merely a dance around this old tree."

"A dance? Around this tree?"

"Indeed. You and your papa and I. We must simply hold hands and dance around this willow and say a number of simple words together. It is a magic tree, you know. It will do precisely as I ask of it."

"You are mad," declared Artemis. "Papa, this gentleman is one cup short of a set. Let us depart from him at once."

"Dance around the tree?" Breckenbridge asked of Lanningsdale, his eyes wide. What could the lad be thinking? To make Artemis act like a fool was no way to disabuse her of Mrs. Paxton-Dalrymple's ideas. And yet, Lanningsdale gazed at him with the most puzzling expression in his eyes. "Well," harrumphed Breckenbridge. "Well, I can see no harm in it."

"Papa!"

"Perhaps a bit of silliness will do us good, Artemis.

We have not been silly together, you and I, since you were a child."

"Men," muttered Lady Artemis under her breath as her father rose from the ground and assisted her to rise as well. "Really, if the lot of you are not busy being loathsome, you are busy being impossible. Mrs. Paxton-Dalrymple is exactly right in her ideas on the male of the species."

Bertram could not understand why his lordship had not yet returned. He stood in the chamber his lordship had taken at the Blue Lady and stared hopefully out into the afternoon sunlight. "Ought to been back by now," he muttered. "Gone a good four hours, he has been. Ought to come driving up any minute." The little valet began to pace the room, his sensibilities atoss upon a sea of imagination. What did keep his lordship? Gone to Roebuck Hall to investigate the situation was all he'd done. Gone to see how he could be of assistance. Surely his lordship had not succumbed to the temptation to place that accursed spell on the gel. No. His lordship had more sense than that. Enough sense to be certain, at least, that Bertram was nearby in case something should go amiss.

But where was the lad, then? "I will take a stroll in Roebuck Hall's direction," Bertram sighed to himself. "Mayhap one of the horses has gone lame or a wheel of the curricle broked. Aye, I will take a stroll up the road and see what I can see."

So saying, the valet checked himself in the looking glass, straightened his cravat the merest bit, tugged on his gloves and left the chamber, taking the stairs to the main floor two at a time. Without gazing to left or right, Bertram stalked hurriedly through the public room and out onto the porch, hopped down three steps and set off down the road in the direction of the Earl of Breckenbridge's estate. Dust swirled around Bertram's shoes and dulled their shine; the sun bore down on his uncovered head and caused his hair to grow wet with perspiration; birds swooped at him out of the trees and fluttered about his shoulders; but none of this he noticed, so intent was he on discovering what could have happened to his master. Bertram's mind was so preoccupied with notions of disaster, in fact, that he did not notice the fiddler who stepped directly into his path, and the valet bumped square up against the beggar.

"Play ye a tune?" asked the fiddler in a voice that sounded a good deal like notes crumbling. "Any tune fer a pence, gov. Y'name it; I plays it."

"No, go away," grumbled Bertram, shoving at the man. "I be looking for a curricle, not a concert."

"But ye be frownin' so angry-like, m'fine sir. A curricle kinnot set yer spirits ta dancin' like what m'fiddle kin."

"Go away," Bertram replied, and reached out to give the filthy beggar another shove.

The fiddler dodged aside, placed his instrument beneath his chin and drew the bow across the strings. "Cheer ye up, I will, m'lad," he said as the fiddle burst into a joyful little song. "Set yer feet ta tappin', I will. Change yer whole outlook on the world, Bertie."

The little valet took a step back. His wide green eyes blinked slowly once and then again. His nose twitched to the left and then the right. "B-Bertie?" he whispered hoarsely and stared directly into the fiddler's face. "Lordship?" he asked with great hesitancy. "Lordship, does that be you?"

"Kinnot tell, kin ye?" replied the beggar, his dirty face creasing into a smile. "Didn't not so much as notice me, ye dinnit, Bertie."

"It do be you!" exclaimed Bertram, one hand going to cover his lips. "Oh, lordship, where be your curricle and team? Where be the elegant togs what I done sent you out in this very morning? How does your face come to be so dirty and odd-looking? What is it that you have gone and done?"

"I have gone an' changed m'self inta a beggar, Bertram. I dinnit intend ta, mind, but it appears how I have done. An' a splendid job I've done of it, too. Even you dinnit reckernize me."

"Oh, I be in for it now," murmured Bertram behind his hand. "I be going back to my pond in the blinking of his late lordship's eye."

"No, why?"

"Onaccounta," mumbled Bertram. "Onaccounta I have done failed him. I have promised to serve you and protect you my whole life long, and just see how I have failed!"

"Fiddle!" protested Lanningsdale and proceeded to do just that on the instrument he carried. His music was delightful, charming. It reached the ears of every person in the coach just then passing them by and sent them to hanging out the coach windows to hear all the better. Still fiddling, Lanningsdale did a bit of a dance step and, laughing, strolled off in the direction of Roebuck Hall, Bertram hurrying along beside him.

Faith, thought Bertram, my lordship has gone and taked a new voice for himself and put his old voice into that fiddle. The birds will be flying down to sit on his shoulder next, and the bees will be buzzing around him soon enough. But he do *look* so dreadful with his nose so big and his hair gone white and his eyes turned brown and dressed in them rags what he be wearing. And he do smell dreadful, too. Oh, but were my lordship's papa alive, he would have me back in that pond on the instant. And no telling but what he willn't do it, even though he be dead!

Six

Bertram ceased to hurry along beside his earl and raised his eyes, his gaze encompassing the whole of Roebuck Hall with rapid-blinking amazement. "It be in the same place as the house what we passed coming to Brecken three days ago," he murmured in wonder, "but it do not look the same at all."

"No. Dinit I say as it got changed?"

"Aye, lordship, but I did not reckon on such an enormous alteration."

"No. I dinit reckon on it, either, but there it be. A reg'lar, actual Hall. Roebuck Hall. Jus' as it were built cent'ries ago. A feast fer yer eyes, ain't it?"

"I do wish you would not be speaking like that," grumbled Bertram, tearing his gaze from the impeccably restored structure and pinning it upon his incredibly decimated earl. "I cannot like it to hear you speak in such a manner. You be a gentleman."

" 'Fraid not, Bertie. Don't be no gen'leman no more. I be a beggar now, through an' through. Done changed m'self inta one, speech an' all. Done a regal-right job of it, too." Lanningsdale grinned widely, sniffed, and wiped his nose on his sleeve. "But I be a happy sorta beggar at the least. I feels m'self smilin', Bertie. An' ye ain't ta fret over it. I ain't goin' ta remain a beggar long. Jus' until I kin figger out how I done it an' change meself back. Course, I reckon as how I'll be hitched by then."

Bertram stared at him in horror. "Hitched, lordship?"

"Aye. Married. Ta the Lady Artemis."

"Surely she will not marry a beggar!"

"She will. I heared her pa say as much wif m'own two ears. I meaned ta change the time, Bertie. I meaned ta press years o' poverty tagether inta four weeks er so, so as Missy'd have the 'sperience wifout me havin' ta wait too long. But somehow I gone an' set back the time instead of makin' it shorter. I gone an' set back the time on all of them what lives in that there house. I figgered ta fit seventeen years er so inta them four weeks. Time enuf, ye know, fer Missy ta gain all the 'sperience possible, just like ye suggested. But I reckon I dinnit say somethin' right. 'Parently I done set the whole o' Roebuck Hall right back inta the seventeenth century, I did. Seventeen years, seventeenth century, mucked it up somehow. Set Breckenbridge an' his household back two hunnerd years."

"You cannot have done, lordship!"

"Did. Moved 'em. All the same age they be, but livin' in the sixteen hunnerds now. An' Missy a screechin' unner that willow tree at her pa as how he be a fool ta be atrustin' o' me, an' proclaimin' as how no man were worth a grain o' salt, him included. An' good ol' Breckenbridge ashoutin' right back at her like he never done afore, declarin' as how she were a shrew an' a tyrant an' vowin' as how he'd be amarryin' her off ta the first beggar what came abeggin' at his door. An' poof! No sooner does he say that perticuler thing but I be a beggarman wif a fiddle in m'hand walkin' down that there road what ye foun' me on. Breckenbridge kin marry the mort off ta a beggarman, too, Bertie," added the fiddler gleefully. "It be 1618 in Roebuck Hall, b'gawd! He kin marry Missy ta anyone he likes an' no laws agin it!"

"I wish you will not be calling me Bertie, lordship," mumbled Bertram, visibly shaken by the sight of the restored Roebuck Hall, by Lanningsdale's account of what had occurred and by the obvious intentions of his earl. "I were Bertie when I were a frog, but never since."

"I knows it. I don't be awantin' ta call ye Bertie, Bertie, but I kinnit help m'self. Comes with being a beggar, I guesses. At any rate, m'dear, I do be a beggar, an' I means to be the first beggar ta be abeggin' at Roebuck Hall this day so that Missy'll be amarryin' of me. Breckenbridge done vowed it!" And with that, Lord Lanningsdale strolled confidently up the drive to Roebuck Hall with Bertram scurrying behind him, tucked his violin beneath his chin as he took up a stance beneath one of the windows, and began to play.

"But why marry the girl?" whispered Bertram distractedly, coming to a halt beside the earl. "What good be it to marry the girl now? You are not yourself, lordship."

But Lanningsdale the fiddler answered not, intent upon his music.

The door of Roebuck Hall sprang open abruptly and a number of male servants came to stand on the doorstep; girlish faces, young and elderly, materialized at windows thrown eagerly agape; and from all about the park doves, thrushes, sparrows, came spiraling down to land on Lanningsdale's shoulders, balance upon his hat, and dance in the most peculiar way at his feet. Never before, not even in the very finest of drawing rooms, had such enticing melodies been played and everyone in and about Roebuck Hall was stunned to hear them.

"Who is it plays such music?" queried Lord Breckenbridge of his butler, who was even then standing with the front door wide. "By Jove, it is some beggar placed himself beneath my windows!"

"Shall I send him packing, my lord?"

"What? Send him packing? No, no, not a bit of it. When he has ceased to play and begins to pass his hat around to all and sundry, then you must bring him to me. Until then, we will listen to the fellow. I have never heard such intriguing music in all of my life.

"This is the man will have my daughter," he whispered to himself, the fiddler's music setting his feet to tapping. "I have vowed to give her to the first beggar come abegging, and so it will be."

And so it was that Lanningsdale—ragged clothes, enormous nose, hair gone white, brown eyes and all— was led before Lord Breckenbridge and played once more, this time inside the Great Hall, for the earl, Miss Waithe and Lady Artemis. And when he had finished, he asked for a trifling gift. "I has been gived a bit by all o' yer servants, gov," he said. "I wunner willn't ye give a poor ol' fiddler a token as well?"

"Your songs have pleased me," nodded Lord Breckenbridge, not for a moment recognizing the beggar as Lanningsdale. Well, who could have recognized him, so changed was he. "They have pleased me so well that I will give you as a token my daughter, who stands so silent there, to be your wife."

Lady Artemis shuddered violently. "Papa!" she cried. "You cannot! Oh, please, Papa, you cannot!"

"I can," declared Breckenbridge. "I have vowed to do it, and I will. Will you take her?" he asked the beggar, cocking one noble eyebrow to urge him to it.

"I kinnit think why not," replied the fiddler, eyeing Lady Artemis up and down in the most appalling manner. "I reckon as how she might be a bit o' help ta me. Course I'll have her."

All that Lady Artemis could say against it proved to be in vain. All her protests were ignored. Her papa was quite aware of the time in which they now lived and knew his rights in the matter. The chaplain of the house was sent for; the words were said. And despite Miss Waithe fainting dead away in the midst of it; despite Bertram choking near to death in the farthest corner of the hall; despite Lady Artemis kicking the chaplain in the shin when he queried if she would have the beggar, Elias, as husband, the fiddler and the earl's daughter were ultimately wed.

"Now," declared Lady Artemis's father, a rush of righteousness and power overwhelming him. "Now you must leave this house and go with your husband to be his helpmate. It is not proper for you to remain in Roebuck Hall—not now that you are a beggarman's wife. Begone from here, gel, and thank God that this man, at least, will have you."

Thereupon, the beggar took the earl's daughter by the hand and led her from the Great Hall. "Don't be afeared," he whispered. "Bertie'll git what clothes he kin from the gen'leman fer ye an' bring 'em along after us. Ye'll not be forced ta wear that fancy dress ferever. We be goin' atravelin', Bertie," he added in a loud voice. "Grab what they'll give ye o' the gel's fixin's an' come lopin' after us, eh?"

It proved to be the most lowering thing. Lady Artemis was actually forced to walk beside the fiddler as they trod the dusty road. "Have you not a dog cart at the least?" she queried petulantly. "A lady ought not be expected to walk all over the countryside."

"Why not?" asked the fiddler. "Ain't ye got sturdy 'nuff shoes 'pon yer feet? They looks fine an' dandy."

"Yes, but it is difficult to walk so far and so long."

"Ah, we ain't near begun as yet," said the fiddler. " 'Tis miles an' miles ta m'house. T'our house, I means. I reckon as you bein' m'wife an' all, I ought ta start referrin' ta it as our house, eh?"

"You actually have a house?" asked Lady Artemis.

"Indeed. It ain't large, mind ye, but it gots a roof an' a door an' one winnow."

"One window?"

"Aye," smiled the fiddler, thrusting out his chest proudly. "I be more 'n a mere beggar, I be. I kin afford a winnow, I can."

Lady Artemis, dismayed at the thought of a house with only one window, trudged along beside him in silence for a goodly while until they chanced to pass beside a shady wood. "What a lovely little forest," she said. "Can we not rest a bit in the shade of the trees?"

"Don' see why not," replied the fiddler. "Give Bertie a opportunity-like ta catch us up, it will." And he plopped down beneath one of the oaks, leaving Lady Artemis to take her own seat, unassisted, on the bare ground.

"I wonder whose wood this is," murmured Artemis, wrinkling her nose and seating herself a goodly distance away from the beggar—beneath another tree entirely. "I cannot recall having ever passed it before."

"Oh, it belongs ta King Thrushbeard," replied her newly acquired husband.

"King Thrushbeard? There truly is a King Thrushbeard?"

" 'Deed," nodded the fiddler. "Leastways, that be what ye called him when he come acourtin' of ye. I done heared 'bout that. Ever'one what knows the gen'leman done heared about that. He be well-known hereabouts, yer King Thrushbeard. Had *he* married ye, these woods would have been yers. But they ain't," the beggar pointed out helpfully. "You done gived up all hope of havin' 'em." Whereupon he tucked his fiddle safely between two tree roots, lay flat upon the ground, tugged his ruck-ety old hat down over his eyes and went to sleep.

Lady Artemis stared about her in gloom. She had never come so far north of Roebuck Hall and Brecken in all of her life that she could remember. Of course, she had lived a deal farther north when she was a child, but she had long ago forgotten most things about that time and her papa's estate at Willodean. King Thrushbeard owns these woods? she thought. Ah, what an unhappy woman I am. These woods might have been mine. But no longer. I have tossed away *that* opportunity and am wed to a smelly, ugly brute of a beggarman with naught but a tiny house that boasts a roof, a door and one window. Had I known such a horror would come to pass, surely I would have been a deal more kind to King Thrushbeard. No, I expect I would not, she thought then, for he is a man just as beastly as this horrible husband I have got. I would hate being married to him as much as I do to this Elias person. I am certain of it.

At last, the fiddler was aroused from his nap by the arrival of Bertie, whom he welcomed with a slow grin and a snap of his fingers. Sitting up and setting his grimy hat on the center of his head, he studied the little man a moment in silence. "That's all what ye got?" he asked then in astonishment.

Bertram, in consternation, stared down at the small portmanteaux he carried and sniffed.

"Aw, I dinnit 'tend ta offend ye, Bertie, but that ain't much fer a lady."

" 'Tis all I could carry, lordship," replied Bertram. *"Walking.* I cannot find the curricle and team," he whispered hoarsely in Lanningsdale's ear. "It has disappeared along with your clothes and all else connected with you but me, lordship."

"Pardon me," ventured Lady Artemis, studying the little valet with great consternation, "but why, husband, does this little man call you lordship? And how comes he to follow you about, him dressed like a fashionable dandy and you in rags?"

"Calls me lor'ship ta make hisself feel uppity, wife. A bit mad, he be. Taken it inta his head that he be m'servant. Likes the idea o' servin' a lor'ship, he does. Likes the idea o' servin' me. So he's gone and maked me a lor'ship.

An' his clothes is dandified 'cause he fetched 'em off a dandified corpse what we found in a gutter. His own size, they was."

"A corpse?" shrieked Artemis at the precise moment that Bertram's face turned a stunning shade of putrid green.

"Aye. But I ain't near so brave as what Bertie be. I ain't got the stomik fer awearin' dead men's clothes even were the bloke the same size as what I be. Come along, then," he urged Lady Artemis, tugging her to her feet. "We gots a ways ta go, we do. Best get on about it."

Just as the sun began to set, the three of them came upon a meadow lush with wheat. "What a beautiful meadow!" exclaimed Artemis. "I wonder to whom it belongs."

"B'longs ta King Thrushbeard," answered her husband offhandedly.

"Ah," sighed the very exhausted Lady Artemis, her thoughts having undergone a definite alteration because of her weariness. "Ah, unhappy me. I might have had King Thrushbeard to wed, you know. He courted me most assiduously. And what have I gained by turning him away?"

"Me," grinned the fiddler, taking her hand into his own and urging her onward. "Come on, Bertie, keep up, keep up. We ain't got much farther ta go."

Late into the evening the three entered a very large village, its houses and cottages asparkle in the night.

"What village is this?" asked Artemis wearily. "Might we find an inn here and rest the night?"

"The village of Wentforth on Wrong, it be," offered Bertram, exhausted. "And if we do not rest the night here, lordship, I shall perish."

"Aye, Bertie. Git us a bit ta eat an' drink an' lay up fer the night here," agreed Lanningsdale heartily.

"Wentforth on Wrong?" yawned Artemis. "I have never heard of it. To whom does it belong?"

"To King Thrushbeard, I expect," answered Bertram before Lanningsdale could reply.

"Oh, what an unhappy woman am I. I might have been King Thrushbeard's slave. He might have taken all that I had, but at least I would not be wandering through all his possessions beside a beggar had I married the man," sighed Artemis. "All men are loathsome beasts, but he, at least, is a loathsome beast with properties."

"And carriages. And teams to pull them," muttered Bertram over his shoulder as he limped awkwardly toward the porch of a posting house.

"I done had enuff," grumbled the fiddler, tugging his wife over before him with one very dirty hand. "It don't please me ta hear ye always sighin' away over another man an' wishin' it be him what ye had fer a husband. Ain't I good enuff fer ye?"

"I—you—I—" stuttered Artemis unhappily, unsure how to answer this odd fellow.

"I were plannin' ta git ye a room in this here postin' house, I were," grumbled the fiddler. "But I ain't agoin' ta do it, soes ye spend the night wishin' ye were hitched-up ta another. No, I ain't."

"How will you get me a room in a posting house?" asked Artemis scornfully. "You've not a penny in your pocket."

"Yes, I has. Any number o' pennies an' a way ta gather any number more," declared Lanningsdale, tucking the fiddle up under his chin right where they stood in the middle of the road. He drew his bow across the strings once, then again. And in less than a minute the windows of the posting house began to open, and heads with hair in various states of undress poked out. Up and down the street doors opened, and men and women alike, in myriad states of nighttime dishevelment, stepped out of their houses and began to smile and laugh and tap their feet. "Take me hat, Bertie, an' pass it around," ordered Lanningsdale. "An' you, wife, doff yer bonnet an' beg a penny er two of them ladies what be a grinnin' at us on that doorstep there."

"I could not possibly!" declared Artemis in horror.

"Does ye be wishin' ta sleep in this postin' house er in its stable?" asked her husband plainly.

With a shudder and a tear, Artemis doffed her bonnet and stumbled wearily forward toward the women her husband had pointed out to her, her head bowed with weariness and humiliation.

Seven

"He did what?" gasped Lady Lanningsdale, her face grown pale. "How could you have allowed him to do it? How could you? You—you—FROG!"

Bertram stood, visibly shaking, on the bright Aubusson carpet of Lady Lanningsdale's morning room. Sunlight beamed in at him through the casement windows, but he had found one spot of shadow in which to stand, and there he remained.

"When did he do this thing? How long ago?" Lady Lanningsdale asked, lowering herself into the lyre-backed chair that sat before the broad bank of windows.

"It will be t-t-t-t-two days ago, ladyship. I think t-t-t-two days. It were a dreadful accident. He did not intend for it to happen quite that way. He c-cannot go to Rosehill, ladyship, the way he b-be. No one there will recognize him and let him in, not even do I say who he be. Think I have gone 'round the bend, they will, do I name him Lord Lanningsdale as he looks now. Bound for the late Harry Barker's hut, he be. Used his last bit of money from his begging to rent me a hack and send me here to beseech you to remove to Rosehill as soon as possible."

"Oh, I cannot believe it," moaned the countess, rubbing at her temples with the tips of her fingers. "I told Elias not to use wizardry. I warned him over and over to beware of his papa's books. He actually married the girl, you say?"

"I believe so, ladyship. There were a parson said all the right words. There were a entry made in the register."

"Yes, but did his lordship enter his true name? No, I cannot believe that he did. Not if he had changed himself into this—this—beggar person, as you said, and did not tell Lady Artemis and her papa otherwise. He is not truly married, then. The ceremony was naught but a disgraceful sham, and the girl will be ruined because of it. Elias is honor-bound to marry her now even if he did not actually marry her then."

"Yes, ladyship."

"Yes, indeed. Well, he was correct to send you to me, Bertram. Did he tell you the name of the volume from which he took the spell which misfired?"

"Yes, ladyship."

"And it is here?"

"In lordship's chambers, ladyship."

"Go and fetch it down to me, and then tell Kathleen that she must pack my things, for we must start for Rosehill as soon as humanly possible."

Bertram's nose quivered the merest bit, for he took the countess' use of "humanly possible" as an insult to himself. But I be deserving of it, he thought as he turned to exit the room. I ought to have stopped lordship from using a spell. I ought to have known he would and stopped him on the spot.

"You do not think, Bertram," Lady Lanningsdale asked just as the little valet reached the door. "You do not think that there is any chance his lordship will abandon his idea of residing in Harry Barker's hut and take the girl straight to Rosehill? He will not hold out hope that Harbinger can be convinced to see him as his true self despite the alteration he has undergone? Harbinger has known him for his entire life, after all."

Bertram thought of the weary couple he had abandoned two nights before and shook his head. "I do not reckon as he will go to Rosehill, ladyship. Even could he convince Mr. Harbinger of who he be, I cannot think that lordship wishes to have the lady reside at Rosehill immediately. Delighted he be with himself at present. Thinks them both being beggars is just the thing, though he do wish for you to help him change back when he deems it time. Plans on making life hard for the girl, I gather. He will not be forcing her to walk all the way into Norfolk, but he will not be hiring a post chaise to carry her in, neither. Might take the mail, perhaps, for some of the distance. Or perhaps hitch a ride upon a hayer's cart. Or borrow an old donkey. Plans upon living like the beggar he looks for a time. 'Tis what he told me. 'Tis why he intends on living in Harry Barker's old hut."

"But why? Why place himself and the girl in such hardship?"

"Experience," stated Bertram flatly.

"Experience?"

"Lordship be wishing to change the lady into a caring human being, and I said to him oncet that to do that he would not need magic, that she would need to h-have ex-experience."

"No, did you? I said as much myself. I could cut out my tongue! And yours," added the dowager, glaring at Bertram. "But he does intend to take her to Rosehill soon?"

Bertram nodded. "But I do not be knowing when, ladyship. Soon, he told me. After he had done what must be done."

Artemis stared at the little hut, appalled. "We have traveled by foot and cart and donkey-back to get *here?*" she asked in consternation. Her face was covered with the grime of travel, her brow furrowed with weariness, but her eyes blazed. "It is nothing but a hovel!" she declared. "I have no doubt that the inside is worse by far than that hot, smelly room in the attic of the posting inn. I know it is smaller yet than the woodcutter's cottage where last we spent the night."

"It be m'home," offered the fiddler quietly. "An' now it be yer home as well. I be willin' ta share all I gots with ye, now ye be m'wife."

Artemis had to stoop to go in beneath the low door. She gazed around her in dismay. There was, as promised, one tiny window and no more. "Is there not one other room at least?" she asked. "Where is the cooking to be done? Where am I to sleep? How am I to wash the dirt of the journey from myself?"

"There be another room most as big as this un right behind them draperies. And as ta sleepin'," offered the fiddler, entering behind her, "there be a perfeckly good mattress stuffed wif hay back in there. And as ta cleaning up oneself, that be simple as a wink. Here," he said, lifting a lump of soap from off a shelf beside the door. "Come an' I'll show ye where a stream lies. Ye may warsh yerself in that. What's this, tears?" he added, his voice growing very soft as he placed the lump of soap into Artemis's shaking hand. "Aw, wife, don't be acryin'. I ain't as good a bargain as King Thrushbeard, but we'll be muddlin' through, m'dear."

For the very first time the fiddler put his arms about Artemis and held her like a babe against his chest. "Hush now," he whispered, his breath stirring wisps of hair that clung with perspiration to her cheeks. "If only ye'll trust in me, ever'thin' will work out ta the best. I promise ye that."

If she had not been half so weary or half so sad, Artemis would have pounded her fists against his vile chest, attempted to free herself from his arms, railed against the beggar and her papa and fate itself. But she was very, very tired and the fiddler's chest was wide and strong. And the arms that enclosed her, though they rippled with muscles, were somehow gentle and comforting. And if the stench of his rags did put her off, nevertheless, the solidity of him, the unexpected tenderness of his touch and the soft whisper of his words were enticement enough to make her linger in his arms for a long moment. "Must I wash in a stream like some Gypsy woman?" she asked him quietly. "Have I come to such an extreme? Am I never to be a lady again?"

"Ye be a lady," whispered her husband in her ear. "Ta my mind, ye'll always be a lady does ye wash yerself in a stream er in a big bronze tub. An' washin' in a stream ain't so dreadful, wife, if ye don't be lingering so very long as ta freeze ta death, fer the water be cold even this time o' year."

"Will you wash as well?" asked Artemis, stepping out of his arms and looking up at him.

"Me?"

"Yes, you. And will you wash your clothes? There is the—the oddest odor about you, and—"

"Pleased ta do it," interrupted the fiddler with a chuckle. "I bean't one ta fear a bit o' soap an' water now an' then. Long as it bean't forced upon me ever' month, I ain't."

For a week or more, Artemis and the altered Lanningsdale lived together in a vague sort of truce in the small hut. Each day the beggarman went off to one or another of the villages nearby, and each evening he returned with bits of this and scraps of that which he cooked over a small fire he made upon the ground outside their door. But one evening he stepped inside the hut and sat down beside Artemis in a chair that listed decidedly to the right. "Wife," he said, taking one of her hands into his, "we kinnit go on as we are much longer—eatin' bits and scraps from other's tables. We needs money, m'dear. I has got ta go out an' earn our keep, an' you has gots ta help me do it or the two of us will starve ta death or freeze come the winter."

"I am to help you earn our keep?" asked Artemis. "And how, pray, am I to do that?"

"Well, I have been athinkin' on it an' I have decided that I shall go off an' cut some willows," declared the fiddler, "an' ye'll weave 'em inta baskets ta sell in the villages while I'm gone off aplayin' m'fiddle."

This idea did not appeal to Artemis at all, but she looked into her husband's eyes and saw a great deal of worry there. She reminded herself, as she studied his large nose and rough face, that this particular man, ugly and poor though he be, had been most considerate of her in every way he could. He had given her his only mattress to sleep on in the back room while he, himself, slept out on the cold, hard ground under the stars. He had cooked and cleaned when he had discovered that she knew how to do neither. And he had not demanded of her his husbandly rights or demanded anything else for that matter. In fact, he had only asked her once, and very nicely, too, to fetch some water from the stream. And she was certain he would not have done that except that he had returned home so exhausted that he could not get up again to do it himself once he had sat down.

"I will attempt to weave baskets," she replied quietly. "But I have never done so before."

"Sure, an' it ain't hard, wife. An' it will be of a great help ta us both ta have a bit more of the ready."

"I will try," Artemis assured him with a wavering smile. "I will try my best to weave baskets from willow." And try she did, but the weaving of willow into baskets proved a hard task. Time and time again the tough wood wounded her delicate hands.

"I reckon as how this willn't do at all," sighed her husband taking her hands into his own one evening and studying them closely. "I kinnit abide fer ta see yer hands all swolled up an' hurtin'. P'rhaps ye ought ta spin? Do ye think ye can spin better than ye weave, wife? D'ye think it will hurt ye less?"

"I do not know," Artemis replied. "I have never found it necessary to spin before."

"Never?" asked her husband. "Not oncet in yer whole life?"

"I was born a lady," Artemis replied, her eyes flashing brilliantly at the remembrance of the life she had long been accustomed to live. "Ladies do not weave baskets or spin wool into cloth. Ladies do not cook or clean or go about begging for bits of food, either."

"I reckon as I done made a bad bargain," sighed the fiddler. "I've gone an' got me a lady instead o' a wife. I expect as how you ain't good fer much o' nothin'."

"I will spin," said Artemis, nibbling at her lower lip with some perturbation, for it *did* disturb her to hear that her husband thought her a bad bargain. "Only find me a wheel and some wool. How difficult can it be?"

Unfortunately, spinning proved to be most difficult. Though she did her best to succeed at the task in her husband's absence, the hard thread soon cut into her soft fingers, and blood ran down on all her work. "I cannot do it," she sobbed as her husband at last returned from his fiddling and stepped inside the little hut the next evening. "I cannot do it, and I should not have to do it! I am a lady born! I am no man's slave!"

"Hush," murmured her husband, taking her hands into his own, wiping the blood from her fingers with the sleeve of his jacket and kissing each tiny cut. "Hush, m'dear. Ye ain't no slave, I promise ye." And when he had torn up the tails of his one good shirt to bandage her fingers, he led her to the chair that listed to the right, sat down upon it, and took her up onto his lap. There he cradled her as though she were a babe and sang to her in a voice almost as comforting as the voice of his fiddle.

Artemis could not think what to do. Tears streamed from her eyes. How she hated this man and this hut and this life! And yet, when he held her so, she could not say as much to him. No, she could not. It was simple to think of him as a loathsome beast while he was gone and she worked her fingers bloody, but she could not think of him as such now while she sat with her head resting against his cheek, his arms holding her so very gently and his song lulling her into calm.

"I don't intend fer ye to suffer, wife," he whispered when his song had finished. "I'd spin if I could an' send ye out to play the fiddle an' beg fer a penny here, a shillin' there. But ye kinnit play the fiddle, an' I've not the time ta teach ye. An' ye'd not be safe upon the roads nor able ta walk the great distances I must ta git from town ta town. Still, I'll not have ye hurtin' of yerself. That I'll not. Perhaps we kin think o' a way ta survive, the two o' us, on what I gits abeggin'. 'Twere enuff fer me alone. Perhaps 'twill be enuff fer us both if I but travels farther an' plays all day an' all night, too."

"You cannot travel farther without a horse," Artemis replied. "We have no money for a horse. And you cannot play all day and all night. Your fingers will grow tired, your playing will suffer and no one will wish to hear you play at all. You have made a bad bargain, husband," she added with a sob. "You have taken a wife who cannot help to provide for herself."

"Never a bad bargain. It were cruel o' me ta say it at the first. Ye be a lovely wife—an' willin', too. Ye have attempted to do ever'thin' what I have done suggested. 'Tis not yer fault as ye was borned a lady."

"N-no."

"No, an' I'll travel farther, an' I will play all day an' all night, fer I'll not see ye starve, nor will I see ye freeze come winter. We has joined are hands an' become as one, an' now ye be a part o' me. If ye kinnot help ta care fer yerself, then I will care fer the both o' us no matter how hard I mus' work ta do the thin'."

"You are most kind," murmured Artemis, swiping at her tears. "You are the kindest of all men, I think."

"No. I reckon as I be cruel," her husband sighed. "Ye'd not be cryin' now had ye married King Thrushbeard instead o' m'self. He'd be af'er takin' great good care o' ye, King Thrushbeard would. He'd not be amakin' ye suffer so, like I be doin'. No doubt ye be wishin' ye was his own ladywife this verimost minit."

"N-no. N-no. It is only his money I wish to have. I have wished for it from the moment we broke our journey in his woods. Then I wished to have it only to better my own existence, but now I wish to have it to help you as well as myself."

"Ye do? Ta help me?"

"Indeed. I would not be happy, husband, to eat well myself, knowing you must starve. I would not be happy to live in a fine house, knowing you must live all alone in this dreadful hut."

"Y'be spouting balderdash," grinned the fiddler down at her. "I reckon as ye be lightheaded-like from not havin' enuff ta eat. Wife!" he exclaimed abruptly, standing straight up with her in his arms and spinning her about. "Wife, I got an idea! I know what we kin do!"

"Wh-what?" asked Artemis, startled by his enthusiasm and smiling at the way he spun her about with him.

"Ye kin sell pottery!" he exclaimed. "Ye kin sell pottery ever' marketday in Doddermeane. I'll take what little I got in me pocket an' buy us some wares from the potter in Tushing, an' ye'll sit in the market in Doddermeane an' sell 'em fer a bit more than what I has done paid. That willn't hurt yer fingers nor harm yer hands. An' ye need not be thinkin' o' yerself as a beggar, neither, fer ye'll be givin' people wares in return fer what ye git! People'll buy yer wares. 'Deed they will, 'cause ye be lovely. They'll be wantin' ta buy jus' fer that reason alone!"

The Countess of Lanningsdale peered down at the handwritten words for the one thousandth time. Her index finger trailed beneath each one of them. Her lips trembled as she read the lines. Over her shoulder Bertram peered down at the words quite as intently, though he could not actually read them. His large green eyes did not blink once. His lips opened and closed and opened again. Beyond the library door, the Earl of Lanningsdale's remarkable home of Rosehill lay silent amongst the shadows of the night.

"I cannot think what he did to change the spell so very greatly," sighed the countess. "Truly, I cannot. It is a very simple sort of spell. Nothing ought to have gone wrong with it."

"No, ladyship," Bertram replied.

"No. And yet, Roebuck Hall has been set back centuries in time, and my son has become a beggarman, a fiddler. How could it have happened?"

"Does it matter how it happened?" asked Bertram with some surprise.

"If we are to reverse the spell, it matters a great deal."

"Perhaps we do not need to reverse the spell, ladyship. Perhaps there be a way to just plain undo it."

"Yes, I have thought of that. But if there is, it is not written in this volume. Fetch me another of my husband's books, Bertram. Fetch them all. I shall change Elias back into himself if I must read every book on wizardry in this entire library."

They worked long into the night, the frog and the countess. And if Bertram could not read precisely well, he proved most adequate at climbing up to reach the top shelves and fetching volume after volume down to her ladyship. And if he could not quite understand what good it would do to know how the first spell had gone wrong, still he cudgeled his brain over it all the while the countess read.

"Her papa grew angry and vowed that he would marry her to the very first beggar who came along!" cried Bertram just as the long clock in the vestibule began to chime three.

Lady Lanningsdale looked up at him. "And so?" she queried.

"Well, I will bet it be like the pig," Bertram replied excitedly. "Yes, exactly like the pig. Lordship began to long for a pork pie, and instead of making Lord Hardin into the man of his beloved's dreams, lordship popped him into a pig!"

"And this time, he began to long so for the girl that he popped himself into the beggar to whom Lord Breckenbridge vowed to give the girl!"

"Precisely, ladyship."

"But what went wrong with the time, Bertram?"

"Well, he could not have had her in this time, ladyship. He could not have. In 1818 a father cannot marry his daughter to anyone against her will, but in 1618—"

"In 1618 it was done!" exclaimed the countess. "Yes, yes, you are a devilish smart frog, Bertram, to think of it. Devilish smart! Now if only we can find a spell to turn time forward once again and then get Lord Breckenbridge to denounce his vow. This particular one does seem appropriate," she added, reading again the words upon the page before her. "But Lord Breckenbridge must be present, and Lady Artemis and Elias as well. We cannot do it without them here before us at Roschill."

Eight

Artemis sat on the corner of the square in the village of Doddermeane with her pottery spread out before her. Though at first she was quite annoyed at being placed in such a lowly position, she remembered quite vividly the weaving and the spinning. And she remembered, too, how it had felt at the very end of her first day with her husband to actually beg. Truly, the selling of pottery was so very much better than all those others that a smile began to flutter about on her lips.

I have much for which to be thankful, Artemis thought, gazing about her at the other sellers. My hands no longer hurt; my fingers do not bleed; and I need not approach strangers with my bonnet in my hand to beg for a penny. I have wares to sell and I ought to be proud of it. I am a woman of business.

Once, she would have scorned any woman who involved herself in the business of making money in any way. She would certainly have thought a woman sitting in the marketplace with wares to sell was quite beneath her. But she held such an opinion no longer. As one by one shoppers came to look upon her wares, to remark on their fineness and to purchase this piece and that, Artemis grew quite proud of herself. I am doing it, she thought as she happily tucked her profits away into the reticule beside her. I am helping my husband to keep us fed. And if these pieces of pottery continue to sell as well as they have been, we shall neither of us freeze to death this winter. If I am able to sell a great many more, perhaps we will be able to purchase a little cottage and leave that dreadful hut behind us before winter even comes. I shall like to live in a cottage. I shall like to have my husband live there with me. He is such an odd man, Elias, but so very kind. I do believe I have grown fond of him, she thought, amazed. I do believe I have.

With such a pretty face and such a fine figure, Artemis could not help but be successful. People wished to buy pottery from her. Some even came and gave her the price of a bowl or a pitcher or a fine vase and then left the article there so that she might sell it again and make a double profit on it.

"Only see what I have got, husband," she cried as the fiddler came at the end of the day to help her pack up her wares. "I have made us a good deal of money."

"So ye have," grinned the fiddler, his eyes shining. "An' ye've a smile upon yer face as well. It's proud I be of ye, m'dear wife!"

That night the fiddler's tiny hut was filled with talk and laughter, and as the evening grew late, Artemis went so far as to ask her husband not to sleep out on the hard ground under the stars but to come into the little room in the back and share her mattress with her. "I will come for a bit," he agreed. And when she had donned her nightrail and slipped in under the blankets he had provided her, he did come and slipped in beside her. "Ye be a reg'lar wizard at sellin' pottery," he whispered, putting an arm around her and hugging her near. " 'Twon't be long afore we own more thin's than King Thrushbeard."

"I expect we shall never be as rich as King Thrushbeard, but soon, if we but save enough, my dearest husband, we will be able to afford a real cottage with a tiny garden and roses growing near the door. And it will have a kitchen. And I will learn to cook and clean and care for you."

"Ye will?" asked her husband, startled. "I thought as how ladies did not cook an' clean. An' I thought as how men was loathsome beasts an' not ta be liked at all, much less cared fer." And then he chuckled and bestowed the softest kiss upon the tip of Artemis's nose.

"You are not like other men," Artemis replied, stroking his bewhiskered cheek with one slim finger. "You are my husband and I find that I wish to care for you very much."

The following day, at Artemis's urging, the fiddler took all of their money and carried it to the potter's where he bought a great many more pieces for his wife to sell. Artemis clapped her hands to see the loveliness of his purchases and stood on tiptoe to kiss his chin. "I will make us so much money next market day that you will never have to travel the roads with your fiddle again," she promised him. "You will play only when you please, for whom you please, just as a fiddler with talent as great as yours ought to do!"

"I cannot do it, ladyship," Bertram replied woefully. "Only look at me. I be not at all convincing."

"It is because you are so short," Lady Lanningsdale observed, studying the odd little cavalryman before her.

"I were taller as a frog."

"Indeed you were. I remember you well. A very handsome, tall sort of a fellow."

"Yes," murmured Bertram wistfully. "I were the handsomest frog in the stream. But this will not work, ladyship," he added, studying himself in the looking glass again. "She has already seen me oncet. She will remember and be highly suspicious."

"Perhaps you will look more military once you are upon a horse, Bertram. A cavalryman, after all, is seldom as handsome and intimidating in a parlor as he is upon his steed. And you must do it, Bertram. You must do it for his lordship. We know now that day by day his memory deteriorates. Did you not say that it took him a full ten minutes to remember you when you went to him yesterday? Did you not say that he actually believes himself to be this fiddler and to live in Harry Barker's hut?"

Bertram nodded sadly. "And he could not so much as recall my name. No, nor would he believe me when I reminded him that he were the Earl of Lanningsdale. If I had not seen the lady selling pottery at Doddermeane, I doubt his lordship would have confided such in me. But she will remember me, ladyship. She did but meet me only oncet, and that be already after the spell fell upon them."

"Yes, well, you must take that chance, I fear, Bertram. We will not get his lordship to come to Rosehill else. I can think of no better way to make it necessary for him to do so. And he must come here if we are to restore him to himself."

The little valet nodded slowly. "I will do it, ladyship. I will do anything for lordship."

Lady Lanningsdale smiled the most tender smile. Well she knew this to be true. Disgusted as she sometimes became with the knowledge that her son's valet was, somewhere deep inside, a FROG, she nevertheless had observed over the years the extent of Bertram's devotion to the lad and had often been grateful for it. "You shall have Satan to ride, Bertram. He is the largest and grandest horse in Rosehill's stables. Most certainly his size and appearance will add to your stature. Once you are up on his back, no one will doubt that you are a true cavalryman."

Her words struck Bertram to the very core. Satan. The little valet began to shake and shiver.

"You are afraid to ride Satan," observed Lady Lanningsdale gently, stepping up to Bertram and taking both of his hands into her own. "Well, you need not ride him, then. It was merely a thought that occurred to me."

"I w-will ride him, ladyship. You be correct in your thoughts. Not one person will doubt that I be a true cavalryman do I be on Satan's back. And everyone will be certain that all were an accident."

"Just so," nodded Lady Lanningsdale. "Just so. And I shall never forget your bravery, Bertram. Never."

The very next market day, as Artemis sat smiling brightly amidst her pottery, the thunder of galloping hooves echoed throughout the square. Like everyone else, Artemis looked up at once, only to see a red-coated cavalryman on a most enormous black steed galloping around the corner and straight in her direction. Artemis screamed and gained her feet at once as the horse charged toward her. In but an instant the enormous animal's hooves were amongst her wares. Pottery popped and cracked and crackled. Shards flew everywhere. Not one bowl, not one cup, not one little vase survived the great, iron-clad hooves as the cavalryman galloped by and disappeared in the direction of the Doddermeane bridge.

Artemis stared about her in horror. Gone. All of her pottery destroyed. Tears sprang to her eyes and dribbled down her cheeks. Everything destroyed—everything in shards—everything, including her hopes and dreams of the little cottage. "What will I tell Elias?" she sobbed, one fist pressed against her quivering lips. "What will I tell my dear husband? He used all of our money to purchase this pottery, and now all is lost. Oh, surely he will beat me and send me from his door. Most certainly he will never wish to see my face again. And rightly so. Rightly so. For I have taken the food from his stomach and the wood from his fire and he will have to walk the roads to the ends of England to gain enough money to replace all I have lost." With a heavy heart, Artemis began to gather up the shards of pottery into a pile. By the time her husband came to fetch her home at the end of the day, the pile of broken pottery leaned like an evil mountain over her as she sat in tears on the ground.

"What's this?" asked the fiddler, looking first to Artemis and then to the mountain of broken pottery. "What's happened?"

Haltingly, Artemis told him of the cavalryman and the great black horse and how all had been broken by those iron-clad hooves. "We are poorer now than ever we were," sobbed Artemis. "And it is all my fault. I ought to have known better than to set my pottery about so near to the street corner. Oh, husband, I have taken your last penny from you and thrown it away."

"Nah, ye never did," her husband replied, offering her his hand and tugging her up from the place where she sat sobbing. "Ye dinnit 'tend fer ta break the pottery, m'dear. Ye dinnit 'tend fer ta waste are money. Do not be sobbing as if yer heart will break," he added, placing his strong arms around her and kissing her most tenderly. "It jus' dinnit work out like we figgered is all. Ye must cease sorrowin', m'dear, an' be grateful."

"Be grateful?" Artemis could not believe her ears. "What have I to be grateful for, husband? What have you to be grateful for? You have married a stupid wife who has destroyed all your hopes of bettering yourself."

"P'raps. But I still does have that wife. Only think if them hooves had come down upon ye, m'dear. I kin always be a playin' of m'fiddle ta git us a pittance here an' a pittance there, but how would I git another you? Aye, we've a deal ta be grateful fer. Ye be alive an' unhurt an' in m'arms."

This reaction was so far from any that Artemis had imagined that her heart rose up nearly into her throat and tears sprang afresh to her eyes. "Y-you are the sweetest person in all the world," she stuttered, burying her head against his shoulder. "H-how have I c-come to deserve you?"

"I does of'en wonner jus' that," chuckled the fiddler, bestowing a kiss upon her brow. "I reckon as how 'twas fated from the first that we be tagether. Mus' have been. An' I be grateful fer that too, I does."

He took her home to their little hut and fed her on bread and beans and water from the stream. Then he sat with his arms around her and pointed out to her the stars twinkling in the sky above them. He named them all, one after the other. "That un be George," he said with great authority. "An' there be Tommy an' Henrietta an Lady Lucy."

Artemis, who had thought never to smile again, giggled girlishly, turned in his arms and kissed him full upon the lips. "You are the best and kindest person in all the world," she told him with great seriousness. "I love you, husband, with all my heart."

"Even if I do be a man? A ugly fella wif a big nose an' hair all white like a billy goat's? Even do I be a loathsome beast an' cruel?"

"You are not a loathsome beast," declared Artemis ardently. "You are not cruel. I shall never believe another word that Mrs. Paxton-Dalrymple told me. Never again. And for my papa's sake, I am gravely sorry that I ever did so, for I hurt him sorely in the doing of it."

It was very late in the evening, two entire days after Artemis's disaster at the market, when her husband came walking wearily up to the hut and spun down into the dirt beside the door. "I kinnit do no better," he said quietly when she appeared from inside. "I have tried an' tried, an' I kinnit make enuff ta feed ye like I ought an' still put some away fer ta go t'wards a little cottage. I kinnit walk fast enuff an' far enuff ta do it."

"Oh, my dearest," whispered Artemis, sitting down beside him. "You have worn yourself to cinders. You have been gone so long that I feared I might never see you again. Where have you been?"

"I have done walked as far as King Thrushbeard's house an' even begged 'neath his winnows."

"You have walked all the way to Rosehill and back?" asked Artemis, aghast.

"Aye, an' playin' all the way. Stoppin' here an' there all along the road. But still I kinnit git enuff ta keep ye from havin' ta spen' the winter here."

"Oh, Elias," she said, for the first time truly daring to taste his name upon her lips. "Oh, my dearest Elias, you ought not to have done such a thing."

"Ye wish fer a little cottage. I knows as ye does."

"Yes, but it is not of any great import, my dear. I shall not die for want of a cottage. We have a fine hut in which to spend the winter. A hut with a door and a window, and we shall go about, you and I, and gather a great stack of wood to burn against the cold. And then we shall be snug and cozy—"

"But ye wants a cottage," interrupted the fiddler, and even Artemis could hear that he was on the very edge of tears. "Ye wants a cottage, an' I wants ta give it ta ye, an' there be no way. There be no way unless—"

"Unless what?" asked Artemis, smoothing his hair from his brow. "What is it has occurred to you?"

" 'Twere told ta me," offered the fiddler. "At King Thrushbeard's house, they be in need of a extra kitchen maid fer a bit. A little man what comed out an' gived me a whole entire guinea fer m'playin', he said as much ta me. 'I know you has a wife,' he done said. 'P'rhaps she'll consider the position. Does she consent ta come, I'll see yer paid ta play yer fiddle fer King Thrushbeard's ball.' "

Artemis, her arm through her husband's and her fingers entwined tightly with his, gazed up at the evening sky and thought. "Do you wish to play your fiddle at King Thrushbeard's ball?" she asked at last.

"Aye. 'Twould be astoundin' profitable, I thinks. But I kinnit do it wifout ye come along wif me an' be a kitchen maid. An' ye be a lady, so ye kinnit do it."

"I have learned to clean the pots and pans here in our own little hut," said Artemis, giving his hand a squeeze. "I have learned to keep things clean and to scrub what must be scrubbed. If I can do so here, why can I not do so at King Thrushbeard's house as well? If it pleases you, my husband, to play for King Thrushbeard's ball, then it will please me well to be King Thrushbeard's kitchen maid for a time."

Her husband looked at her, his eyes wide, his lips parted in wonder. "If ye truly means ta do it," he said, "p'raps we kin make enuff atween us ta git that cottage!"

"Perhaps we can," nodded Artemis, smiling. "But even if we cannot, perhaps we can earn enough to replace the money we spent for the pottery, and that, my dear, will take us through the winter without fear of starving or freezing, will it not?"

"Aye, 'twill."

"Then we must take advantage of the little man's kind offer. We will walk together to Rosehill, you and I, and see what bargain may be made."

And so the daughter of the Earl of Breckenbridge became a kitchen maid in the house of the Earl of Lanningsdale. Willingly she placed herself at the cook's beck and call. She worked from morning till night for three days running, doing all of the dirtiest work in preparation for the upcoming ball. Never once did Artemis think to complain about a thing. She only worried a bit, and that was not about herself but about what King Thrushbeard's little man—a most familiar looking little man—might be doing to her husband. The man, who called himself Bertram, had come and taken her husband away from her at once, saying that the fiddler must be cleaned up and dressed properly for the occasion and taught how to behave should King Thrushbeard be so impressed with his playing that he would have a word or two to say to the fiddler in praise of it.

"I can certainly understand," murmured Artemis to herself as she scrubbed away at the most enormous pot, "that Elias must be dressed properly. But how on earth that man intends to teach him to speak properly in so short a time as is available to him, I cannot imagine. But certainly that must be what he intends or my husband would be with me by now and not hidden away in some room in the attic."

The fiddler was not, however, hidden away in the attic as his wife supposed. He had been, instead, taken directly to the master's bedchamber where Bertram had taken the rags from his back, helped to scrub the grime from his body, and dressed him up in the very best of King Thrushbeard's togs. Then the little valet had led his charge down the stairs to the first story and into the silver saloon to stand before Lady Lanningsdale.

"Elias," the countess said, a catch in her throat as she gazed upon her son. "Elias, I am so very pleased to see you. Do come and sit here beside me."

The fiddler stared in horror at Lady Lanningsdale. "No, ma'am, I couldn't not do that," he whispered. "It wouldn't be proper-like, a fella like me hobnobbin' wif a reg'lar flash mort."

"Oh," sighed Lady Lanningsdale, her hand going to her creamy white neck. "Oh, Bertram, have not Lord Breckenbridge and Miss Waithe arrived yet? We must begin soon—very, very soon—or there will be no saving him. No saving him at all!"

Nine

"It is his lordship's betrothal ball," the cook advised Artemis quite haughtily. "His lordship is to be married within the week to the young lady of his dreams."

"He is?" queried Artemis, taking no offense at the cook's haughtiness, for why should cook not think herself of greater importance than a mere kitchen maid? "Is she very beautiful, the lady of his dreams?"

"They say she is the most beautiful woman in all England."

"Oh," murmured Artemis, turning back to her pots. She thought for a moment of the handsome King Thrushbeard and how she had treated him in London and hoped that this lady of his dreams, beautiful or not, would treat him a good deal better than she had done. "He is kind, your master, is he not?" she asked quietly.

"Indeed."

"He is not some loathsome beast seeking to take all the lady has and make a veritable slave of her?"

"What? My Lord Lanningsdale? Good heavens, girl, he is the gentlest, finest human being upon the face of the earth. He knows my name, he does, and comes sometimes to sit and have tea with me here in my own kitchen. At least, he was accustomed to do so. I have not so much as set eyes upon him since he rushed off to London. But he will arrive this very day, and tonight we shall all celebrate his good fortune. He is a gentleman deserving of all happiness."

Yes, so he must be, Artemis thought. It was I who acted like a loathsome beast. It was I who was cruel and unfeeling and treated him like a slave. What a dreadful person I was. But I shall be no longer. "I would like to wish him happy," she said aloud, "though I expect I shall not be afforded the opportunity."

"Wish him happy? You? Why you are not even truly one of his servants. You are only here because her ladyship wishes your husband to play his fiddle at the ball."

"Yes, I know," Artemis replied. "It was a stupid thing for me to say. His lordship would not care whether I wished him happy or not. I am quite certain of that. Yet I *should* like to wish him happiness."

"Well, then you shall," the cook replied quite unexpectedly. "You are an odd little creature, but pretty as a picture and with a manner of speaking that belies your position. And you are a hard worker as well. You have been scrubbing away here for hours now without one complaint. And if we did not have you to lend a hand, we should all of us be out of sorts. I will speak to Harbinger, and he will find you a place on the stairs where you may peek in at the ball and see my lord and wish him happy, though he will not hear you do so."

"Oh, I should like that very much," smiled Artemis, pleased at the opportunity to see her onetime beau for one last time and perhaps to catch a glimpse of the lady to whom he had at last given his heart. "And perhaps I will hear my husband play for him as well. He is a fine fiddler, my husband."

The ballroom at Rosehill glistened and sparkled and glowed with the light of a hundred candles reflected over and over by the crystal drops of the chandeliers. Blue and white bunting hung from the cornices, dipped from the drapery rods and played over the mantelpieces of the fireplaces at either end of the room. The dance floor shone golden and invited all who entered to come and dance upon it. As the guests gathered within, Lady Lanningsdale could not but smile distractedly and play with the golden locket that sparkled at her throat. Upon the balcony that circled the ballroom, a little group of musicians began to play and Lady Lanningsdale gasped the tiniest bit to hear a fiddle join them. "He plays," she whispered to the gentleman beside her. "Listen but a moment."

"Aye," said Lord Breckenbridge, "that will be the same fiddler to whom I gave my daughter. I ought not to have done that. But I vowed I would, and I could not unvow it."

"And now we shall never see our Artemis again," added Miss Waithe, peering up at Lady Lanningsdale from almost behind her brother-in-law. "She is lost to us. Gone forever."

"Oh, no, she is not," replied Lady Lanningsdale kindly, stepping forward and taking them both by the arm. "It is the reason I have invited you here tonight—to see Lady Artemis again and to meet her betrothed."

"Her betrothed?" asked Lord Breckenbridge, an eyebrow cocking in suspicion. "The gel is married. How can she be betrothed?"

"Well, that is rather hard to explain, but I shall attempt it. Join me for a moment in this antechamber, away from the others, and I will tell you all that I know."

Lord Breckenbridge's face grew flushed. Then it grew pale. Then it grew flushed again. His cheeks puffed out. His chin quivered. "A spell?" he gasped. "The rascal cast a spell over us? How dare he to do such a thing!"

"Oh!" cried Miss Waithe, clutching at her bosom. "We have been misused—gravely misused! I knew there was something quite odd about it all. I did. I could not re-member Roebuck Hall ever having had a Great Hall when we stayed there before."

"I shall take this up with Lanningsdale directly. You may believe I will," stated Breckenbridge angrily. "Of all things! To use witchery upon us!"

"His intentions were good," explained Lady Lan-ningsdale hastily. "He meant only to dispel the hateful ideas that this Mrs. Paxton-Dalrymple implanted in Lady Artemis' head. That was all. But Elias—Elias is not quite the—the—wizard—that his papa was and—something went amiss."

"I should say something went amiss," cried Brecken-bridge. "I have married my only daughter off to a beg-gar!"

"No, no, you have not. As a matter of fact, Lady Artemis is not actually married at all."

"What?" gasped Miss Waithe. "Artemis gone off with a man and not married to him?"

"No, my dear, but she will be married, and within the week, I promise you. My son will offer for her just as soon as he is himself again. And he will see that most of the monies you have lost are restored to you, Lord Breckenbridge."

"Well, he need not do that. That had naught to do with him, did it?"

"No, but he has always intended to make you a very generous offer for the opportunity to become your son-in-law. And he will do it, too, just as soon as he remem-bers who he is."

"Lord Lanningsdale does not know who he is? Well, by Jove, why not? He has caused my daughter to live with a beggar to whom she is not even married and swept Gwenyth and myself into another time, and now he pre-tends that his wits have gone wandering? Lead me to him and I will remind him who he is with my good right fist."

"I will lead you to him," said Lady Lanningsdale. "But when I do, we must all be certain to say just the right thing, together, at just the right time. Only hear me out and I will explain every bit of it to you."

It was not Harbinger who came down into the kitchens and led Artemis forward and up the staircase where she might gaze in at the ballroom and glimpse Lord Lanningsdale in his finest hour. It was a little man in an emerald-green jacket with a pristine neckcloth tied elegantly about his neck and wide green eyes that blinked at her in the most peculiar way.

"I hope you will not think me forward," whispered Artemis as he led her up the staircase, "but I do think that I have seen you somewhere before, sir."

"Good," replied the man. "It begins to work already, and we have not even done the most of it yet."

"What begins to work?"

"You will see soon enough, my lady."

"Oh, I am not a lady. I was a lady once, but now I am merely a kitchen maid and only a temporary one at that."

"Yes, temporary," murmured Bertram. "Please God that it be so. Temporary." And without another word of explanation he left her to stand on the stair where she could see into the ballroom and hurried away.

Several of the Rosehill footmen, carrying wine and glasses from below, passed her as she stood gazing up into the ballroom. She felt them stare at her as they passed by, but she would not look at them, for she was dressed so raggedly and they were quite above her in their fine livery and their exquisite wigs. She was certain that they were laughing at her as they passed, remarking upon her poverty and the inappropriateness of her peering in at the ball.

But it was such a fine ball, and her husband's music danced through the crowd with such love and joy that surely every heart must be filled with both. And as she glanced up at the balcony to see him there among the other musicians—all of whom had ceased to play and sat listening in awe to her husband's fiddle—she caught the glint of his eyes in the candlelight and the hint of a grin upon his lips. "Oh, but he looks so very fine," she whispered to herself, smiling up at him. "They have dressed him up in such fashion that he is almost beautiful."

"He is very beautiful," answered a voice from the step below her. "As odd as his face may be, the beauty of his soul shines through. Such a man as he cannot help but be beautiful. One need only open one's eyes to see it. Come with me, my dear, and dance with him."

"Oh, I could not," protested Artemis, hiding her hand beneath her skirt, appalled that the graceful woman in silk and satin who had come up behind her should even think to take hold of it. "I am naught but a kitchen maid, madam, and Elias, a beggar. Such as we may never dance at so fine a ball as this."

"So you know his name at least."

"Yes, madam," Artemis answered. "He is my husband."

"Come, then, and dance with your husband."

"I cannot. I cannot show my face amongst such a grand crowd as is gathered here. They will laugh at me and chase me from the place."

"They will not," declared the lady. "This is my son's house, and if I say that you and your husband may dance upon the ballroom floor, there is no one here will gainsay me."

"Oh, your ladyship!" gasped Artemis, and trembled a

tiny curtsy. "I did not recognize—I did not realize—I shall return to my duties at once."

But as she turned away, Lady Lanningsdale seized her hand, turned her back around and led her up the last of the servants' stairs and into the ballroom. The fiddle ceased to sing as she led Artemis through the guests. The dancing stopped and the dancers moved from the floor to stare in amazement at the begrimed little creature that Lady Lanningsdale tugged into the center of the dance floor. "Fiddler, come down from your perch and dance with your wife," Lady Lanningsdale called.

"Aye, fiddler," added Lord Breckenbridge, stepping up to take Lady Lanningsdale's other hand in his own. "Come down at once, sir, and dance with your wife."

"Yes, do," Miss Waithe said as loudly as she dared while she clasped Lord Breckenbridge's left hand.

"It is a reward for the joy your music gives us," continued Lady Lanningsdale. "Come down, fiddler; take this woman in your arms and waltz with her."

And the fiddler did come down, abandoning his fiddle and rushing down the steps at the back of the alcove. At the very bottom of the steps, the little valet stopped him and placed a twig of willow in the fiddler's buttonhole. "It is for good luck, lordship," he said.

"First ye be dressin' me up like a lor', an' now ye be addressin' me as one? Ye be a odd little fella, don'tcha?"

"Indeed," said Bertram. "Odd. Go now and dance as her ladyship requests of you. Her heart does be set upon it."

Lady Lanningsdale smiled a most worried smile as the fiddler made his way through her guests to the center of the dance floor. Bertram had placed the willow twig correctly. She, herself, had schooled Lord Breckenbridge, Miss Waithe, all of the servants and the invited guests in precisely what to do and say. The musicians were at the ready on the balcony. "It must work," she murmured.

"It is the very best spell in all of Giles' volumes for unraveling what has been done."

"Spell?" asked Artemis, overhearing but that portion of her ladyship's speech.

"Yes," Lady Lanningsdale replied adroitly. "A bit of dizziness. But it will leave me shortly, I have no doubt. Only see, my dear, here is your husband come to lead you in a waltz."

"I do not believe he knows how to waltz," protested Artemis, once again aware of all the guests who stared at her. "We shall make perfect fools of ourselves."

"No, we willn't," answered the fiddler confidently, taking her hand. "A little fella by the name o' Bertram done showed me the steps this very af'ernoon, an' I be good at 'em."

"But Elias, my gown is old and dirty from working in the kitchen. My hair has come loose some from its knot, and there are smudges on my face. I can feel it is so. You look exquisite in the clothes they have given you, but I am not fit at all to be standing among such people as these, much less dancing among them. They will laugh at my audacity and ridicule me for being the kitchen wench I am."

"They willn't," protested her husband. "They be nice people, these. Pleasant to me they been an' kind. An' there be any number o' servants here, wife. Any number jus' a standin' lookin' on."

Artemis gazed about the ballroom and discovered that he told the truth. There was cook, in her apron still, standing near the servants' staircase, smiling. And all of the footmen were scattered 'round about, and the butler, and the little man in the green coat and any number of maids and serving girls peering down from the balcony.

"Come, wife," whispered the fiddler, taking Artemis into his arms. "Waltz with me."

Lady Lanningsdale, Lord Breckenridge and Miss

Waithe slipped quietly back among the crowd at the edge of the dance floor, urging them all to join hands until they formed a circle, ladies, gentlemen and servants together, around the couple. In the little alcove on the balcony Bertram told the musicians to begin.

The fiddler smiled down at Artemis, and she knew in that very moment that she would do anything to see that smile for the rest of her life, even make a veritable fool of herself before all these people.

"Will ye waltz?" asked her husband. "Will ye waltz wif me an' be m'love in fronta all o' these Swells?"

"If it pleases you, Elias, indeed I will." And the two of them began to dance, swirling most gracefully around the floor. And together, the onlookers began to chant in time to the music the odd words that Lady Lanningsdale and Bertram had taught them.

Artemis gazed up into the dear face she had come to love and then could not take her eyes from it. For it was changing. It was changing. The fine brown eyes were turning the most lovely shade of blue. The large nose steadily dwindled. The chin became the least bit crookedy, while his lips became sweeter, more alluring.

"Something is very wrong, Elias," she gasped looking up at him. "I am—I am—seeing things."

"Are you, my lady?"

"Yes, yes!" And then she noticed his lank white hair begin to curl, dark and enticing, about his face.

"I love you, Missy," he whispered. "I have always loved you, from the time we were children." And that whisper thrilled her, lifted her heart with joy and sent her nerves to shivering and shuddering all through her, just as the voice of his fiddle had been wont to do.

"King Thrushbeard!" Artemis cried as he led her through a turn. "Lord Lanningsdale! Elias! My love!"

"I like the very last the best," whispered Lanningsdale.

"Will you be my love, Missy? Will you marry me and be my love?"

"I have already done so, have I not? But how can I have done so? When we began this waltz, you were the man I married, but now you are not. It cannot be. And yet, you are the man I love no matter the shape of your face, the color of your hair, the richness of your dress. You are my dearest love, and my heart will recognize you do you change into the Prince Regent himself next. We are already man and wife, Elias, are we not?"

"Well, no, not quite. I remember now how it came to be. There was the least bit of irregularity about that wedding, but we shall mend it this time around and live most happily ever after, I promise you."

Around about them, as Lanningsdale became himself and waltzed Artemis from kitchen maid to the lady that she was, her drab, dirty gown whirling magically into silver satin, the smudges flying from her face, her hair sparkling and pristine in the candlelight, the guests and servants of Roschill ceased their chant, unclasped their hands and began to applaud. Lord Breckenbridge grinned from ear to ear as he lent the support of his good right arm to a Miss Waithe who trembled with joy. Lady Lanningsdale's eyes glistened with tears of happiness as she made her way around the room and up the stairs to the balcony. Bertram started and swiped at his eyes as she came to a halt beside him.

"We have done well, you dear frog," she said, taking his hand into her own and leaning forward to peer over the balcony rail at her son and his ladylove waltzing below. "We have set everything right, you and I. And only see how she loves him now. It is clear in her eyes even from here."

"Just so, ladyship," whispered Bertram hoarsely.

"Just so," replied the countess. "And thank goodness that tomorrow not one of the servants or guests will remember a thing but how wonderfully Lady Artemis and my son waltzed this night to celebrate the occasion of their betrothal."

"I hope they do not remember anything else," gulped Bertram. "We did be doing everything correct, ladyship, did we not?"

"We did," smiled Lady Lanningsdale. "We did everything correctly, just as Giles did everything correctly when he took you from Elias's hands and made you into a perfect valet."

"But I do not be perfect," murmured Bertram, embarrassed by her praise, his palm sweating in her grasp.

"I know, Bertram," she laughed. "You were taller as a frog."